THEODORE TERHUNE STORIES

And a Bottle of Rum

A THEODORE TERHUNE MYSTERY

BRUCE GRAEME

With an introduction by J. F. Norris

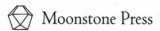 Moonstone Press

This edition published in 2022 by Moonstone Press
www.moonstonepress.co.uk

Introduction © 2022 J. F. Norris

Originally published in 1949 by Hutchinson & Co Ltd

And a Bottle of Rum © the Estate of Graham Montague
Jeffries, writing as Bruce Graeme

The right of Graham Montague Jeffries to be identified as author of this work has
been asserted in accordance with the Copyright, Designs and Patents Act 1988

ISBN 978-1-899000-38-8
eISBN 978-1-899000-39-5

A CIP catalogue record for this book is available from the British Library

Text designed and typeset by Tetragon, London
Cover illustration by Jason Anscomb

Printed and bound by CPI Group (UK) Ltd, Croydon, CRO 4YY

Contents

INTRODUCTION

Of Books and Ships and Smugglers, Too

Books take a step back to make room for the spectre of "the Scarecrow of Romney Marsh" in this final adventure in the Theodore Terhune series. Less of a traditional detective novel than others featuring our favourite bookseller turned amateur sleuth, *And a Bottle of Rum* (1949) finds Bruce Graeme indulging in his gift for action sequences. Combining the conventions of a pursuit thriller with those of a detective novel, the story begins with the mundane yet cruel crime of a hit-and-run, leading to a battle of wits between the police and a gang of clever smugglers who use the quotidian routines of village life to mask their crimes.

Graeme does not forsake his love of books altogether. The opening scene has Theodore and Julia MacMunn (sadly making only a cameo appearance) headed for a remote estate where Terhune will inspect a vast library of antiquarian volumes that he might end up purchasing. On the way home they are nearly run off the road by a lorry and discover a man in a ditch who has been knocked down and killed by the same vehicle. What appears to be an accident will, however, prove to be something more sinister. Having initiated this adventure, books continue to feature when the victim's widow approaches Terhune to peruse her husband's collection, modest in comparison that of the Stallybrass home, but nonetheless holding one huge clue that helps Terhune get to the root of the death of P.C. Tom Kitchen and solve the mystery of the speeding lorry.

Among the books in the policeman's rather odd library are several on the history of smuggling in the Dymchurch region of Kent. Readers as knowledgeable as Bruce Graeme may raise their eyebrows at once, for they will certainly recognize the village of Dymchurch as the home of Dr. Syn, aka "the Scarecrow of Romney Marsh", a fictional series character created by Russell Thorndike and the protagonist of several books of crime and adventure inspired by Kent's infamous history of smuggling.

The early nineteenth-century writer and poet Richard Harris Barham, who used the more recognizable pseudonym Thomas Ingoldsby, wrote in his seminal collection of Gothic short stories and poems *The Ingoldsby Legends*: "The world, according to the best geographers, is divided into Europe, Asia, Africa, America and Romney Marsh." In that hyperbolic quip Barham manages to evoke the strangeness and singularity of this region, which he came to call "the fifth continent". (Antarctica was still a vast anonymous and unexplored land of ice and snow in Barham's day, and North and South America were conveniently clumped together for the writer's purposes.) He goes on in the story "The Leech of Folkestone" to describe a realm of witches on broomsticks and enchanted cows, one where the uncanny seems to have permanently taken root and uses men in the service of all that is evil.

Due to its unique geography and fickle climate, the Romney Marsh has for centuries been known to be perfectly suited to the purposes of smugglers and criminals, who exploit the frequent smothering fog and rocky coastline to carry out their wicked deeds. Writers inspired by both their landscape and their history of criminality have doomed the Romney Marsh region and the surrounding towns and villages, from Dymchurch to Hythe to Folkestone, to be locked for ever in their notorious past. Graeme reminds us of this when he has Terhune examine the history books that P.C. Kitchen has obviously read several times and annotated with curious marks and abbreviations.

Ever the erudite book-lover, Graeme selected actual historical volumes to include in Kitchen's small but noteworthy library. *The Smugglers* by Lord Teignmouth and Charles G. Harper, subtitled "Picturesque Chapters in the History of Contraband", was published in 1909 by Cecil Palmer in Britain and in 1923 by George H. Doran in the United States. This vast, two volume-history was reprinted by a Yorkshire publisher in a single volume in 1973. I trust that the several passages cited in *And a Bottle of Rum* are quoted verbatim—Graeme was nothing but thorough in his research.

Also found in the dead man's collection is *Smuggling Days and Smuggling Ways* (1892) by H. N. Shore, reprinted in 1929 by Philip Allan, a publisher known for his interest in the outré, especially supernatural and horror fiction. Uncannily, just as with the Teignmouth and Harper history, Shore's book was also revived in a much later reprint in the 1970s. The undying curiosity and interest in Romney Marsh and Dymchurch serve to keep the past alive. A simple Google search for "smuggling" and "Romney Marsh" turns up numerous websites with a wealth of history and lore. These latest contributions in our age of information saturation signify an apparently never-ending desire to cement this region of Kent into its criminal past. Graeme is conscious of this when he writes: "so many writers had been lured by the strange remoteness... using it as the locale for stories: it lent itself so readily as an insidious spur to the conflict of human passions."

The bulk of *And a Bottle of Rum* reads like a manic thriller. Indeed, with its many action-oriented incidents, Graeme might have eschewed numeric chapters in favour of evocative chapter titles like "The

Adventure of the Accidental Stowaway" for the episode in which Terhune finds himself locked inside the smuggler's truck headed for destination unknown, or "Darts and Detection" for the scene in which he travels to local pub the Load of Hay to take part in a darts competition while simultaneously gathering information from the garrulous drinking crowd, whom he suspects of belonging to the gang of smugglers.

This adventure finds Terhune dealing with professional criminals rather than the devious murderers of his previous escapades. The gang takes advantage of the relatively unsophisticated forms taken by rural crime in order to create havoc while they run their smuggling operation. Following the nasty hit-and-run murder, Terhune confronts haystack arson and cow-rustling, misdemeanours used as distractions and cover for the smugglers. No less devious or clever than the murderers he has dealt with in the past, this band of criminals are probably more ruthless and dangerous than any villains he has met before. They are smart enough to know that a hit-and-run can be easily forgotten in a week when car crashes, burglary and an attempted rape are also keeping the police hectically busy.

One of the most interesting passages in the book has Terhune observing two suspects and comparing their personalities. Just as his love of books defines him as a detective, Terhune's love of language finds him examining the subtle differences between two types of criminal:

> Two dangerous men; each in his own way. Terhune could not decide which would have to be the more feared in case of trouble. If there were a shade of difference—not admitted by most dictionaries—in the definition of cunning and crafty, he would have described Matcham as cunning; the other as crafty. Each in his own right a dangerous opponent in combination...

In the final chapters of *And a Bottle of Rum*, Terhune is in full detective mode. Never fear that this seems less of a bibliomystery than the other books in the series. When our hero stumbles across an inscription in a copy of *The House of Arden* by Edith Nesbit he realizes that Tom Kitchen's miniature library has secretly held the most damning piece of evidence—one that was patiently waiting for Terhune to find it. A savvy and assiduous reader will latch on to the inscription's significance quicker than Terhune if he or she has made note of a single passing remark made very early in the book. Once again Bruce Graeme has planted a clue rather ingeniously in his story, later coming full-circle in order to allow his detective hero to lead the police to the guilty party. Tom Kitchen is vindicated by his own book collection and we as readers cheer for Terhune, who has done it again. *And a Bottle of Rum* is a fine ending to his adventures, wrapping up the saga of one of the best literary-minded sleuths in the world of Golden Age detective fiction.

Graham Montague Jeffries (1900–1982), better known as Bruce Graeme, was married and had two children: Roderic and Guillaine. Both his son and daughter went on to write books and interestingly also used their father's alter ego surname for their own pen names. Guillaine Jeffries, as "Linda Graeme", wrote a brief series of books published between 1955 and 1964 about a girl named Helen who was a ballet dancer in theatre and on TV. Roderic Jeffries followed in his father's footsteps and turned to writing crime fiction, using his own name and the pseudonyms "Roderic Graeme" (continuing his father's series about the thief turned crime novelist Blackshirt), "Peter Alding", "Jeffrey Ashford" and "Graham Hastings". In addition to more than sixty crime, detective and espionage novels, Roderic wrote a number of non-fiction works on criminal investigation and Grand Prix racing.

Late in life Graeme gave his Elizabethan farmhouse in Kent to Roderic and his wife. Graeme moved up the road to a bungalow and would have lunch with his son and daughter-in-law once a week. According to Xanthe Jeffries, Bruce Graeme's granddaughter, he remained in Kent while his son's family moved to Majorca in 1972. They remained close even while apart, and Graeme would visit in May every year, on his birthday.

When I asked for any family stories she might share with Moonstone Press readers, Xanthe very politely complied with an anecdote-filled email. I learned that her grandfather kept a couple of marmosets as pets and had inherited a Land Rover from his son when Roderic moved away. She also wrote of his annual visits to Majorca: "If the weather was not to his liking," she reported, "we never heard the end of it. On his last trip to us he became very worried about having to travel back to the U.K. via Barcelona." Apparently he was concerned about Spanish customs law. "When asked why he told my parents that his walking stick was in fact a swordstick!" Clearly, Graeme was something of an adventurer himself.

J. F. NORRIS
Chicago, IL
December 2021

Chapter One

There was no threat of fog when Julia called one evening about seven, to drive Terhune to *Pennyfields*, a house on Romney Marsh half a mile north-west of Dymchurch. On the contrary, the early evening was both warm and pleasant enough to make it a tempting one for a swim.

"I suppose you positively must go tonight?" she asked in a deceptively casual manner, as they followed the winding road down to the Marsh.

He grinned, suspecting what was in her mind. "Tonight's the night fixed by the old boy for the doings."

"You could telephone him that something had turned up to prevent your keeping the appointment."

"I could, but what for?"

"Any cold, rainy night is good enough to go pottering among a lot of silly old books."

"Good enough for me, old girl, but not for old Stallybrass. He's moving in less than a month's time."

"It might be raining by tomorrow," she wistfully commented. "It would not take us long to run back for my costume—"

"Nothing doing," he firmly interrupted. "To quote the classics— Business is Business."

"It's after business hours."

"Not for me, Julie. Besides, the Parkinsons are expecting you."

"I could 'phone them—"

His "No" was adamant. So Julia, with a sigh of regret but not too much disappointment—for she knew her Theo too well—resigned herself to spending a boring evening with an old school friend living in Folkestone. A short while later she dropped him by a pair of handsome wrought-iron gates, the entrance to *Pennyfields*.

"I'll call for you about—"

"Say…" He reflected. "Ten-fifteen?"

She nodded. "I'll be here." He knew that she would be, too, for Julia had a rare sense of punctuality. She waved a hand. "See you later," she called out as the car drove off.

He waited until the car had passed out of sight round a near corner before turning to enter the iron gates. They were closed; but there was no lodge nor any bell that he could see, so he turned the solid iron handle and pushed. The right-hand gate opened easily and without noise. He entered, closed the gate, and began walking up the gravelled drive which forked two ways. He automatically took the left-hand fork, which soon began to curve to the right.

Because of the massive hedge which bordered the road on both sides, he could see nothing of the house, nor anything of what lay beyond the hedges. This knowledge made him realize that, in spite of his having passed and repassed the property many hundreds of times, never once had he had a glimpse of the house. Wondering how this had come about, he decided that there was only one answer. A simple one. The house was not to be seen from the road. Doubtless it was hidden by trees. Otherwise, he would certainly have seen it; if not on one occasion, then on another. Especially when cycling or walking.

The carriage-way continued to curve, still to the right. It seemed to him that it must be circular in shape; and, judging by the distance, probably surrounded the house. This deduction was presently proved right, for when he reached a wide gap in the right-hand hedge he saw the house for the first time, and appreciated that it was situated in the middle of a large, bowl-like depression that was entirely bordered by the right-hand hedge of the drive. Within the outer border of the hedge was a screening belt of trees which ran parallel. No wonder the house was not to be seen save from where he stood.

A second drive, in the shape of a horseshoe, proceeded from the break in the bordering hedge as far as the house. The left-hand prong bore a discreet notice board marked *Tradesmen*, so Terhune took the other.

As he advanced towards the house he saw that he would arrive at one of those porticos that are a feature of Georgian architecture. Neither the portico nor the house itself impressed him as being in any way artistically beautiful. The building was square and ugly, and possessed nothing of the elegance which often accompanies simplicity. To Terhune's eyes it more resembled the officers' quarters in a barracks than a home. Especially as attached to the main building, was a large, and equally barrack-like, range of outbuildings.

He knocked; then grinned, for the knock produced just that sort of dull, echoing sound he had anticipated. While he waited for someone to answer, he tried to picture the type of man who would receive him. He had never met Stallybrass; all the preliminary dealings, which were culminating in the present visit, had been conducted by correspondence, or over the telephone. If the style of letter were in any way indicative, or the dry, formal tones of a somewhat high-pitched voice, then he expected to meet a smallish man of advancing years, probably one with a scholar's stoop, a minimum of grey hairs, thin bloodless lips and pale blue eyes. But, of course, there was nothing more deceptive than a voice, he told himself. B.B.C. news readers and commentators were living examples of that particular generalization.

The door opened without sound or warning. When he saw the man who peered near-sightedly at him from within the gloomy interior he gaped with amazement. For the tiny, stooping grey-haired man was the personification of everything he had idly imagined Stallybrass to be. It was too absurdly miraculous; it was as if, in fact, the other man had stepped out of his own imagination.

He presently realized that the other man was beginning to look somewhat startled. He tried to disguise what he felt sure must be an inane grin, and asked hastily, "Mr. Stallybrass?"

The little man nodded. "Mr. Theodore Terhune, I presume." Without waiting for confirmation, he went on, "Will you come in?"

Terhune stepped inside. Stallybrass closed the door with deliberate care. "You came by car, I see. Have you left it in the road?" He rightly interpreted his visitor's expression. "No, the road is as invisible from the house as the house is from the road. But your shoes would have been dusty—which they are not—if you had walked. You would not look as cool as you do if you had ridden a bicycle. No bus passes through this district. Therefore, unless I am greatly mistaken, you came here by car."

There was not the vaguest suspicion of humour in the dry, even voice. Nor of patronage. Nor of anything to suggest that he was being personal at the expense of Terhune, whose detective novels were in ever-increasing demand. "You should have driven it up to the house—"

"I was driven here by a friend, who is on her way to Folkestone and will call for me on her way back."

"Good." The exclamation was disinterestedly polite, no more. "Shall we go into the library?" He led the way across the large square hall towards a door at the far side, which he opened; then stood aside for Terhune to enter. "I shall leave you here, if you will excuse me. I have some work in the kitchen to do. I live alone except for a male servant to attend my simple needs. It is his night off. Perhaps you will ring the bell beside the fireplace when you have finished your work, or if you should want me before then."

"Thank you." There seemed nothing more for Terhune to say; Stallybrass did not appear to be a man who would patiently exchange civilities, or waste time in meaningless chatter. He passed into the library and cast a quick, appraising glance about him. He did not hear the door close behind him, or the sound of any movement; but when he turned back to the door it was shut. So, with shining eyes, he approached the nearest bookshelf: his first glance had already assured him that he was a lucky man to have the opportunity of making an offer for the complete library.

2

Time ceased to be of consequence to him as he inspected the crowded bookshelves, and jotted down compendious notes of the more important titles together with the prices he could afford to pay. Some of the expensive titles he examined in closer detail to ascertain the date of the edition, and the overall condition; the cheaper books he accepted on trust—not a particularly risky course, he felt, for it was easy to see that the collection was a well-preserved one, and belonged to a man who was unlikely to be satisfied with spoiled or incomplete books.

In between times, while he paused to refill and light a pipe, he wondered why Stallybrass was selling his library. True, he had announced that he was moving away from the neighbourhood in consequence of having sold the property; but that was no explanation for selling the library as a whole. If it were a case of moving into a smaller house, with less room for books, the likely course would have been to keep the most treasured books and sell the surplus. But no; he had made it perfectly plain to Terhune that no offer would be considered for a part of the library; it would have to be for the entire collection, a condition to which he was only too willing to agree, for his business was continually expanding. Perhaps Stallybrass needed the money, was the next reflection. Or perhaps he was going abroad to live, and did not want the expense and trouble of taking his library with him.

Terhune finished writing his last note with a sigh that was more of regret than relief; where books were concerned his energy was inexhaustible. He glanced idly at his watch, then leapt to his feet with dismay: the time was already ten-forty.

He hurried across to the fireplace and looked for a bell-push. He wasted nearly two minutes before realizing that there was none, and that the purple silken cord which descended from the ceiling was the only bell in the room. This he pulled with an impatient jerk which would have been disastrous to a weak link anywhere. Though he listened carefully he heard no echoing jangle; he was scarcely able to prevent himself from giving the cord another tug just to make sure. Fortunately, he left it alone; the door was opened as quietly as it had been closed; Stallybrass entered the room.

"Have you finished, Mr. Terhune?"

"Just. If you will excuse my hurrying off—my friend promised to meet me at ten-fifteen—"

"Ah! Then indeed you must hurry. You are very nearly thirty minutes late already. You have everything you want?"

"Yes, thanks." Terhune stuffed the mass of notes into his pocket.

"Come along then." Stallybrass's small legs twinkled across the floor. "Thank you for coming here tonight," he flung back over his left shoulder. "But, as I explained to you, tonight is my only free night."

He reached the front door, hastily opened it and waved his hand. "Don't wait on formalities, Mr. Terhune. Good night." Then: "Ah! How unfortunate! Fog!"

Terhune reached the open door and saw the white filmy cloud which clung to the splash of light that was spread, in a small circle about the main entrance of the house, by a lamp which hung from the roof of the portico. His sense of guilt deepened for having kept Julia waiting for so long; waiting in any circumstances irked her, he knew, for she was far from being a patient person; but with fog to add to her misery the thirty minutes' wait must have been particularly depressing.

With a hurried, "Good night, Mr. Stallybrass, I'll telephone you tomorrow morning," Terhune ran down the few stone steps into the slow-drifting fog; but as he reached the fringe of the spreading light from the porch, Stallybrass's voice arrested him.

"Have you a torch, Mr. Terhune?"

He hadn't; and, as he peered into the darkness, he realized that if he were not to keep Julia waiting longer than was necessary, he would need one to help him keep to the drive.

"No," he called back.

"I will lend you one. I have one handy."

Evidently, the old man's statement was literally true; within a matter of seconds the tiny figure was twinkling down the steps and across the gravelled drive.

"It will be easier with this. You can return it at your convenience; I have several. Good night." The little man hurried back into the house as if anxious not to catch cold.

Terhune was soon grateful for the torch; even with its help he was not able to hurry. The fog, which was salty to the taste, had evidently rolled in from the sea; though it did not reduce visibility to nil it restricted one's vision to little more than a matter of yards: Julia was in for an unpleasant drive home, he reflected miserably.

It took him, he estimated, just about double the time to complete the journey to the road that he had taken to cover the same ground earlier on. But there were no reproaches from Julia as he approached the car; only a relieved laugh.

"Don't tell me, my pet, let me guess. You forgot to look at your watch."

"Right first time," he gasped. "I'm terribly sorry, Julie. I should have had more sense—"

"I never look for sense from you once you get sunk in your old books," she jested. Then her voice sharpened. "You are panting, Theo—"

"I've been hurrying. How is the fog?"

"Bad enough. It started coming in from the sea as I left Folkestone. It's been steadily getting worse ever since."

"Isn't it too thick for driving? If so, I'll walk ahead."

"I'll switch on the fog-light." The light, low-slung, spread an orange carpet across the road for a short distance ahead of the car; with its help it was just possible to distinguish the edge of the grass verge.

"I'll just be able to see," she assured him. "As long as it doesn't get worse. I'll probably have to keep in middle gear. Coming, Theo?"

As he passed behind the car in order to take the near-side front seat beside her he heard the throb of a motor exhaust from the direction of Dymchurch.

"Don't move for a few moments," he warned, as he entered the car.

"Why not?"

"There's something coming up behind us: it might be safer to let it get past before we start off."

She laughed softly. "Good! I'll let the other fellow do the work by following his tail-light."

She pressed the self-starter. At first the sound of the engine blotted out the noise of the car behind, but soon afterwards they heard it; simultaneously, they saw, through the rear window, the spreading white glow of approaching headlights.

"Here she comes," he warned, as the glow rounded the corner.

The lights came, but as they approached the gates of *Pennyfields* the hum of the engine slackened.

"Don't say he is going to wait for me to lead *him*!" Julia exclaimed, as her car was enveloped in the white glare cast by the other's headlights.

She received a direct answer before her companion could think one up: the whine of the engine behind rose to a louder key as its driver pressed heavily down upon the accelerator. To the accompaniment of a loud, deep rumble which was possibly accentuated by the fog, the second vehicle thundered by; as it reached the orbit of the orange beam sent out by their own car they saw that it was a closed five-ton lorry.

Julia revved-up and swirled forward on to the crown of the road. But when she peered through the fog for a glimpse of the red tail-light she was unsuccessful. She accelerated slightly; and almost at once found herself in imminent danger of colliding with the lorry. She allowed the car to fall back just enough to keep the vague, uncertain outline of the lorry within the limit of her fog-light.

Then she waxed indignant at the carelessness of the lorry-driver for having no rear light.

"He ought to be reported to the police," she exclaimed, but with no intention of doing so herself. "It would have been so much easier to follow—"

The back of the lorry vanished from sight as it rounded a bend; Julia had to brake hard to avoid driving straight into the far hedge; the car rocked as it swirled round the corner. Her headlights picked up the outline; but only for a matter of seconds: the lorry disappeared again; once more Julia had to pull hard on the steering-wheel to keep the car on the road. The brakes squealed as they skidded round another bend, this time a right-hand one.

"The man must be mad to drive along these roads at speed on a night like this," Terhune exploded.

Julia leaned forward, and peered at the uncertain outline of the lorry. "At any time these roads are not fit for speed." A note of grudging admiration underlined her next words. "He must be very sure of himself."

The speedometer crept slowly upwards. If the lorry-driver's skill was superb, Julia's was scarcely less, although she did have the advantage of seeing the back of the lorry swing out of sight as it rounded a bend or corner, and so had just enough warning not to crash into the verge one side or the other. But even though she was ready to acknowledge the skill of the man in front, she wondered how much longer he would be able to keep up such a reckless speed: in all the many miles of roads which wound inconsequently about the Marsh she doubted where one could find a straight stretch of more than one hundred yards.

"He must know the roads very well," she commented as, in cornering a right-angled bend, the bumpers of her car grazed the off-side hedge.

He grew alarmed for her safety. "Let the swine break his fool neck," he urged. "We can find our own way back."

She laughed with more excitement than he had ever known her betray. "If he can keep it up, my pet, I can."

When the speedometer crept forward another point her expression turned grim, but she managed to keep the lorry within the powerful beam of her fog-light. Because of this they were eye-witnesses of what happened. One of the flaps at the rear opened; and, for a few seconds, they saw an orange-tinted face grimacing at them through the flowing stream of fog which swirled about in the lorry's wake. Then two hands appeared, each holding several objects which they were unable to identify. Something flashed in the orange glow. There was a thunderous report. The car lurched about like a drunken man, mounted the near-side verge and crashed into the thick hedge: the engine spluttered, and faded out. The sound of the lorry's exhaust gradually died away; its deep roar seemed to hum a paean of triumph.

3

The shock left them feeling temporarily stunned and helpless. Terhune was the first to speak.

"Did that man throw a bomb?" he asked in a shaky voice.

"It was a tyre-burst, Theo," she answered unsteadily.

"But I thought I saw him throw something out."

She nodded. "He did. Perhaps it was something made of glass."

"The devil!" He made a snatch for the torch which Stallybrass had lent him, and made a move to leave the car. But he could not open the door more than three or four inches. "We're in the hedge this side, Julie. What about your side?"

Julia's door was similarly unusable; but the rear door opened to its widest extent. So he scrambled over the back of the front seat, and left the car by that door. It did not take long to discover the cause of the accident. Scattered across the width of the road was a quantity of jagged-edged glass; it was a miracle that only one tyre, and not all four, had burst. No sooner had this reflection occurred to him than he realized that he had no reason for being confident that only one had burst. He took a few hurried steps back to the car and shone the torch on all four tyres in turn. He was relieved to find that a miracle had, in fact, occurred: only the front near-side tyre was flat.

He straightened up to the sound of an anxious, "Well?"

"We're lucky; only one tyre caught it."

"Only one?"

"The swine threw out a load of empty bottles."

"Theo! Why?"

"In the hope of causing a burst."

"I don't mean that. Why did they want us to have a burst?"

"My guess is that there were crooks in the lorry who thought we were chasing them. Probably thought this was a police-car."

"They might have killed us."

"They might," he grimly agreed. "Do you remember their number?"

"SKK 164."

"That agrees with what I remember... I shall not forget it in a hurry. But if there were crooks in that lorry, the chances are that it was stolen, or that the registration plates are false. The point is, are we going to get home tonight?"

"I'll get out."

"Try the engine first."

The engine purred as smoothly as ever when Julia pressed the self-starter button: she turned it off again, and got out of the car. Together they surveyed the damage. Julia exclaimed sadly when she saw to what extent the paintwork of both front wings and doors had been scratched by the thick, hawthorn hedge, but beyond that no other damage was visible at first inspection, the strong bumpers having taken the impact of the collision.

Their next consideration was the possibility of shifting the car back on to the road there and then, for there was little hope of a stray car—or a stray person, for that matter—coming to their aid so late, and in the present circumstances Terhune was afraid that there was nothing to be done without a bill-hook to slash a large gap in the hedge, but then he was prejudiced by a desire to see as little further damage done to the car as possible.

Julia, on the other hand, had less scruples; she was convinced that the engine was powerful enough to pull the car back on to the road; and as for damage—what were a few more scratches more or less to the car which, in any event, would have to be re-cellulosed as a consequence of the mishap?

She had her way; and, with the help of his strong arms at the off-side front wheel, the car rolled back on to the road. There they substituted the spare wheel for the one with the burst tyre: once again he felt grateful to Stallybrass for the kindly thought which had prompted the loan of the torch; without it the job would have been exasperating, and probably filthy.

They continued their journey a little shakily, but with a feeling of gratitude to a kindly fate that they were still alive and unhurt. Their speed was in accord with this humility; they crept cautiously along the narrow, winding road—more or less a necessity, this course, with nothing ahead to lead the way. Her unwilling admiration of the lorry-driver's skill and daring increased.

Twisting and turning, they progressed what seemed to them a matter of miles, but which the speedometer registered as less than one. There they entered an even thicker belt of fog. Terhune began to despair of their being able to complete the journey, but Julia's streak of obstinacy refused to let her admit defeat. She reduced speed to a mere crawl; although she had frequently to brake hard and wrench the car round to avoid running into the hedge for a second time, she kept doggedly going.

Suddenly she braked so hard that the car rocked to and fro. Before he could question her she waved a shaky hand in the direction of the road ahead. He had been focusing his eyes for a longer distance; they took time to adjust themselves.

"The devil!" he exclaimed.

Stretched across the road was the body of a policeman.

Chapter Two

T hey scrambled out of the car and ran towards the still body. There was an ominous look of death about the ruddy face; but that might be the uncanny effect of the fog and the orange light, Terhune reflected. He took hold of the limp wrist in the hope of feeling the beat of the pulse; but, as far as he could make out, it was still. But, again, it might be that his own nerves were jumping too much. In spite of having fought in battles, he still had not conquered his distaste of the dead.

He looked up at Julia. "I can't feel anything, Julie…"

She understood the reason for his uncertainty; but, not sharing it, she bent over and placed cool, steady fingers on the other wrist. She soon shook her head.

"He's dead, Theo dear. There is nothing we can do."

They straightened up, and gazed down upon the dead policeman. Terhune pointed to the broad band of dust which traversed the blue chest. "That looks like the mark of a tyre, Julie—a heavy tyre…"

"The lorry?"

"I shouldn't be surprised. The body isn't cold yet."

"The beasts!" After a pause: "What ought we to do? Telephone the police?"

"Yes."

"Murphy?" referring to Detective-Sergeant Murphy, attached to the Ashford Division of the Kent C.I.D.

He nodded. "I think so, though I believe that this district is part of the Hythe area. The point is, where is the nearest telephone?"

They looked at each other. "It might be miles away."

"Do you know whereabouts we are?"

She shrugged. He grimaced. "I thought I knew this road well enough, too. But we can't be a long way from Farthing Toll."

"Shall we drive there?" Even in the uncertain light his expression of hesitation was unmistakable. "Is anything the matter?"

"Everything. If it was the lorry that killed the poor devil, then his death may be no accident, but downright, brutal murder."

"You mean, if the driver had deliberately driven into him after being ordered to stop?"

"Yes."

"What difference does murder or accident make to our driving on to Farthing Toll?"

"In either case the police wouldn't want the body to be moved, but particularly so if it is a case of murder. You can't get the car by without moving the body."

"Oh!" A quick glance assured her that he was right. "Then one of us must stay here."

"I'm not leaving *you* alone with those murdering swine loose in the countryside," he stated firmly. "Nor am I going to let you walk alone to Farthing Toll. Do you mind leaving the car, Julie?"

"Of course not."

"Then we'll take a chance, and both go. I only hope nothing comes along while we are away."

"We can stop anything that is coming this way," she sagely remarked.

As soon as Julia had turned the fog-light off they started out for Farthing Toll, where there was a public call-box outside *Toll Inn*. In fact, they never reached there, for, half a mile on, Terhune recognized presently where they were, and recollected the existence nearby of a farmhouse which was on the telephone.

Julia remonstrated. "They are sure to be asleep, Theo."

"I don't doubt it, but they can't object to being awakened for a call to the police. It will give them something to talk about for the next six months."

They found the five-barred gate which opened into a yard, of which the house formed one side. Directly the gate clicked shut the silence was disturbed by the frantic barking of a watch-dog, tied up at the far end of the yard, which was taken up and echoed by a second dog either inside or tied up on the far side of the house.

"I don't think we shall have to knock on the door to wake the family up," Julia commented.

She was right. They heard the noise of a window being thrown open. Then a gruff voice shouted out: "Who's there? What do you want?"

"To use your telephone, please." A loud growling mutter warned Terhune to hurry on: "There's been an accident just down the road, a policeman has been killed. We want to 'phone the police."

There was a startled gasp in a female voice from inside the room. The male voice bellowed back: "Did you say a policeman, mister? Not poor old Tom Kitchen?"

"I don't know. He's a tall, thin man with a red face and brown hair."

"That's him. He was out on duty tonight. His missus told us so not two hour ago. Poor old Mill! Tom's death will fair upset her; her with two kids and another coming. Stay where you are, mister; I'll be down and let you in."

The barking of the dogs did not cease even when the farmer angrily bellowed at them to "Shurrup, you noisy brutes." There wasn't much fear of this house being burgled, Terhune thought, as he lifted the receiver and dialled O; it wasn't much of a life for a dog, to be chained up day and night; but dog-like both were unstinting in their duty to an unsympathetic master.

Exchange answered him. He asked for the Ashford number with an uneasy feeling that he would be disturbing Murphy's first sleep; he was relieved when the call was almost immediately answered, and he heard Murphy greeting "Hullo" in a voice that was not in the least sleepy.

"Terhune here. Hope I haven't disturbed you from your slumber?"

The sergeant laughed. "Not by ten minutes. I was just having the last fag before turning in." His voice grew businesslike as he realized that a call at that time of night denoted a matter of urgency. "Is there anything I can do for you, sir?"

"I have some bad news for you, Sergeant—official, I mean; not personal. Miss MacMunn and I have just found the body of a policeman on the Dymchurch road. He was run over, I think, but I suspect that there's a complication about the accident which you should investigate."

"What sort of a complication?" the sergeant sharply asked.

Terhune was aware that at least two pairs of ears, possibly more, were listening with morbidly avid interest to everything he said.

"I'm telephoning from a farmhouse half a mile from the scene of the accident. The farmer very kindly offered to let me use his 'phone."

Two and two made four for Murphy. "I understand. Whereabouts is the body?"

"Hold the line a minute." Terhune turned to the farmer, who was standing a few feet away, holding an oil-lamp. "The police want to know the name of this farm."

"Appletree Farm. Tell them John Summers's place. Everybody knows me."

"About half a mile south-east of Appletree Farm, John Summers's place," Terhune passed on.

"Then it's a matter for the Hythe people to take up. I'll get on to them."

"Will you be coming out here yourself?"

"Do you think I ought to?"

The eagerness in Murphy's voice made Terhune chuckle. "If it's permissible. There may be a tie-up with Ashford."

"That's good enough for me. I'll get on to the Super."

"By the way, there's a thick mist down here. Visibility practically nil."

"Is there? It's almost clear here. Thanks for 'phoning me. See you later."

Having expressed their apologies to the excited farmer for disturbing the family's sleep, Julia and Terhune left. A few moments before the full-throated barking had at last died away to an uneasy growling, but Terhune's voice, as he called out good night, roused the dogs to a renewed frenzy, which continued for as long as the echo of their footsteps was within the hearing of the dogs.

Terhune chuckled. "I don't think a thief would stand much chance of stealing anything from here. What a racket! I'll bet it can be heard from the next farm."

Julia's thoughts were elsewhere. "I'm glad Mother is away."

"Why?"

"I also should have had to ask Mr. Summers for the use of his 'phone."

"Which would have supplied a spicy tit-bit of gossip for the village... 'Would you believe it, my dear, but that *nice* Miss MacMunn—you know, the daughter of the Hon. Mrs. MacMunn what lives at Willingham Manor—telephoned to her mother *at nearly midnight* to say she was out with a young man and wouldn't be back for *ever so many hours*'!"

She laughed, but made no comment; for her original remark had been prompted by a reflection that had progressed along somewhat similar, though less racy, lines. She had lived all her life in the country, and knew that gossip, not necessarily malicious, was the breath of life to anyone, male or female, whose existence was circumscribed within the restricted limits of farm or village life.

They arrived back at the car, to find everything as they had left it. With a hasty glance at the body they turned towards the door.

"We may as well sit inside," he suggested. "You needn't turn on any more lights until the police arrive."

She nodded, entered the car, and relaxed in the driving-seat. He sat next to her. In silence they lit cigarettes and gazed out of the side windows or down at their feet: anywhere but ahead of them where the body lay: although it was cloaked by darkness and fog, and not visible, their imaginations were vivid enough to picture the crushed, bruised body as they had last seen it, and the sensation was not a pleasant one. So they maintained a silence which made the night even more eerie and mysterious; almost frightening.

Outside the car there was noise of a kind. From the direction of the sea came the mournful wail of a buoy's fog-horn: from a nearby copse the harsh shriek of an owl: from the hedge, nearby, the rustle of a disturbed animal; a rabbit, perhaps. But, apart from these sounds, the quietness was oppressive, even ominous: they experienced the strange sensation of being isolated in a damp, small world of their own.

"How can men be so horribly coldblooded?" she asked, in a strained voice which warned him that she was talking for the sake of talking.

He did not believe that she really wanted an answer to her question; in any event, he could not think of an intelligent answer. He did not know.

"Try not to think about the matter, old girl," he urged gently. "The risk of violent death is one which every bobby takes when he joins the force. I don't say that many die in the course of a year—not a fraction of the number of coal miners who are killed in the mines—but it's a chance he takes—"

"What about his wife, Theo? And the two children—a third on the way…" There was a catch in her voice which surprised him; occasions when she was emotionally disturbed were extremely rare; normally, she was so annoyingly self-possessed.

He did not know what to say—to think too much about the tragedy gave him a squeamish feeling inside, he found. An awkward silence followed; but fortunately it was not of long duration. He heard faintly the distant throb of an automobile engine.

"A car is coming, Julie. You'd better turn on the fog-lamp."

She did so, listening. "Which way is it coming?"

He tried to identify the direction, but the distorting effects of the fog made this difficult; the sound seemed to vary from east to west.

"I think it's coming from Ashford, but I couldn't swear."

All the same, he was right. As the noise of the engine grew slowly louder it became certain that it was coming from the north-west. At last, after an infuriating interval, they saw a white curtain approach and round the bend in front of them; presently, they were able to distinguish two round discs of light; but no more, for the other car stopped some distance short of the body. Then the vague figure of a man emerged from the white curtain, moved towards the dead policeman, stood there for a few seconds, then carried on in the direction of Julia's car.

"Hullo, there!"

Although conditions made recognition of the face impossible, the voice was unmistakable.

"We're in the car, Sergeant," Terhune called back. "I'll join you."

Murphy approached the off-side door. "Good evening, Miss MacMunn." His tone was sombre. "A nasty business, this. Poor devil!" As Terhune joined him: "Good evening, sir. I telephoned Hythe Division: they are probably on their way here. I also spoke to the Super. In view of what you said he agreed that it might be as well if I came along." There was an enquiry in his voice.

"I have an idea that the death of Tom Kitchen wasn't accidental."

"Glory be! And how are ye after knowing his name already?"

The comic note of surprise in the sergeant's voice made Terhune grin. "I haven't been anticipating the police—"

Murphy hastily interrupted. "You don't need to be telling me that, sir," he denied with warm friendliness. "But I've niver come across such a man for finding corpses. Niver at all, at all. If I didn't know you so well I'd say that you spent your time looking for 'em."

As well the sergeant might, for this was now the fourth occasion on which Terhune had come across the body of a murdered man; either by mere chance, or, as in the case of the disappearance of Andrés Salvaterra from the House with Crooked Walls, as a consequence of intelligent anticipation.

"Farmer Summers gave me his name directly I told him that a policeman had been killed just down the road—at least, my description apparently fitted."

"I forget sometimes that everyone knows everyone else in the country, even the local bobby," the sergeant commented. "That's what comes of having lived and worked in towns all me life. But what makes you think that Kitchen's death wasn't accidental? It looks as if he was run over: there's a tyre mark across the poor devil's chest."

"Run down might be a more correct description than run over, Sergeant. And what makes me suspicious of his death is the fact that the driver of the lorry which I think ran him down damn' near killed Miss MacMunn and myself."

"What's that?"

It was reassuring to hear the sharp note of interest in the sergeant's voice: it reminded Terhune of a terrier's bark as it first sights a rabbit. Without further delay he gave the detective a full account of all that had happened from the time he had left Stallybrass. As usual, Murphy proved himself a good listener: not once did he interrupt the story.

When at last he did speak it was to ask, "Did you do anything about the rest of the broken glass, Mr. Terhune?"

"Swept it, as best we could with a folded newspaper, into the ditch."

"Do you think you could find it again?"

"You mean tonight?"

"If you have time, and think there is a chance." Murphy's voice was apologetic.

"If Miss MacMunn is willing—"

"Of course!" she interrupted. "The man who killed that poor fellow deserves to hang. If there is anything I can do, Mr. Murphy—anything—"

"We have only to find the break in the hedge where the car crashed in," Terhune went on quickly, to cover up Julia's distress. "The glass should be nearly opposite. Do you think it might afford a clue, Sergeant?"

"Who knows? What kind of bottles were they? Beer—spirit— vinegar, for instance?"

"I didn't trouble to take any notice."

"It doesn't matter much. But many bottles have a label with the local seller's name printed on it as well as the brand label. How far back from here would you say the bottles were thrown out?"

"About a mile, I'd say."

"We'll go there after the Hythe people have arrived."

Some minutes later two cars arrived from the direction of Dymchurch. Three men stepped into the area of light.

"Hullo, Murphy," hailed one of them. "I was told you would probably be here." He looked down at the corpse. "Poor old Tom Kitchen! One of the keenest men we've ever had on a rural beat. Wait till I catch the—" He hurriedly swallowed the word as he caught sight of Julia. "The swine who ran into him." He half turned to the man who stood on his left. "This is Doctor Anderson—Detective-Sergeant Murphy, of the Ashford Division."

Anderson and Murphy shook hands. Then the doctor knelt on one knee to examine the body. While he did so Murphy introduced Julia and Terhune to Detective-Sergeant Raines from Hythe.

"Have you met Mr. Terhune before, Raines? If not, you've heard of him."

"The Mr. Terhune from Bray-in-the-Marsh?"

"The same."

The pressure of Raines's hand increased. "It's a pleasure to have the opportunity of meeting you, sir," he warmly declared. "Every policeman in Kent has heard of your name, if you don't mind me saying so." His manner turned brisk. "Am I to understand that you being here means there is more to this business than meets the eye?"

Murphy answered for Terhune. "Mr. Terhune found the body."

"I see." This with a suspicion of disappointment.

"But Mr. Terhune thinks there is, for all that." Raines picked up. "Why?" he snapped.

"A short time before he came across Kitchen here, some men in a lorry, which Miss MacMunn had been following to make for easier driving through the fog, emptied some empty bottles out on to the road to give them a burst."

"And did they?"

"What do you think? It's lucky they are still alive. Luckily for them the glass only pierced one tyre."

Raines glanced quickly at Julia's car. "They must've thought a police-car was following 'em. That put the wind up 'em for a start; so when they saw Kitchen they thought they were in some sort of a trap and deliberately ran him over. Is that the idea?"

"It's Mr. Terhune's. And mine also, for that matter."

Terhune turned to the man from Hythe. "There's one point which puzzles me, Sergeant. Had you a general warning out for a lorry of any kind?"

"Not that I've heard of. Had you heard of one, Day?" Raines spoke to the third man, who, all this time, had been standing close by.

"No."

"Why did you ask, sir?" Raines questioned Terhune.

"Judging by the present position of the body, Kitchen must have been standing roughly in the middle of the road when the lorry struck him. I was wondering why. Unless he was waving to the lorry to stop, so that he could ask for a lift home."

"I don't think that's likely. It's less than a mile to his home from here. Besides, what about his bicycle? Speaking of that—have a look about for it, Day. Have you a torch?"

Day had: he moved off towards the near-side hedge. As he did so the doctor stood up.

"Death was instantaneous, Sergeant."

"And the cause—a motor vehicle passing over his body?"

"In non-technical language, yes."

"Thanks, Doctor. I'll take what photographs I can in this light, then you had better let the ambulance take you back; Day and I will probably be here some time."

Anderson nodded agreement, so Raines went back to his car and presently returned with the necessary apparatus for taking photographs. As soon as he had exposed six plates, and taken a series of measurements, he shouted for 'Thomson'. Thomson and a companion soon appeared, carrying a stretcher. They and the doctor transferred the body into an ambulance that was hidden by the fog; the others heard the sound of the car's engine being started, the whine of gears, the slow fading away of the exhaust.

Day came back into the aura of light, wheeling a perfectly sound bicycle.

Chapter Three

"Where did you find it?"

With a nod P.C. Day indicated the far side of the road. "Just inside the field, leaning up against the hedge."

"Inside!" Murphy's sharp exclamation was one of surprise. "Then he must have been waiting about in this neighbourhood for some time."

There was a query in his voice that his fellow sergeant was quick to answer. "I've heard of nothing, Murphy. But Kitchen was a keen man, as I told you just now. I worked with him on that bungalow affair eighteen months ago. Although he didn't say so in actual words, it struck me then that his ambition was to get into the C.I.D. I should say that if he was on to something he would have kept it to himself as long as possible, in the hope of getting the credit. Don't blame him, poor devil."

"You may find some notes in his book."

"I'll look when I get back." Raines gazed about him with keen eyes. "The point is, what was he doing in the middle of the road? The obvious answer is—he was waving to the lorry-driver to stop. Why? He couldn't have known that the man was a wrong 'un: he wouldn't have been able to see the lorry's registration number; and I very much doubt whether he would have been able to distinguish anything about it to recognize even if, for argument's sake, he had been on the look-out for it. At the moment it looks as if coincidence killed him: it was his damn' bad luck that the men in the lorry thought that a police car was chasing them, and seeing him, put two and two together and made five of it. What do you say, Murphy?"

Murphy shook his head in doubt. "I don't put much faith in coincidences—"

"What about the Stake House burglary?"

"Yes, I know. I could mention others. But if it was just coincidence that made Kitchen try to stop the lorry Mr. Terhune had been following, there is still the question you asked just now: why did he want to stop a lorry—or any other vehicle, for that matter?"

A thought occurred to Terhune. "Do you think he wanted to warn the driver that he was driving dangerously? Which he was, on this road and in this fog. He might even have had the intention of charging the man. He was a keen man—"

Raines gestured a denial. "He wouldn't have had enough evidence to support a charge. But there might be something in your warning idea."

"That still doesn't explain why he left his bicycle *behind* the hedge," Murphy pointed out.

There was a long pause during which everyone waited for someone else to put forward other suggestions. When nobody did so Murphy went on: "If there's nothing more to be done here I suggest that we try to find the remains of the broken bottles which Mr. Terhune swept into the ditch. I was telling him, Raines, that if any of the bottles have labels on we might find a clue from them where they've come from."

"Good idea. There's a gateway a few yards down the road where you can reverse, Mr. Terhune."

The fog made the job of reversing a tricky one, for there was little room to spare, and bends in the road to cope with. But with the help of the rest to shout directions to the driver, first Day backed and reversed the police-car, then Julia did the same with hers. As soon as she had done so Raines invited her to lead the way. With Julia leading, the Hythe police car following, and Murphy bringing up the rear, the three cars proceeded slowly in the direction of Dymchurch. Julia kept to the wrong side of the road so that the headlights of her car could pick out the details of the hedge on that side; Terhune watched ahead for oncoming traffic.

They were actually passing the spot where they had smashed into the hedge before Julia recognized it. By the time she had brought the car to a gentle stop they were well past it. The two following cars stopped; their occupants joined Julia and Terhune. He led the way to where he had swept the glass into the ditch, and found the place without too much difficulty. While he and Julia held torches the two detectives knelt down, and began to examine each jagged piece of glass with eager interest. Their hopes were soon disappointed. Piece after piece was devoid of label of any sort: Raines picked up the last piece with a muttered 'Damn!', smelled it as he had smelled the rest, and stood up.

"If you ask my opinion, Murphy, the men had prepared these bottles ready for chucking out in a case of emergency. To judge by the lack of smell every one of 'em has had the label washed off. Somebody was wise to the danger of leaving a clue behind."

Murphy nodded. "All the more proof, if we need it, that professional crooks were in the lorry. They even took care to use every kind of bottle there is, from Gordon's Gin to an ordinary beer bottle."

"Sure. I don't think there's much doubt about crooks being behind all this business." Raines shrugged his disappointment. "That's that! There's nothing much more to be done tonight. Tomorrow we'll check up on the number you gave us, Mr. Terhune; ten to one it's a false plate, though. Thanks for all your help. Sorry to have kept you up so late. Now we shall have to find a place where you can reverse again."

They all walked back to their respective cars. As Terhune opened the off-side door his toe touched something on the road which tinkled musically. He shone the light of his torch down and saw the bottom half of a bottle which had apparently escaped his previous sweeping. He picked it up, for it was a menace to any self-respecting tyre; but as he turned to carry it to the ditch on the other side of the road he grew aware of the fact that the inside of the dark brown bottle was moist, and emitted a pungent odour that was vaguely familiar to him. He raised the piece of bottle to his nose; after a second or two he recognized the smell as that of rum.

"Sergeant."

Murphy's voice came from behind the dark curtain of fog. "Yes, sir."

"I have just found something."

Raines as well as Murphy joined Terhune. Murphy took the half of the bottle and smelled. He recognized the liquor immediately. "Rum," he confirmed, but the word was all but drowned by an excited exclamation from Raines.

"A piece of a label, Murphy!" He flashed his own torch on to the side of the bottle which was farthest from Murphy's nose. There was not much printing to be seen, for the portion of label was very small; what there was of it was torn and grimy. "R—H—U—" he spelled out. "Underneath that N—E—G—R—The rest is torn off. What's *rhu* and *negr* stand for? They aren't parts of any word I've ever heard of—they can't be—"

But they were for Terhune. "It's R-H-U-M N-E-G-R-I-T-A," he finished off. "R*hum* is the French word for rum; Negrita, the name of the maker."

"A French rum!" Raines repeated with indignation. "Can't we damn' well import enough rum from our own West Indies without buying from France?"

Enlightenment spread across Murphy's face. "The divil!" he exclaimed.

"What's up?" Raines demanded.

Murphy's reply was short, and to the point.

"Smugglers!" he answered.

2

Raines snapped his fingers. "You may be right, Murphy. If that lorry was filled with smuggled goods you can bet your sweet life that the men in it weren't going to be chased by a police car if they could do anything about it. Nor were they likely to stop at the first wave of a village bobby's hand."

Murphy turned to Terhune. "It's no secret that smuggling came back into fashion with the world shortage of goods, and the existence of black markets: the newspapers have been running accounts of the smuggling business for months past, drat them! Strictly between ourselves, sir, they are not so wide of the mark as they often are. There's a divil of a lot of smuggling going on; especially in the Marsh here; it's always been a smugglers' paradise. We've been on the watch for months; we've captured a few consignments, and made a few arrests; but we've only landed the little fellows—the amateurs—so far: you know, ex-naval types and the like who can't settle down to a decent way of life because it's dull and monotonous. The trouble is, there are some big fellows in the game as well, and they've organized the racket, the same as they're organizing all crime these days."

Terhune knew Murphy too well to suspect him of exaggeration; but, on this occasion, his explanation failed to convince.

"Would there be enough money in smuggling rum to satisfy the big fellows, Sergeant? Wouldn't they be more likely to smuggle stuff with less bulk and of greater value?"

"I'm not suggesting that they are specifically smuggling rum. What I think happened is that one of the smugglers bought a bottle of rum to drink on the way across, and having emptied it, chucked it among the other empty bottles without thinking."

"I wouldn't say that they weren't bringing in bottled stuff, Murphy," Raines argued. "They wouldn't have wanted a thundering great lorry just to run nylons."

"Is it true that smugglers are using landing-craft to bring the stuff in?" Terhune asked.

"They are using every method known to smugglers, and then some. We have reason for believing that landing-craft are being used. Why?"

"I think there is something in what Sergeant Raines says, Murphy. If the smugglers are using L.C.s as well as five-ton lorries to make their runs they don't have to worry about bulk."

"Perhaps not." Murphy sounded disappointed. "For one moment I had had hopes that the presumed tie-up between the lorry and the gang of smugglers might supply a lead. But it doesn't."

"On the contrary," Raines added. "If the run was organized by our big fellows, the chances of laying hands on the driver of that lorry are pretty slim. Your hunch about coming down here tonight was a good one, Murphy. I have one that nearly every Division in the county will become involved before long. I suppose you'll make a check on whether the lorry was seen passing through Ashford?"

"Sure."

"Meanwhile, I'll get in touch with Maidstone." Raines turned to Terhune. "Thanks, sir, for the second time. Murphy says you're his lucky mascot: I'm beginning to think he is right. Good night." With a friendly wave of his hand he disappeared into the fog.

3

The rest of the journey home was very quiet. Julia seemed disinclined to talk; but whether on account of tiredness, or because of the sombre events of the past hour, Terhune could not decide. Perhaps both reasons applied, he reflected. Whatever the cause, he was glad of the opportunity to ponder on the death of P.C. Kitchen.

He could not remember any crime which had shocked him more, both for its meanness and for its brutality. He could not believe that the smugglers—if they were smugglers, of course—had really found it necessary to kill the constable. Surely, if the driver had sounded his horn in warning of his intention to drive straight on, Kitchen would not have been fool enough to stand his ground? He must have believed that the lorry intended to stop. Was it possible that the driver had pretended to stop; and then, when it was too late for the policeman to jump out of the way, that he had accelerated and deliberately charged the unsuspecting victim?

The thought disturbed him; caused a nasty feeling in his stomach. But he was honest enough to admit that this was not entirely on account of the way the policeman had been killed.

Mingled with his natural horror at such a brutal crime was a vague disappointment that, as such, it would be essentially and wholly a police affair. There was no place in this crime for his assistance; no likelihood of his expert knowledge of books being called in. No doubt Murphy would keep in touch with him—the sergeant was a sport in that way—and would probably keep him acquainted, within reason, with the progress of investigations. But that was not like having a personal connection with a crime; second-hand, it lacked the morbid fascination which is so often associated with a man-hunt.

Not for the first time did this feeling of regret torment him. He had tried previously to shame himself from dwelling upon that particular aspect of investigation, but he had failed; chiefly because he had the disconcerting habit of being honest with himself.

In its own way, the thrill of investigating a case of murder was comparable, he had decided, with the writing and selling of a book. To be faced with a blank page one of a new book could be almost as disheartening as the beginning of a new investigation—the frantic groping for the opening paragraphs was no less fatiguing than the anxious hunt for the first clue: the satisfaction of finishing the first two or three vital chapters no less acute than the establishing of a definite trail to follow up: the gradual building-up of plot, atmosphere, characters, no less exciting than the slow building-up of evidence against the unknown criminal: the completion of the final chapter no less soul-satisfying than the knowledge of a duty well done in the bringing to the bar of justice the robber of another man's precious life.

That there were exceptions to this generalization he was well aware. Even if Murphy had not told him of such cases, he was intelligent enough to realize that circumstances could—and did—often arise when a policeman, plain-clothed or uniformed, was compelled to do his duty with a sad heart; in cases, for instance, where the criminal had been tempted beyond reasonable limits, into the execution of a crime which, in happier circumstances, he would never have contemplated.

But, in the case of Kitchen's death, it did not seem likely that any mitigating circumstances could possibly exist. Passion, starvation, desperation—none of the usual emotions appeared to have any place in the crime: the heartless running-down of an innocent, helpless police constable seemed to constitute as beastly a crime as any he had heard of; even if no secondary motive of fascination had existed he would have been glad to help in bringing about the arrest of the evil man who had killed P.C. Kitchen.

After a tiring three miles the road began to ascend; gradually, the hedge on the left was more clearly outlined, then the road ahead, and lastly the opposite side of the road. As they neared Willingham the last vestige of fog disappeared. At the Wickford crossroads Julia, who would have had to turn right for Willingham, where she lived, turned left for Bray, in spite of all his remonstrances and his plea that he could easily walk the odd mile or two to Market Square. She merely trod more firmly on the accelerator. A few minutes later she left him outside the door of the flat in which he lived above the business, bade him an unusually sombre good night, and left—with a roaring exhaust which was not likely to find favour with his neighbours, he guiltily reflected.

He wasted little time in getting into bed, for he felt more than usually tired. He had spent most of the evening poring over books; and, of course, the hour was extremely late—or early, according to which way one cared to regard the hour of 2.10 a.m. But what had tired him mostly had been the constant staring at the white blanket of fog.

In spite of all these reasons for dropping off to sleep as soon as his head touched the pillow, to his extreme annoyance he found himself restless from overtiredness. He turned, and turned again; he straightened up one moment, curled himself double the next; but he could not fall asleep. The gruesome picture of a limp, blue-uniformed body spreadeagled across the road shimmered before his eyes. Death could be damnably ugly, he thought. He had written of death several times in his books; but not one of his fictional murders had been as ugly in its callousness as the real one which had taken place on the Dymchurch road an hour or so ago. The longing to do something to help in the arrest of the slayer was too intense to let a man sleep, he reflected ruefully.

4

Terhune eagerly awaited news of the crime, but three days passed without a word from Murphy. He looked through several newspapers, but only two of the three London evening newspapers mentioned the death of the police constable, and then only in short paragraphs which conveyed no suggestion of its having been other than an accident. The B.B.C. broadcast a request from the police for the driver of the lorry, or anyone else who had witnessed the accident, please to report by telephone to the Chief Constable at Maidstone. He concluded that the police were wisely keeping a secret the possibility that death had been due to the deliberate intent to knock the policeman down.

On the afternoon of the fourth day following the death Murphy telephoned to say that he would be along that evening. He duly appeared, a few minutes before nine. He looked tired so Terhune concluded that Kitchen's death had been keeping him busy. This was only partly true, as he soon revealed.

"Something must have been wrong with the weather the night P.C. Kitchen died. At any rate, something seems to have affected a lot of people living hereabouts. As well as Kitchen's death there was a burglary at Ashford, an attempted rape at Hothfield, and a car smash on the Folkestone road just this side of Ashford. Incidentally, there's more than a suspicion that the car smash was caused indirectly by a lorry, which may or may not have been the one that killed Kitchen.

"Unfortunately, the only person who could have given us any reliable information on that point was the driver of the car which caused the accident—he turned off the main road without slowing up, without any warning, on the wrong side of the road, and ran smack into another car that was just slowing up to turn into the main road. Unfortunately, the first driver was so tight that his evidence can't be relied on."

"What makes you think that the lorry was concerned?"

"Because the first driver swears that he turned into the side road to avoid an accident. According to his story, he was leaving Ashford after visiting friends when he saw a huge animal with a pair of glaring eyes come round a corner and charge straight for him, roaring like thunder. So, frightened out of his life, he says, he swung round the corner into a side road in an effort to escape. The eyes could have been headlights; the thunder, a car horn—it might have been that the lorry-driver saw that the car was being steered all over the place, and sounded his horn in warning. Anyway, the driver of the second car thinks he saw something on the large size pass along the main road; but he can't be sure because he was so busy trying to avoid the first car. The time element is why we think that the lorry was the one we are after. It could have been in the neighbourhood of the accident roughly about that time."

"What about Kitchen's death?"

A troubled frown made Murphy's weariness more pronounced. "Except for the accident I've just been talking about, we've not a clue to work on... we checked on the registration number, of course, but it was false. I was talking on the 'phone to Raines just before coming along to you; they are stumped good and proper. They carried out tests to see whether the death could have been accidental, but everything points to the fact that it wasn't."

"Do you think the stuff had been landed that night—assuming that there were smuggled goods in the lorry—or was it being conveyed from one hiding-place to another?"

The disconsolate twitch of the sergeant's mouth forecast the reply. "We just don't know what to think, sir. On the one hand, there has been nothing reported by anyone to make us think that any unauthorized vessel approached our shores; no ditto at sea was sighted by any local coastguard, or by the special coastguard patrol vessel. Nor has any ship reported having seen one, although there is no special reason why any report should have been made."

"You haven't asked for one, then? Mightn't it be worth while to do so?"

"You mean, by radio?"

"Yes."

Murphy shook his head. "The smugglers might pick the message up which would put them on their guard."

"They must realize that you are aware of what they are doing: the newspapers have said as much."

"Perhaps," Murphy agreed doubtfully. "But the Chief Constable has ruled against any broadcast message to ships at sea. As regards your question about whether there was a run the other night, there is the fog to remember. Provided the crew were willing to take a chance of a collision, the fog might have been used as a cloak to cover up the ship's movements: it could have come in with the fog, and gone again, without anyone else being wiser. The tide was about right, too."

"The swine aren't going to get away with killing Kitchen, Sergeant?"

Murphy shrugged. "Every man in the force is on tip-toe to get the people who were in the lorry that night, sir; but the problem of hit-and-run drivers is the hardest problem we have to tackle. Unless they leave part of their own vehicle behind, or are unlucky enough to have a crash in front of witnesses, half the time there's no trail for us to follow. Suppose you had been the ones to hit Kitchen, suppose you kept your mouths shut, the two of you—how do you suppose we should ever have caught up with you?"

"Mr. Stallybrass might have read about the accident, and have reported to you that I left his house in a car a short while before it happened."

"That's true, and so he might have—though most of us don't get in touch with the police because we are so sure that our friends wouldn't be such bad drivers; or, even if we were, that we would be sure to get in touch with the police in the case of an accident." Murphy shook his head. "Take it from me, sir, that we don't get much help from the general public in hit-and-run cases. No, the only clue we have, apart from what you already know, is of the negative kind. We have good reason for believing that the lorry did not enter or pass through Maidstone."

"Could that mean that the stuff might have been delivered in Ashford?"

"It could, but I don't think so. Personally, I think it is hidden in some place between Ashford and Maidstone, waiting the next stage of the journey to London; probably in small lots."

"Then there doesn't seem to be much hope of tracing the lorry?"

"Not unless a miracle happens," Murphy gloomily replied.

Chapter Four

L ocal interest in the death of the police constable was not long maintained. The verdict of the inquest was reported in the local press,
but not anywhere else—accidental death in the course of duty was far
too prosaic to earn valuable space in any of the national newspapers.
Only people who personally knew the unfortunate man experienced
more than a fleeting emotion—after all, anyone was liable to die on
the roads in these days, so there was nothing particularly sensational
or heroic in the passing of P.C. Kitchen.

In the days which followed Murphy's call, Terhune heard nothing
more from the sergeant—one case, he knew, in which no news was not
good news; for he needed no assurances that the police were keeping up
an intensive campaign to identify and interrogate the driver of the lorry.
Nor did anyone else ever mention the matter to him, except Julia. She
did no more than ask if he had heard any more from Murphy; when she
was told that he had not, she quickly changed the conversation—but
not before he had seen bitter disappointment in her dark brown eyes.

One day a woman entered Terhune's shop in Market Square. The
pallor of her drawn face was intensified by the black hat and black
overcoat which she wore over a dark brown dress. She clutched a child
in either hand; a boy and a girl, neither being more than six years of
age. Once inside the door, she gazed about her with an awed, rather
indeterminate air. When she caught sight of Terhune sitting at his desk
in the far corner she seemed to grow still more timid: she half turned
towards the door as if to leave again before completing her business. At

that moment Anne Quilter—Terhune's young assistant—approached her. A rather lengthy conversation followed, which ended by Anne's moving across the shop to Terhune's desk.

"There is a woman here who insists upon seeing you, Mr. Terhune. About some books, she says. She won't let me deal with her. I told her that you were very busy…" Anne was apologetic.

Terhune grinned. It did not often happen that anyone got the better of Anne: she was so very efficient. And, on this occasion, he was genuinely busy. Still, he was too good-natured to refuse anyone a personal interview—a few minutes wasted would not make very much difference to his work.

"What is her name?"

Anne's pink-and-white face expressed indignation. "I asked her. She wouldn't tell me."

He frowned: he always felt suspicious of people who refused to give a name. He felt inclined to tell Anne that he would not speak to the woman until she gave her name. Then it occurred to him that, if she were there with ill-intent, she would probably have been prepared to give a false name.

"All right. Send her over."

Anne went back to the woman. After some more conversation the stranger reluctantly moved across to his desk, dragging two equally reluctant children with her. He rose, and offered her the spare chair which stood beside the desk. As she nervously sat down he saw that she was probably not quite so old as he had believed her to be—just about on the right side of thirty, he estimated.

He tried to put her at ease. "You wish to speak to me?"

She swallowed. "Yes, sir, if you please, sir." She came to a stop.

"Well?"

"Some'un was telling me yesterday as how you buy books from people as want to sell them, sir."

"Yes." After a pause, to encourage her, "You have some you wish to sell?" He saw how sad were her eyes. "You have them with you?" he asked, glancing down at the string bag which the older of the two children carried.

She shook her head. "They aren't mine in a manner of speaking, sir. They was my husband's." Her eyes filled with tears. "He was quite a one with books, was my Tom. Fair loved 'em he did, sir, and wouldn't let nobody set 'ands upon 'em but himself. Once a month, reg'lar-like, he took 'em off the shelves, dusted 'em and put 'em back again. Wouldn't let neither of the children touch any on 'em to save his life, he wouldn't, though he would read to 'em by the hour, poor dear."

There was tragedy in her eyes, her voice, her black coat and hat. "Your husband—"

"He's dead." Her lips quivered. "Now he ain't got no more use for 'em, and I needs money bad, for to keep a roof over our heads while I finds work. Me pension which I'm going to get, won't go far with three kids to feed…"

She gazed at the children with such obvious distress, he began to feel suspicious that she was acting a part in order to get a better price for the books by appealing to his sympathy—it was an old trick which he had had twice played upon him.

"My assistant tells me you refuse to give your name," he began sternly.

She forestalled what he was about to say. "Not to you, sir," she denied eagerly. "Not if you promise not to tell nobody I'm selling poor old Tom's books."

An unconvincing excuse, he thought. "Why shouldn't anyone know?"

"You see, sir, I've allus used to boast as how my poor Tom were a fair one with saving his money. 'Tweren't true, but it didn't do nobody no harm me saying so. It used to make him feel good and important, which was good for 'is work, him being a policeman. But now I don't want any of 'is friends to know, now he's gorn—"

The word 'policeman' supplied a clue to the mystery of her identity.

"Are you Mrs. Kitchen?"

"Yes, sir. It was me poor dear husband what you found dead in the road last week."

He started. Neither he nor Julia had mentioned their gruesome find to anyone; he was quite sure that the police had not done so.

"How do you know I found the body?" he demanded.

The question seemed to astonish her. "But everybody knows it. John Summers heard what you said on the telephone to the police."

"Of course." Inward amusement at his own slow-wittedness quickly vanished at the thought of her sorrow.

"I'll make a point of calling in to see the books as soon as I can," he promised. "And when I take them away it shall be at night so that nobody can see what is happening."

"Thank you, sir," she said in a dull voice. "Will you be coming soon?"

"Before the end of the week." A thought struck him. "If a pound or two on account would be of use to you, Mrs. Kitchen—"

She shook her head. Quickly, perhaps with pride. "I have enough to go on with." Her flat voice tailed off; instead of moving, as he had expected, she sat still and stared at the pile of books which stood on the corner of his desk. Her infants apparently shared Terhune's impression that silence denoted an early move on her part, for first one and then the other began impatiently to tug at her arms.

She shook them both. "Be quiet, you little fidgets," she snapped. "Can't you see I'm busy with this gentleman?"

This was his cue. "Is there something else, Mrs. Kitchen?"

She looked embarrassed, nervous. She opened her mouth to speak, closed it, then tried again.

"I was wondering, sir, if you wasn't to pay me nothing for poor Tom's books, whether you would do something for me instead." She galloped on, stammering. "I know it ain't right to ask such a thing, sir, and I wouldn't take the liberty if it weren't for what happened to my Tom." Her dull eyes unexpectedly blazed with determination; her flabby lower lip turned rigid. "But I don't care what I does to see that them what killed him is punished. Even if me and the kids have to starve afterwards."

Her obvious sincerity offset any hint of the theatrical in her manner; in any case, he was too surprised to be critical. He could not imagine what could be the meaning of her strange outburst.

"What do you want me to do?"

"Help to catch them what killed my poor Tom."

"Good lord!"

She thought she detected criticism in his astonished exclamation. "It's true that you're a detective, ain't it, sir?" she appealed. "Tom used to talk a lot about you. He says it was practically you what caught Charles Cockburn what killed that sailor man in Windmill Woods, and also that there foreigner what did in Mr. Harrison of *Twelve Chimneys*." She would not let him interrupt. "Everybody talks about what a fine 'tec you are, sir: they says as how you ought to be in the police force instead of selling books. If you'll help to catch them what murdered Tom I'll give you every one of 'is books, and if that ain't enough I'll sell the furniture. Please say you'll help, sir. Please."

It was pitiful to hear her agony; but he was scarcely conscious of it: the whole of his attention had been attracted by one word of her impassioned plea—the word *murdered*.

"Murdered, Mrs. Kitchen! The verdict of the coroner's inquest was accidental death," he pointed out in a sharp voice.

A look of sullen contempt forecast her answer. "Them coroners never can see what lies beyond the tips of their noses. It didn't make sense, my poor Tom just standing still in the middle of the road waiting to be run over. He would have seen the lorry coming in plenty of time for him to jump out of the way, wouldn't he? Even if somebody had switched off its lights, he would have 'eard it getting too close to him for comfort."

There was a sly uneasiness in her eyes which convinced him that she was still concealing something from him.

"He might have been signalling to the driver to stop but wasn't seen until it was too late."

"I don't doubt he was signalling to the driver," she agreed. "But the man saw Tom right enough and ran 'im over purposeful to close his mouth."

It seemed that he would have to wheedle information from her in spite of her plea for his assistance. He assumed an air of scepticism.

"You mustn't allow your grief to make you morbid, Mrs. Kitchen. There could have been no reason for the lorry-driver to close your husband's mouth."

"That's just where you're wrong, sir," she denied with a snap. "I happen to know that Tom were on to something big—something to do with lorries, too—" She paused abruptly, as if realizing she had said more than she intended. Then she looked about her with eyes which only lost their look of fright when she saw nobody else in the shop save Anne Quilter; and she was too far away to have heard anything.

"Go on," he urged. "You were saying—"

"More'n I ought, unless I want to go the same way as Tom."

"Come, come!" he remonstrated. "I am sure you are exaggerating."

"Maybe I am, but I can't be sure of that—especially after what happened last night."

"What happened?"

The fear in her eyes increased. "It wasn't nothing to speak about, sir—just footsteps—but it ain't usual to hear footsteps at the back at that time of night—"

"What time?"

"Nearly one o'clock," she replied, in a whispering voice.

"Have you said anything about your suspicions to the police—"

"No," she interrupted in agony, "I ain't, and I ain't going to."

"But why? After all, your husband was a policeman. You can't possibly be afraid of men who knew and worked with him."

"It ain't them I'm afraid of. It's the others."

"What others?"

"Them what he was after. If they was to hear that I'd tell the police what I could tell, they'd be after me and the kids, sure as pigs is pigs."

"Oh! come—"

"They killed Tom, didn't they?" she challenged.

"That is your idea," he prevaricated, just in case she had laid a trap for him—into which only a quick second thought had prevented his falling. "Then you don't intend to tell the police either of your suspicions, or pass on to them what knowledge you have?"

"No," she stated with determination. "That's why I've come to you. Nobody won't never dream I've told you instead of them, especially if they thinks I'm only seeing you to get you to buy Tom's books."

He began to feel respect for the woman's cunning, if not for her intelligence or courage. But, before he could speak, she went on with desperate urgency:

"You won't say nothing to the police, will you, sir? If you do they'll know I've told you, and then they'll do somethink to me for splitting on 'em. Promise me you won't, sir."

He began to lose patience with her for making a melodramatic mountain out of what was obviously a commonplace molehill.

"I am sorry, Mrs. Kitchen, but I am sure there is nothing I can possibly do to help in finding the lorry-driver that the police cannot do. I am not a detective, and if I were to do something in the matter as a private individual it is quite likely that I should find myself in the dock charged with obstructing the police in the course of their duty."

Her eyes misted with despair. "But everyone says you are a detective—Tom used to talk about you—"

"Nonsense! I have been able to help the police now and again, thanks to a sound knowledge of books and the book trade. There is no question of that knowledge being of the slightest use in this case."

Tears rolled down her tanned cheeks: her thin lips trembled. "It was something in one of his books which first put Tom on the track," she whimpered.

Instinct, spurred by desire, reacted more quickly than commonsense. "What book? On the track of what?" he questioned promptly, before he could check himself.

She answered promptly. Too promptly for his peace of mind, for he instantly had a shrewd suspicion that, in spite of his precautions, he had fallen into one of her traps.

"I don't know which particular book, sir. He didn't trouble to tell me. All he says that night was, 'Lil, old girl,' he says—that's me, sir; Lily is me first name—'Lil,' he says, 'I've just read somethink that's given me an idea,' he says. 'An idea about what?' I asked him. 'An idea why old Newdick's haystack caught fire last week,' he says. 'And why somebody drove Jim Davis's cattle into the road a fortnight afore that,' he says. 'And blast me!' he says, 'now I comes to think on it, if it don't explain why that there private car were slewed right across the road, a fortnight afore that. Lil, old girl,' he says, 'I'm beginning to think your Tom's on to somethink big.'"

She paused; although he deliberately refrained from glancing directly at her, he felt convinced that her heavy-lidded eyes were anxiously studying his face in the hope of obtaining from it an ink-ling of what impression her words were making upon him. He tried to express unconcern, but was not at all sure that he was successful. Inwardly he was beginning to feel excited; although he suspected that she was dramatizing her story for the purpose of capturing his interest, there was a ring of sincerity in her actual words which made him believe them.

He drew a series of geometrical designs on the scribbling-pad before him. "How long ago was this?" he asked in a casual manner.

The note of hope in her voice warned him that he had not deceived her in the slightest. "Nearly two months ago," she quickly replied. "Ever since that night he's been acting mysterious-like, going out nights on his bike when he weren't on duty, and coming back later nor he need to when he was. Then, three days afore he were killed he says to me, after looking up in a diary what he had bought the day after the night what I've just been telling you about, he says to me, 'Lil, old darling,' he says, 'if I don't have somethink to tell the Serge less than a week from now, my name ain't Tom Kitchen.' That's what he says to me, sir, so help me God."

"Didn't he ever give you a hint of what or who he was after, Mrs. Kitchen?"

"No, sir. Tom weren't one for talking about police business to 'is wife. He used to say as how police business weren't no woman's work, except what I had to know, of course, for when the Serge or anyone else might come along when Tom were out on duty. I did arst him once; but he wouldn't tell me. 'Don't fret your head about what I'm doing,' he says. 'Just you remember it's somethink big I'm on to, and if I pulls it off I'll be a detective-sergeant afore many more years is up.'"

"Do you know what caused him to buy a diary?"

"No, sir."

"Going back to the first night when he told you that he had just read something that had given him an idea—what makes you think that the idea had come from a book and not the daily newspaper, or even an article in a magazine?" He was quite unconscious of the fact that by interrogating her, he was already taking the first steps in the course which he had refused to take.

"Tom never read no newspapers in his free evenings, sir. Always books. He used to read the *Daily Mail* weekdays, and the *Sunday Express* and *The People* most Sundays, but always in the mornings, and then only as a duty, he used to say, 'cause he reckoned a policeman should keep up-to-date."

"Have you no idea what book he was reading that night?"

"No, sir. You see, I'd gone up to bed, not feeling up to the mark, like, being as I'm not too far off my time."

"Had he remained below?"

"Yes, sir."

"Had he bought any books recently?"

"He was always buying books whenever he saw any cheap enough of the kind he liked."

"What kind did he like?"

"Thrillers, mostly, but he was fond of books about Kent."

"What was peculiar about the stack fire, and the cattle which strayed?"

She looked vague. "I don't know, sir. He didn't tell me."

"Nor about the car which was slewed across the road?"

"He did mention something about that to me. As he was cycling along the Dymchurch road about one o'clock in the morning, he saw a car slewed right across the road in such a way that nothing could pass by one way or the other. Just when Tom was beginning to wonder what had happened, 'cause he couldn't see nobody about, he heard movements the other side what was away from him. He managed to squeeze by the bonnet, and saw a man changing the wheel after a burst."

After a long pause he prompted, "Well?"

"That's all, sir."

He was disappointed; he had anticipated that the burst had had something to do with broken bottles, dropped from the rear of a speeding lorry. He was also astonished; he could not feel that there was much about the incident that was significant—except that the driver had left the car slewed across the road instead of straightening it to leave room for others to pass.

When he mentioned this to Mrs. Kitchen she nodded. "That's what Tom said, but all the man said was that it didn't take him two shakes of a dog's tail to change a wheel, so he hadn't thought it worthwhile to straighten the car at that time of the morning, when it weren't likely that anything would want to pass by on such a deserted road."

Because the commonplace reply was convincing in its reasonableness he was puzzled to account, first, for why Kitchen had told his wife about the incident; and secondly, what connection it could have, if any, with the burning haystack and the wandering cattle—particularly so as all three incidents had taken place on different nights, two weeks or more apart.

His perplexity did not last overlong; Mrs. Kitchen's own words supplied a clue to a possible solution. She had said that her husband had seen 'a car slewed right across the road in such a way that *nothing could pass by* one way or the other'. Had that been the purpose of its presence there, at one o'clock a.m.? To prevent the passing by of a chance police-car, for instance? Or pursuit by a police-car after a lorry filled with smuggled goods?

Although his intellect was imaginative and unconventional, he was not impulsive. Sometimes, though rarely, these contrary influences came into conflict with each other. This they now did. Imagination, fifed by excitement, tempted him to accept the widow's invitation to investigate the circumstances of her husband's death: a very normal, matter-of-fact prudence warned him that he was already allowing himself to be prejudiced by his desire to assist in the discovery of the killer's identity.

Prudence won with the sage reflection that nothing was likely to be lost by sleeping on the proposition. He turned to the widow.

"I'll call tomorrow evening to make you an offer for the books, Mrs. Kitchen."

She looked at him with sullen, disappointed eyes. "What about poor Tom's death?" she whined. "I thought you was beginning to be interested…"

He could find nothing about the woman to like; but he felt sorry for her; for her loss, her condition, and her understandable wish to see her husband's killer punished.

To the devil with prudence… "I'll do all I can," he promised in a rash moment.

Chapter Five

Having agreed to investigate the several curious circumstances related by Mrs. Kitchen, Terhune wasted very little time in beginning his task. That same afternoon, as soon as he had finished tea, he took out his bicycle and set off for Manor Farm, the home of Jim Davis. He knew Davis; at one time the farmer had been a subscriber to the circulating library that had been the foundation-stone on which Terhune had built up his business. Davis was no longer a subscriber; as soon as he had exhausted every Western in the library—the only type of fiction he would read—he resigned; from that time Terhune only saw him through the plate-glass windows in the Square on market days.

Manor Farm was a mile south of Farthing Gibbet, a village half-way between Farthing Toll and Dymchurch. The farmhouse itself was an ugly building which had been built by an essentially practical man; but the land which surrounded it was rich, and bred fine sheep that were famous even in a district which had a world-wide reputation for quality sheep.

Jim Davis was at home, and relaxed after the last meal of the day. He gave Terhune a respectfully warm welcome in a voice that failed to disguise the question-mark in it.

"Good evening, Mr. Terhune. 'Tisn't often you visit these parts."

"As a matter of fact it is: I do a lot of cycling in my spare time." Terhune decided not to waste time in preliminary conversation but to get straight to the point. "But tonight I'm here for the particular purpose of asking you something, Mr. Davis."

The farmer chuckled. " 'Tain't no use you asking me to join the library again, mister. I've got out of the way of reading books since I left off borrowing them cowboy stories from you. There's too much ruddy work to be done outside, and in the house, too, what with filling up dratted forms all the time."

"I've come about something quite different. Would you mind my asking you a few questions about how your cattle escaped into the road one night about three months ago?"

The other man took his time about replying: he thrust his hands deep into the pockets of his breeches and stared at some hens that were scratching about in the stackyard. An expression that was shrewd without being suspicious passed across the lean brown face. As soon as he had decided what his reply was to be his gaze shifted back to his visitor's face.

"It ain't nothing extraordinary for cattle to break loose, mister."

"It is, when a farmer has the reputation of being a good farmer."

Davis nodded his head, pleased with the subtle compliment.

"So there *were* something fishy about Tom Kitchen's death?"

Terhune's face must have expressed his astonishment, for a twinkle lightened the farmer's steady stare. "You're not the only man round these parts that can put two and two together, mister, and make four on it." This in a perfectly friendly voice. "Everybody knows that you do a spot of detective work on the side now and again. And it were you what fust came across Tom's body, weren't it?"

Terhune's grin was wry: the country was not a place where anyone could hope to keep his private life a secret to himself.

"Well?" he challenged; his manner—he hoped!—non-committal.

"Tom Kitchen asked me about them cattle more'n two months back. I'll lay you've been talking to Newdick, too, 'bout his haystack catching fire."

"No."

Davis was not deceived. "But you're going to ask him about it, aren't you?"

Terhune was not prepared deliberately to lie. "Yes."

"I thought so. Ted Newdick told me Kitchen had been to see him. Well, it don't need brain to see that, if you're as curious as Tom Kitchen were about my cattle, and Ted Newdick's fire, there were some funny goings-on which probably had something to do with Tom's death. I never did think it were natural for a smart 'un like Tom to stand in the middle of the road and wait for a blasted lorry to knock him down."

For Terhune the farmer's quick understanding of the implications to be drawn from being asked a second time about the cattle was extremely disconcerting. In a matter of days the news would travel round the neighbourhood that 'that there Mr. Terhune of Bray' was investigating the death of Tom Kitchen. The ramifications likely to follow that event were three-fold: one, his chance of obtaining unprejudiced information from local inhabitants would easily be spoiled; two, the news might reach the guilty men, who would thus be put on their guard (and might even avenge themselves on Mrs. Kitchen if her fears were more justified, and less hysterical, than, for the moment, he believed); and last, but by no means least, the news would most certainly reach the ears of the police. Then the fat would be in the fire, was his wry reflection. The local C.I.D. would be justifiably annoyed; Tim Murphy hurt; for a premature revelation that the police were suspicious of Kitchen's death might easily hamper, and even ruin, their chance of arresting the murderers.

He could see only one way of avoiding an awkward situation: he must tell Davis some part of the truth, in the hope that the farmer could be cajoled into maintaining silence.

"I agree with you, Mr. Davis: it struck me at the time that Tom's death didn't look like an accident."

Davis's heavy eyebrows twitched suggestively. "The police think it were an accident."

Damn! Terhune thought. He knows I'm friendly with Murphy. He shrugged. "They are probably right."

"Oh ah!" There was a suggestion of mockery in the exclamation. "But I don't see no connection between some damned swine turning my cattle loose on the road, and Tom Kitchen's death."

"Did anyone have reason for interfering with your cattle?"

"Not that I knows of."

"Or for firing Newdick's stack?"

"Ted says he don't know why anyone should have set the ruddy stack alight. Ted's liked well enough."

"Right. Then doesn't it look to you as though there is someone living round about the Marsh who is a bit soft in the head?"

Davis gave this suggestion long and serious study. At last he nodded. "Tom didn't think of that, but it sounds likely."

"Kitchen probably thought so, too. But he wasn't one for saying more than he had to."

"He weren't; he were close-mouthed, was Tom, 'specially about police matters."

"All the same, somebody talked—at least, that's my idea—"

"It weren't me," Davis hastily interrupted. "I ain't said a thing to nobody about Tom coming to me about them cattle. He asked me not to, and I didn't. If it was anyone it was Ted. Ted's a good chap except when he's in liquor. Then he'll talk a donkey's hind leg off."

"Assume that Newdick talked one night, and that news reached the lunatic that the police were after him. Don't you think it likely that his crazed mind might have seized the opportunity of killing a man who was trying to arrest him?"

"Ay!" the farmer presently agreed. "Likely enough. Do you reckon to catch up on him?"

"I am trying."

"Good luck to you, mister; mad or not, the man who killed Kitchen didn't ought to be free. There's no knowing what he might be up to next."

"That's what is worrying me, Mr. Davis. If it gets around that I have started making enquiries—"

"He might be after you, too," the farmer drily finished.

Terhune reddened. "I was not thinking of myself, but of Mrs. Kitchen."

"Oh ah!" The shrewd eyes twinkled. "So that is who told you that Tom Kitchen had come to me about the cattle? I wondered." Davis grew serious. "But you're right, Mr. Terhune. If Tom was murdered it won't do for it to get around that Lil's been talking. You can trust me to keep my mouth shut, but I'd go careful with Ted Newdick if I was you."

"Thanks for the warning." Terhune was pleased with the success of his stratagem. "To get back to the question of who let the cattle out of your field; were you able to give Kitchen any helpful information?"

"He may have found it helpful; but if he did, I'm blowed if I know how."

"Exactly what happened?"

"Have you time to walk half a mile? If so, I'll take you along to the field and show you for yourself."

Terhune had the time, so the two men set off down the road in a southerly direction. After they had gone some distance Terhune took subconscious note of the existence of another road, on his left, which proceeded in a north-easterly direction after effecting a T junction with the one they were on: a passing reflection occurred to him that it must be one of the few roads on the Marsh with which he was not familiar.

They reached an empty twenty-acre pasture field; its surface was lush, and practically unblemished; no trace of thistles and other noxious weeds; no bracken; no casts. The hedges were thick at the bottom, and trim. The five-barred gate was in good condition; so was its latch, strong and secure.

"See if you can push the gate open," Davis suggested.

Terhune tried to open the gate by any method other than the proper one, but failed. He was convinced that no cattle, in spite of the mischievous cunning possessed by many, could have opened the gate once it had been properly shut. Everything about the field proved that it was worked by an efficient and conscientious farmer.

"There were a dozen cattle in the field that night, and the gate was safely shut just before seven-thirty."

"You are sure of that?"

"As sure as I am of my own name. I was here myself that night. I'm not going by what any of the men said."

Terhune wondered whether coincidence was responsible for the farmer's visit. "Do you look at all your fields every night?"

"Most nights I do. I don't believe in leaving things to chance."

Terhune was prepared to believe that statement; there was something about Davis—his expression, his firm stance, his plain, neat clothes—which spelled efficiency. If the farmer claimed to have left the field and the cattle in good order it seemed safe to assume that some mischievous human agency must have been involved in the animals' escape.

"What happened next—I mean, as far as you are concerned?"

"The following afternoon, just before I sat down to have my tea, Tom Kitchen comes along, looking for me. 'Say, Jim,' he says, 'did you know them cattle of yours in Church Field was loose in the road last night?' At first I thought he was joking; but he went on to tell me as how he were on his rounds the night before and all but ran slap-bang into the cattle, which were feeding all over the road."

"Feeding?"

"Ah, mister, feeding. On some fresh hay what was strewn along the road just as if it had toppled off a cart."

"Had it, do you think?"

"What? Toppled off?"

"Yes."

"Well, mister, any farming man what couldn't load a cart better than have half of it topple off on the way home, or didn't miss it when it got home; or any carter what didn't know he was losing half his cartload, or, if he did know, was too ruddy careless to reload it, wouldn't last long on a farm. Still, strange things do happen in the country, I grant you. If it hadn't been for the cattle I should probably have reckoned that somebody was a fool, and thought no more about it."

"But you did think more about it?"

"Of course. I knew that them cattle couldn't have broken out of Church Field, and that somebody must have opened the gate and deliberately druv them out."

"I suppose it isn't possible that the animals smelled the hay, and made a special effort to get to it?"

"Of course they smelled it, and I don't doubt they would have tried to reach it: cattle like a new bite just the same as us humans do. But they couldn't have got out," the farmer doggedly repeated.

"Perhaps somebody saw the hay in the road and, rather than see it waste, let the cattle out to feed on it."

Terhune knew that the suggestion was a feeble one, and was not surprised when it was accorded the reception it deserved.

"Then that somebody wasn't no countryman," Davis stated with derision. "No countryman would let cattle loose."

"What did you and Kitchen consider to be the explanation?"

"That somebody had a spite against me."

"Did you suspect anyone in particular?"

Davis hesitated. "I did," he presently admitted. "I told Tom the name, and Tom said he would make enquiries."

"Did he, do you know?"

"Ay, but he was satisfied 'tweren't the man I'd told him about. So, if it's all the same to you, mister, I'll not cause anybody trouble by repeating it."

"Do you remember the date, Mr. Davis?"

Terhune judged, by the renewed interest taken in the busy hens, that the farmer was giving the question his usual concentrated attention. For two minutes Davis was motionless and quiet. Then, with slow deliberation, he turned to face his questioner again.

"It wouldn't have been the seventeenth July, which were the wife's birthday: I took her to Folkestone that day to give her a treat; we weren't back before dark. It wouldn't have been the twenty-first, neither: Tinkerbell calved that night, a couple of days afore her time, and I were keeping an eye on her, the men having knocked off for the night. But that were after the night Kitchen found the cattle in the road. I'd say, mister, that it were either the eighteenth, nineteenth, or the twentieth. The nineteenth, most likely; but I wouldn't take my Bible oath on it."

"I suppose you can't remember what sort of a night it was?"

"As regards what, mister? The day of the week?"

"No, the weather."

"I can tell you there weren't no moon to speak of, for I saw the new 'un on the twenty-first, while I was out with Tinkerbell; I turned the money over in my pocket for luck."

"Just two or three more questions, Mr. Davis. I won't keep you much longer—"

"Keep me as long as you like, mister, if it will help to put the man who killed Tom where he belongs—standing on the drop, with a noose round his neck. He weren't a bad bloke, was Tom; though he were keen enough to get on, he didn't go around 'specially looking for to get other people into trouble, if you know what I mean."

Terhune did know. Like many rural policemen, P.C. Kitchen had known when to look the other way.

"Where is the nearest pasture to Church Field, adjoining the road?"

"Up along Rackham's Farm, just past Chestnut Lane." The farmer jerked his thumb in a northerly direction.

"Chestnut Lane? Where's that?"

"Leastwise, that's what it's still called by the older people. 'Tain't a lane any more, but the road to Tapley."

"Is that the road we passed on our way here?"

"Ay. But nearly all the land on the Marsh is used for grazing. If somebody wanted to amuse himself driving animals on to the road he needn't have looked far. I'm not much of a thinking man, but it do seem to me as though there were a reason for driving my cattle out of the field instead of Bob Pearce's sheep, or Alf Collins's sheep, or, come to that, Fred Hopkins's Jerseys."

Terhune detected no undercurrent of querulousness in the farmer's complaint; but just curiosity—any annoyance which Davis might have felt had, it seemed, long since evaporated. But this aspect registered itself but vaguely in Terhune's thoughts: he was far more interested in the possible significance to be drawn from the position of the farm in relation to the Tapley road. The outlet from Church Field was situated in what, looking northwards, was the lower half of an S bend. The junction of the Tapley road with the Wickford-Dymchurch road was just beyond the limit of the bend in the upper half. This meant that the junction was effectively concealed from any point in the lower bend.

The reason for choosing Davis's cattle in preference to Pearce's sheep, or Collins's sheep, or Hopkins's Jerseys, grew clear. In the event of a pursuit, the presence of the cattle in the road could easily have delayed the pursuers long enough for them not to see which road the pursued had taken.

But this solution he discarded as soon as he gave it further thought. If the pursuit were a close one the foremost car might itself be delayed by the wandering cattle, with disastrous result so far as the pursued were concerned. On the other hand, if it were not a close pursuit, the rear car would not be able to see which road had been taken by the other; consequently, previous precautions, such as the driving of cattle into the road, were unnecessary.

All the same, he thought, Davis's question did raise the interesting query—why *his* cattle? Why not the sheep from Rackham's Farm? Decidedly a point worth further examination. But later on, in the peace and quietness of his room.

"The last question, Mr. Davis. Either before or since the night we have been talking about, have any other unusual things happened to you or your farm? Or your neighbours' farms?"

"Meaning am I quite sure that it wasn't spite or mischief?"

"Yes."

"Well, nothing that I can remember, or know of."

The two men walked back to Manor Farm, where, after a few more words of a more general nature—and, from Davis, the offer to assist in any way he could; together with a renewed warning not to let Ted Newdick suspect anything—Terhune rode off in the direction of Ted Newdick's farm. He went by way of Chestnut Lane; not solely for the satisfaction of cycling along possibly the only road on the Marsh unknown to him; for Tapley was on the way to Dymstreet, where Newdick lived.

The road—it was, in fact, little better than a lane—was no less tortuous than any other on the Marsh. But, although it had started off from the Wickford road in a north-easterly direction, its general direction soon changed: after half a mile or so he found himself going towards the south-east.

He passed through Tapley, where he found himself on the Willingham road, and shortly turned east again for Dymstreet. Meanwhile, he tried to devise a plan whereby he could question Newdick without betraying his object in doing so. Several ideas occurred to him; but he discarded them all as being unconvincing and likely to raise suspicion.

While still half a mile from Dymstreet—and a long way from having prepared a likely story for the farmer's benefit—he saw, on the far side of a low hedge, a square mound of ashes. He had seen the remains of burned-out stacks before, and so recognized the ashes for what they undoubtedly were. He dismounted, stared with curiosity at the disfiguring scar, and wondered whether he were alongside Newdick's farm. If so, it seemed risky to try and find the farmer that night, for he had not yet decided on a safe method of approach.

But Newdick found him instead. "Not what you'd call a pleasant sight, eh?"

Terhune turned. A man in gaiters and breeches leaned, arms bent, against a five-barred gate on the other side of the road. Terhune wondered where he had come from: he had not been in sight the previous moment. Hidden behind the hedge, no doubt. Though why...

"That's the sort of thing us ruddy farmers has to put up with. Twenty ton of hay wasted, and me not knowing how I'm going to feed my stock come the winter."

The man could be Newdick—he had spoken of *my* stock.

"Weren't you insured?" Terhune used for an opening gambit.

"Insured!" The farmer spat his disgust. "I've a better use for my money than giving it away to insurance companies. Besides, it's not only the loss of the money. It's the hay I need. The ruddy insurance companies don't pay back hay, do they? Do they?" he repeated, raising his voice in challenge.

"No, but the money they would have paid out would have bought fresh hay to replace what was burned."

"Would it? That shows what little you know about local conditions. If I was to offer you a pound a ton extra for every ton of hay you bought for me, even at the highest price, you wouldn't make enough to buy a packet of fags. There just ain't none for sale for miles around. I know, because I've been trying to buy some."

Terhune tried to look sympathetic. "That's bad luck. How did it catch fire? Spontaneous combustion?"

An expression of disgust spread across the face of the man on the other side of the road. "When I build stacks I builds them to keep, not to catch theirselves afire. I've farmed ever since I were a nipper helping out me father, but I've never had a stack catch fire yet until that one. Besides, that one were last year's hay; not this. It couldn't have catched itself after so long."

"What happened? A passing traction engine, or a tramp?"

"Sabotage. That's what it were. Damn' ruddy sabotage." The farmer shook his fist at some unseen unknown; his face turned purple with anger.

Chapter Six

A few judicious questions from Terhune soon established that Newdick's charge of sabotage—for the man was Newdick, as Terhune subsequently learned—was based on no firmer foundation than his own imagination. At the same time, Newdick's answers made it reasonably unlikely that the stack had caught fire by accident.

As soon as he could escape from the irate farmer—no easy matter, for, like most solitary people, Newdick battened on a willing listener—Terhune started back for home.

Twilight soon spread a dusky veil of mystery over the Marsh, which presently tempted him to stop and look backwards. By then he had reached a point high above: mile upon mile of flat countryside was spread below and before him, seemingly as infinite as the darkling sky above; for the cliffs of Folkestone, the Dymchurch sea-wall, the radar towers at Lydd, the Dungeness lighthouse were hidden in a haze of crimson-shot grey which merged land and sea and sky into one indistinguishable entity.

As always he found the sombre beauty of the scene deeply satisfying. It was not surprising, he reflected, that so many writers had been lured by the strange remoteness of the Marsh into using it as the locale for their stories: it lent itself so readily as an insidious spur to the conflict of human passions. As readily, indeed, as the venue for their illegal traffic to the smugglers of a past century. True, its proximity to the Continent had been a not unimportant detail for the law-breakers, but not the sole one. Looking at the Marsh from the edge of the downs above, one readily realized how easy it had been for them to terrorize the inhabitants into silence; even now, midway through the twentieth century, the few habitations were scattered and lonely, often half a mile or more away from their nearest neighbour.

The roads must have been equally helpful: there were many of them; in tortuous curves they criss-crossed the Marsh from coast to downs; from east and west. To patrol every road effectively, and in sufficient strength to engage the smugglers, had been a task beyond the strength of the preventive officers: no wonder they had been forced to ask for military help in combating the bands of reckless men who had grown rich at the expense of the Government's revenue account.

As he continued to survey the darkening countryside below him, for the first time he began truly to appreciate how, in spite of the advance in mechanical and scientific equipment, it was still possible for a gang of well-organized and resolute adventurers to defy the excise authorities. Each winding road was, in itself, an ally of any reckless driver bent on speed rather than safety: when such roads were comparatively numerous; when so many of them ran roughly parallel to one another; when, in addition, some of those parallel roads were connected with one another by unfrequented, lonely side-roads; it became easy to realize how a clever driver could slip through any police cordon unless it was large enough or strong enough to close every road leading into or out of the Marsh.

Add to those odds against the police the impossibility of knowing beforehand when a run was to be made, and the equal impossibility—on economic grounds—of keeping a cordon permanently drawn round the Marsh, and the prospect of effecting a series of successful runs became increasingly possible.

As more and more distant lights twinkled into existence, the hazy panorama below grew less realistic, more fairy-like. Glowing headlights moved slowly among the now invisible roads; it was hard to believe that they were moving at speeds of twenty-five miles per hour and more. Much further off, a long stream of bouncing lights passed, even more slowly, across the background—the coast road from Dymchurch to St. Mary's Bay, he realized. Away to his right the Dungeness Light intermittently pierced the darkness. Above, disappearing clouds filled the velvet sky with friendly stars, and the silver crescent of a new moon.

The scene was no new one for Terhune, but he did not willingly turn away from it: familiarity had not yet bred contempt for it; nor probably ever would. But, although he did not move, his thoughts stopped dwelling upon the sentimental beauty of the scene: they began to occupy themselves with the problem of why Ted Newdick's haystack had been set alight. The purpose of driving Jim Davis's cattle out of the field on to the road seemed obvious—or, if not obvious, at least it was possible to work out a reasonable explanation.

The same could not be said of the stack fire. Because the stack stood in a field, the fire could not have served to block the road alongside; on the contrary, the flames must have helped very materially to light it up for some distance either way. Besides, the road was an unimportant one, so far as he could see, having little strategic value in so far as helping smugglers to run contraband was concerned.

Then there was one more factor to be taken into consideration. In answer to a question about the state of the weather on the night of the fire, Newdick had replied, with convincing decisiveness, that visibility had been fair; moonless, but with a clear sky above. Not a suitable night for a run, it would seem. The farmer was equally informative about the date: Friday, 25th July. Taking these several facts into consideration, he was inclined to think, in spite of Newdick's conviction that the stack had been deliberately set alight, that the fire had been accidental, and therefore had no connection with the activities of any smugglers.

He resumed his interrupted journey back to Bray. Before he arrived there something occurred which made him change his opinion of the stack fire. It was a very simple happening. A short distance ahead of him a smouldering bonfire burst into flames, which shot upwards for some considerable height. The sight was a fascinating one—especially for one who was still capable of enjoying the boyish thrills of Guy Fawkes Night. With only part of his attention concentrated on the deserted road, he watched the leaping flames for all the time they were before him: not until the bonfire was behind him did he consciously realize with what relish he had enjoyed watching it: he wondered what there could be in a fire to make it such an irresistible attraction for so many people.

This rambling reflection started a new train of thought. Had the stack been fired with the deliberate purpose of attracting and holding the attention of anyone, within a radius of miles around, who might be out and about at that late hour—11.30 p.m.? Such a simple stratagem, and yet so clever: it was so certain that the majority of people seeing it would be too occupied in staring at the fire, and speculating on its whereabouts, its origin, and the name of the unlucky tenant or owner, to pay any attention to a passing motor lorry. Even the patrolling bobbies would be attracted by anything which promised to break the monotony of their lonely vigil.

Later came a doubt, prompted by the memory of what the weather had been that night. Was it likely, he asked himself, that the smugglers would have chosen a night when visibility was reasonably good? The answer was obviously no. And no it remained until he reached the outskirts of Bray. At that point another aspect suggested itself. Maybe the contraband had not been *landed* that night. But it might have been transferred from one cache to the next; Murphy had spoken of the likelihood of there being dumps of smuggled goods hidden up and down the county; just as there had been during the heyday of smuggling, when large quantities of brandies, silks, laces and other treasured goods were to be found hidden in thickets and woods, in the cellars of lonely inns and squires' mansions; even in the vaults and towers of the Marsh churches.

If he were right in his assumption—the more thought he gave to the problem, the more reasonable seemed his solution—then it was obvious that the gang of smugglers was being directed by someone who had imagination and wit in addition to a decided flair for organization. All the more remarkable, then, that the unaided, unorganized investigations of a country bobby should have given him a clue to the probable time and place of the latest run—for Mrs. Kitchen's story made still more likely the deduction that he was lying in wait for the smugglers when they killed him. Terhune's respect for the dead man's acumen and intelligence increased.

2

The following evening Terhune fulfilled his promise to call on Mrs. Kitchen. He found the cottage without difficulty: a low building with a neat little flower-and-fruit garden on one side, a sizable vegetable plot on the other, with a small yard and a newly-cultivated field at the back.

She opened the door to his knock; he stepped into a small sitting-room that was clean even if it was not too tidy. Conspicuous in a room that lacked any other mark of personality were the three shelves of books which he had come to buy—about sixty in all, was his first quick estimate.

"No further trouble last night, Mrs. Kitchen?"

Her dull eyes filled with alarm. "Not last night, sir—but this afternoon—"

"Well?"

"A man came from the police about Tom's pension. He wanted some paper what Tom was supposed to have."

Again he had to prompt the nervous woman. "Yes?"

"When I said that I didn't know nothing about it, he asked where Tom used to keep all his papers. I told him, in an old case what we used to keep under the bed; so he asked whether he might look through the case. He said as how he'd recognize the paper directly he saw it, as it were the same as what all policemen had when they joined the pension fund."

He was puzzled to know what the story was leading up to. "Go on."

"I let him look through the case, but he didn't find nothing, so he left and said as how I should be hearing from the police by letter. After he had gone I had a look through the case to see whether I could find what he had been looking for."

"And did you?" he asked, with impatience that was unusual in him: it seemed that she was incapable of continuing a longish story without constant prodding. Lord! What a colourless, boring woman she was!

"No, sir, but his diary had gone."

This was indeed an item of news. "Are you sure?"

The unintentional sharpness of surprise in his voice made her nervous. "Yes, sir. You see, I—I—" She paused, swallowed.

"You what, Mrs. Kitchen?"

"I had seen it there with me own eyes only this morning."

"What was in the diary? Police matters?"

"I don't know. I never looked at it; I wouldn't dare while Tom was alive, and I haven't wanted to since he's dead." She began to weep—not ostentatiously, to enlist his sympathy, but quietly, with genuine sadness.

He felt awkward, not knowing whether he should try to comfort her or whether it would be a greater kindness to ignore her tears. Chiefly because he could not like her enough to be sincere, he chose the second course, and stared out of the small window. What a fool of a woman, he thought, to allow a stranger to enter the cottage and look through her husband's belongings without taking the simple precaution of challenging his authority. But remembering how easily the average woman is imposed upon by anyone with an authoritative manner, he reversed this over-harsh judgment: not many, he realized, would have the courage to defy anyone claiming to be a policeman.

Then he began to reflect upon another facet of the man's visit. Or, rather, on several facets; not the least important of which was the irresistible conclusion to be drawn from the visit that, if further proof were needed that Kitchen's death had been deliberate, the theft of the diary supplied it. Had the death been accidental, committed by a reckless but otherwise innocent driver, there would have been no reason for anyone's wanting to search the dead constable's belongings. The fact that someone had taken the risk of doing so proved to his satisfaction that the driver of the lorry had belonged to a body of law-breakers—probably a band of smugglers; that those men were convinced that the police constable's appearance on the road was not a coincidence; and that they were prepared to take chances to prevent, if they could, the constable's notes, and anything else of use, from reaching his superiors.

More than ever Terhune regretted his promise to Mrs. Kitchen to say nothing to the local C.I.D. of Kitchen's discoveries. To try and obtain enough evidence to arrest a gang of men was obviously beyond the capabilities of one man; still less a private individual like himself, who could only play at being a detective. From the first words Mrs. Kitchen had addressed to him the previous afternoon he had become increasingly aware how necessary it was for the activities of the smuggling organization to be matched by the police organization.

He realized, too, that Mrs. Kitchen's fears for her own safety were not entirely unjustified. If the smugglers should come to suspect that she had information about them which could be useful to the police, they were possibly reckless enough to see that she was not allowed an opportunity of passing it on. For her own safety she needed police protection.

"Listen, Mrs. Kitchen," he began earnestly, "you're nervous, aren't you, that the men who killed your husband have become unpleasantly interested in you?"

"Yes, sir," she whispered, and glanced with apprehension at the small window.

"Don't you think, for your own sake, that either you or I should tell the police all you know? Especially in view of what happened a few hours ago."

She trembled. "No, sir. The police can't do nothing."

"They could protect you—"

"That's what I'm afraid of. Directly them men should hear that the police was guarding me, they would know for certain that the police don't really believe poor Tom was killed accidental."

There was truth in what she said; but he was surprised that she had enough intelligence to reason it out for herself. She did not appear to possess so much commonsense.

"You think you are safe from them as long as they do not think you know anything; but that, if the police begin to guard you, they would be sure that you know something, which might make them do something desperate?"

"Yes, sir."

"Don't you think that the police are capable of guarding you?"

"I don't know. I don't want to take the chance." Tears began to flow again: her hands trembled. "You won't tell them anything, will you? You promised—"

"Yes, yes." He renewed his promise with a quick nod. "Not without your permission." He did not like the idea of being held to this promise; more especially as there was something about the woman which both puzzled and worried him. It did not seem to him that a normal woman should have quite such a lack of confidence in the police as she seemed to have—more particularly, being the widow of a police constable. On the other hand, he was equally surprised that her undoubted affection for her late husband was not powerful enough to help her to conquer those fears; to take risks—or what seemed to her to be risks—in the hope of bringing about the arrest of her husband's murderer.

"Now, Mrs. Kitchen, the books—"

"They are over there," she needlessly pointed out, adding hurriedly: "There's no need to pay me anything for them, sir. You're to have them—"

"No, Mrs. Kitchen." He tried to keep his dislike for her from revealing itself in his voice. "I am not a professional investigator. Anything I can do to help bring about the arrest of the lorry-driver I shall be glad to do on a voluntary basis. I shall offer you a fair sum for the books. After that it will be for you to decide whether to accept it or not."

"It's very kind of you, sir. I don't know what to say."

The eager note in her voice belied her words. He knew that she would take whatever sum he offered, and gladly. He frowned, feeling more than ever annoyed with himself for his unwilling antipathy. Poor devil! She needed the money, no doubt. But she needn't have looked quite so avaricious...

He crossed the room and inspected the books. At first sight the small collection appeared to be a purposeless one; the property of a man who bought a title merely because it appealed to him at the time. The strangest assortment of titles rubbed covers with one another. Volume 34 of *A Saunter Through Kent With Pen and Pencil*, by Sir Charles Igglesden, was next to Peter Cheyney's *This Man is Dangerous*; Graham Greene's *The Man Within* was neighbour to *Scotland Yard*, by J. F. Moylan; a badly-rubbed copy of Kenny's *Outline of Criminal Law* dwarfed a war-time copy of a thriller by John Creasey: one of the many Toff titles.

A closer examination contradicted this snap judgment: he saw that almost every title fell into one of three categories. One, thrillers and novels of detection by a number of well-known writers; two, books dealing with the history or topography of Kent; and three, books and novels dealing with smuggling.

The discovery warmed him: particularly the third category; a significant pointer to the fact that the investigations which the constable had been conducting had some connection with organized smuggling.

To these smuggling books he paid particular attention. Among them were one or two titles of which he had never heard: for instance, *Chronicles of the Customs Department*, by W. D. Chester, published in 1885. And another, called simply *The Smuggler*, by G. P. R. James, which Simms and M'Intyre of Paternoster Row, and Donegall Street, Belfast, had published in 1850. *The Man Within* he knew, of course: he had another copy at the shop. Also the equally famous *Doctor Syn*, by Russell Thorndyke.

There was also on the shelves another nineteenth-century title: *Smuggling Days and Smuggling Ways*, by H. N Shore. And two from the present century: Alton and Holland's *The King's Customs*, and two volumes of *The Smugglers*, by Lord Teignmouth and C. G. Harper. He was examining this copy when he wondered whether Kitchen had been in the habit of annotating his books. He opened it, and looked quickly through the pages, but saw no pencilled notes. On the contrary, between two pages, he found fresh-looking crumbs of Indiarubber, which would suggest that Kitchen had taken the trouble of rubbing out some pencil mark—left there, maybe, by a previous owner.

It was obvious from what Mrs. Kitchen had said, of the care and attention to the books, that her husband had been a book-lover. Terhune's expression glowed with the ardour of a fellow enthusiast. What fun the constable must have had, searching for the books, he reflected. And what undiluted joy when finding an unexpected title, or an elusive title long sought for. It was a pity, in one way, that he had not annotated his books—Terhune glanced through another—for who knew what clue might have been offered by a note, a simple underlining, a question mark? But, in spite of the difference such a clue might have made in the progress of future investigations, he had a sneaking feeling of gladness that the constable had not committed that most heinous offence.

He estimated the amount he would normally have offered for the smuggling books; then added ten per cent. because he was a sentimentalist, and not as hardheaded a business man as he should be. The total was small enough, but he knew he would be able to offer rather more, per volume, for the topographical and historical books for which there was always a persistent demand. Turning his attention to these, he noted that several volumes in all of Igglesden's *Saunter* were scattered among the other books. Kitchen must have loved his Kent, Terhune reflected. Then memory jogged. Maybe the constable had, but many of the *Saunter* volumes—especially those before him—contained snippets of smuggling history, descriptions of one-time smugglers' haunts.

Always smuggling!

Terhune made a generous offer to Mrs. Kitchen for the books. It was accepted after an insincere protest—but not until she had made him repeat his promise to investigate her husband's death. He paid her the money, made arrangements with her for the local carrier to pick up his purchases for delivery to Bray, and returned home.

He arrived there just in time to open the door for Murphy.

Chapter Seven

U pstairs, in the untidy, book-lined room which Terhune called his den, the two men relaxed before a wood fire, and smoked. The night was not really cold enough for a fire, but Terhune liked the homely cheerfulness of the flames, and the fragrant smell of smouldering oak; he welcomed any excuse for lighting one. Most evenings he found an excuse if he had work to do.

"I suppose you've been wondering what happened, Mr. Terhune?"

"No. I guessed that no news was—well, no news."

"True enough. Until last night."

"Another run?"

"Nothing so exciting. Ever met George Smiles, of Abbotsbury?"

"Never heard of him."

"I didn't think you had, but one never knows. You seem to meet almost everyone. Well, just before midnight last night, George Smiles was found lying in the middle of the High Street, Ashford. One of the police-cars all but ran over him. I don't think the world would have suffered much loss if it had done so."

"He hadn't already been run over, then?"

"Like Kitchen?" Murphy chuckled. "No. He was dead drunk. The drunkest drunk I've seen for years."

"*You've* seen!"

The sergeant nodded. "The desk sergeant got me out of bed because of something that was found in the gutter not ten yards away from him. Like to guess what?"

"Give up," Terhune promptly answered: he was anxious to hear what had been found.

"An empty rum bottle."

"R*hum Negrita* again?"

"Yes." Murphy blew a wispy trail of tobacco smoke at the fire. "What do you make of that?"

"Probably, one of two things, Sergeant. Either George—what's his name?"

"Smiles."

"Either George Smiles is one of the contraband runners, or else he buys his liquor from someone who sells contraband."

The sergeant nodded. "I thought you wouldn't overlook the alternative. Raines reckoned you would. In either case we've got something to work on." For a long time he contemplated the fire; his expression was quizzical. Terhune did not disturb his guest: he was sure that Murphy would speak at the right time.

When at last he did, he surprised Terhune.

"Does a fire ever send you off to sleep?"

"If I stare at it. Not when I'm working."

"There's something fascinating about a fire." Murphy roused himself. "D'you know the *Load of Hay*, Mr. Terhune?"

"At Abbotsbury?"

"Yes."

"I've passed it often enough on my bike. Been inside twice—maybe three times."

"What's it like?"

"Something out of the eighteenth century. Low ceilings, oil-lamps, small windows, fug."

"Humph!" Murphy relaxed into silence again. This time it lasted longer than Terhune's patience.

"Is the *Load of Hay* George Smiles's port of call?"

"It is the only one within two miles of his cottage. He's a small-holder, by the way. But you wouldn't think he could scratch a living from his thirty acres. It's almost the worst-kept farm on the Marsh."

"You think the bottle of rum could have come from there?"

"Could have." The detective scratched his cheek with the mouth-piece of the pipe he was smoking. "I was talking with the Super about you this afternoon."

The remark surprised Terhune. And puzzled him. He found himself unable to follow his visitor's mental gymnastics; or the reason for them.

"Well?"

"You could help us, sir. But the Super—he's doubtful... Not of you personally," the sergeant hastened to add. "You see, there's something you could do to help us—"

"Done!" the delighted Terhune exclaimed with enthusiasm.

"No, wait. I put the idea up to the Super, but he's doubtful, as I was saying. You see, there might be some danger..."

"Danger!"

"There didn't seem to be much hesitation about killing Kitchen," Murphy remarked drily.

"I see!" Terhune's eyes began to shine with an enthusiasm that was characteristic of his natural naïveté, the same naïveté which made so many women long to mother him. "What's the job?"

Murphy looked uneasy. "I'm not taking yes for an answer before you have heard what the Super—and myself—have to say about this smuggling business. The more we investigate it the more certain we are that it is being run by an organized band of runners. And by a band, I don't mean just three or four men. I mean—well, many. How many we can't guess; but we can reckon on quite a few. There are the buyers in France; the transport men there; the crew of the vessel which runs the stuff across Channel; the undercover men on this side; the trans-port men here; the men who store the stuff; and the men who sell it."

Terhune nodded. There were other members of the band that he knew of, but Murphy did not: the men whose job it was to drive cattle out on to a public highway, or set light to a haystack, or block a road by slewing a car across it. Quite a few men, indeed.

"The police are always finding themselves up against organized gangs of criminals—especially the Metropolitan Police, and the forces of Cardiff, Liverpool, Glasgow and other great cities. But, for the most part, those gangs aren't dangerous. But there's something about smuggling which attracts the more reckless spirits. It always did in the past, and there is no reason for thinking that men have changed that much. Remember Prohibition days in America? Anyway, there is a smell of danger about the present investigation. I have an idea that the twentieth-century smugglers will fight as the nineteenth-century contraband runners used to, when the police round them up. The poor devil Kitchen was the first. I don't believe he'll be the last."

"All of which means…?"

"That by helping the police you might be risking losing something which we have no right to ask you to gamble with—your life."

It became the turn of Terhune to stare reflectively at the fire. He had known Murphy long enough to realize that the sergeant was intensely serious: he was not merely disclaiming in advance any responsibility for what might happen; he, and the Superintendent, genuinely believed that the smugglers were reckless men who might not hesitate to kill anyone who threatened their liberty.

The prospect of giving the police a hand with their investigations into the activities of the local smugglers was exceedingly attractive. Not so the chance of being shot in the back, knifed, or run over by a lorry. Terhune knew he was not cast in an heroic mould. Life, too, was attractive and very sweet. All the sweeter because it was treating him so well. Almost too well.

He did not try to delude himself that he would have nothing to fear, because of the improbability of the smugglers finding out that he was helping the police. There was Murphy's belief—intuitive though it might be, for the moment—that someone with brains had organized the smugglers. If this were so, then something might easily link his name with Kitchen's death—if Jim Davis talked too much, for instance!

In spite of Murphy's warning of danger the temptation to join in the man-hunt was irresistible. He turned to Murphy and nodded; while making a mental reservation that, not being cast in an heroic mould, he would exercise every possible caution and precaution in keeping as far away from danger as he possibly could!

The sergeant accepted this decision without much expression. "I thought you would say yes," he murmured. "This is what we should like you to do, sir. Visit the *Load of Hay*, and keep your eyes and ears open. Of course, we shall send a plain-clothes man there as well; but I don't think he will find out anything worthwhile."

"Why not?"

"If we send a local man, like as not somebody would recognize him. As we don't want the smugglers to suspect that we are on to them, that's out. We shall have to borrow a man from Maidstone; but you know what'll happen. The regulars will shut up like an oyster as soon as they see a stranger about."

"What about me?"

"They'll find out soon enough who you are, especially as you've been there before. When they do, they'll open up. Try and make the landlord remember you. That'll help, if he does."

Terhune was less optimistic. "I'll go. As soon as you say the word, Sergeant. But you're overlooking one fact. I have a reputation—"

"That's what I'm banking on. You're on the look-out for some books. Or a plot—"

"And I don't mean for buying and selling books, or writing 'em. I mean, as a sort of local private detective."

"Damn!" The exclamation was almost obscene in its heartfeltness. "I was forgetting. There's been too much about you in the local newspapers—at least, from our point of view," the Sergeant added apologetically.

"And from mine, don't you worry. But I'll do what I can. I'll think up some story for being there..."

Murphy shook his head. "No, sir. You mustn't take the risk. When the Super and I discussed your going to the *Load of Hay* we'd both forgotten that blasted newspaper publicity. Anyone with an ounce of intelligence would guess what you were doing there. You found the body—you've got a local reputation for doing a spot of detective work on the side—why the sudden interest in the *Load of Hay*? Sure, any babe in arms could add that particular two and two together, and make four of it."

It was surprising how completely stubborn an otherwise shy and rather ingenuous face could turn upon occasions. Murphy did not remember having ever seen Terhune in an obstinate mood. The sight brought a grin to his tight lips.

"You've said too much, Sergeant. I'm going." Terhune paused, for an unpleasant thought occurred to him. He continued, hesitatingly, "Unless you think that official investigations might be prejudiced by somebody's putting two and two together."

The sergeant resisted the temptation to take advantage of Terhune's conscience. "I don't think that is likely to happen, Mr. Terhune. In fact, it might prove to be a good red herring if somebody was to think you were there for a particular purpose."

"Why?"

"Because there would be the chance of their overlooking our own man through keeping an eye on you."

Terhune chuckled. "I've often wondered what it feels like to be a stooge."

The detective's face did not reflect his companion's light-hearted spirits. "Frankly, sir, the more this suggestion is talked over, the less I like it. Stooge is the word, though we hadn't meant it to be; and stooges usually get the thick end of the stick."

"Try and keep me away from the *Load of Hay*, Sergeant."

Murphy's mouth tightened before he spoke. "The divil knows! Though it was me own idea in the first place, I don't like it. Not a-tall, a-tall!"

2

During the following afternoon the local carrier delivered Kitchen's books. Terhune at once separated them into two groups. In the first he placed all the thrillers and detective novels which the policeman had obviously purchased for recreation only. These he dealt with in the normal way, by pricing and exposing for sale. The remainder he took upstairs to his den for reading and closer examination—for in one of these books was to be found, if Mrs. Kitchen's story was true, the clue which had put its late owner on the track of the smugglers.

With the end of business for the day he was faced with alternative courses of action, both of which were equally attractive: to remain at home reading, or to visit the *Load of Hay*. The weather gave the casting vote, for the evening was an ideal one for a cycle ride. Besides, there would still be time, upon his return, to read.

He snatched a hasty tea, then left for Abbotsbury. He pedalled slowly, planning to arrive at the inn after dark. Soon, he found that his impatience to be there had made him leave Bray far too soon; and that, unless he made a detour, he would reach his destination before dusk. He therefore took the next turning to the right, and made for the coast. There he sat down by the sea-wall, and watched the horizon close in upon him as it slowly darkened.

The sea was smooth with a contented swell; his imagination drifted away on its slate-grey surface towards and through the horizon, and so to the coast of France. It was not impossible, he mused, that another consignment of contraband goods was there being loaded, preparatory to making a quick dash across the Channel—the latest broadcast report for shipping had forecast fog in the Channel. He glanced on either side of him, then behind him. He was in a deserted spot: two miles from the nearest town, with no more than a mere handful of houses lining the road. Behind him, miles of flat country, sparsely populated; a maze of winding roads leading in every direction save south.

With the high sea-wall to conceal from the road behind it what was happening on the sands, it was easy to understand how, on a foggy or especially dark night, a flat-bottomed vessel, such as a landing-craft, could nose its way to within a few yards of the wall, and discharge its cargo on the beach without being seen or suspected. It was easy to understand how a small number of silent-footed men could manhandle the cargo over the sea-wall into a waiting lorry.

But that one road could well be the danger-spot for the smugglers, he realized. With the sea-wall on one side, and a canal on the other, there were only two ways open for them to go: east or west. Either way, the nearest road over the canal was more than a mile distant. It should be an easy matter, he considered, for the police to block both ends of the road. On the other hand, with so many miles of convenient beach from which to choose, even if the excise authorities should suspect a landing, was it likely that the smugglers would select any one spot until they had made certain that the coast was clear?

The horizon vanished. Then the sea, too, save for the thin line of white spume when the lazy ripples reached their limit. Soon that would disappear from sight, for the tide was out. It was time for him to move on to the *Load of Hay*. Besides, the wind from the east had the chill of autumn in its boisterous caress.

As he leaned his bicycle against the wall of the inn the cheerful noise advised him that he had well timed his arrival. He pushed open a heavy, iron-bound door; oak, and black with centuries of weathering. The hinges squealed. As he bent down to pass under the lintel—although he was not a tall man—a draught of warm, smoky air blew against his face. Its warmth was welcome; not so its staleness, which was beer-impregnated, and acrid from smouldering cigarette ends and fouled pipes.

The room he found himself in was low ceilinged, and lime-plaster walled. The beams, under which a taller man than he would have had to bend, were the colour of pitch; an adze had fashioned them, the years mis-shapened them; the worm had powdered their outer core in places; but their inner core was intact, and would be for many more centuries. The plaster between was cracked, and stained with smoke and greasy soot. So were the walls; which were further disfigured with half-a-dozen hideous monstrosities: conventional Victorian prints that were faded and dirty. Beneath them were ranged wooden forms, shined by centuries of beer-stains and trousered posteriors. Crudely carpentered tables were set in front of the forms; these, too, shone with the patina which is said to come from beer-froth and elbow-grease.

The floor was of old Kent bricks, long ago worn into unevenness by scraping boots. The fireplace was a small inglenook; low, sooty, mis-shapen by sunken foundations. A trunk of a small tree smouldered in the ashes, sullen and smoking; the freshening breeze blew most of the smoke back into the room; it was sweet and pungent to the nose, but smarted the eyes.

One corner of the room was occupied by an apology for a bar, a converted oak dresser; of its three drawers, two were used for packets of cigarettes; the third contained the till. Before it stood a broad-shouldered man with a hawk nose, gross, cruel lips, beetling eyebrows, and only a fringe of oily grey hair. Ranged round the room, on the forms, sat half-a-dozen men: only one wore collar and tie; he also wore gaiters and breeches, and a round, brown hat on the back of his head, had a large paunch, and looked prosperous. Of the others, three looked like farm labourers. The remaining two were less identifiable. They were dressed like farm labourers, but their eyes were less steady, their skins less tanned by the weather: there was an air of the town about them rather than the country.

Light, apart from the red of the wood-ash in the fireplace, was supplied by two oil-lamps, one on either side of the room. They scarcely did their job effectually; their wicks were untrimmed, their chimneys smoke-grimed. In consequence, the room was a place of shadows, eerie and sinister.

So was the silence which Terhune's entrance caused. A resentful silence, to match the stare of the seven pairs of eyes which watched every movement he made.

He nodded genially at the landlord, then at the rest of the company, as is the way in the country.

"Good evening."

The landlord returned a surly "Good evening."

There were only two vacant places: one by the fire and next to the paunchy, hatted farmer; the other near the door. For preference he would have chosen the place nearer the door, but policy dictated a bold front, not lack of confidence.

As he sat down he gave his order. "Mild and bitter, please." He turned to his neighbour. "A freshening breeze outside." At that moment the reflection occurred to him that the weather forecasting had slipped up somewhere—there would be no fog tonight: not in that neighbourhood, anyway. Awkward for the smugglers, if they should rely upon a radio forecast.

"Ay," grunted the farmer.

The embarrassing silence continued. The surly landlord slammed the tankard of mild and bitter down on the table; some of the liquid slopped over. Rather than meet the resentful, watching eyes, Terhune stared at the table, where the spilled beer had collected in a tiny yellow stream that was trickling in the direction of his trousers—a mute commentary on the floor level. There was not room to move his legs out of danger, so he took out his handkerchief to mop up the beer.

"Same again, Alf," said one of the farmers, as he shoved his tankard across the table.

As though the words were a cue to the rest to relax, the men began to talk again. Terhune was relieved, and swallowed a satisfying draught of beer. Then he leaned back against the wall and looked about him.

An imaginative man, he was acutely conscious of the fact that Time had played a strange trick on the *Load of Hay*. Here, in the bar-parlour of an isolated country inn, Time had stood still. He was prepared to believe that only the men had changed during the passages of centuries. Not even the men, perhaps; not their manners, their habits, their conversation. Only their identities, their clothes. Everything else was much as it always had been. The lime-plaster walls, the beamed ceiling with its cobwebs, the brick floor (though more worn), the table, the forms, the tankards, the smoking fire, the atmosphere of secrecy: a secret not to be shared with strangers. It was as if he had turned over the pages of a history book, and was staring at an illustration of a Kentish inn in the time of Elizabeth, or the Regency period.

The feeling was a queer one. And exciting. Here in this inn, he felt, the old-time smugglers had once met to plan a new run, or to drink away the illegal profits of a past one. Here, in their own secluded circle—and in their cups—they may often have shouted defiance at King George's preventive officers; or even dealt, without conscience or remorse, with unwary excise officers and spies. Bloody stories might well be writ in every brick and stone for anyone with the wit to read them.

He remembered a French saying: *Plus ça change, plus c'est la même chose*. The more things change, the more they are the same.

The sullen glances of the men about him made him feel damnably nervous.

Chapter Eight

"Won't be long afore the first frost," said the farmer. "For meself, I likes a nip in the air when I gets up of a morning. Makes me feel fresh."

The remark was specifically addressed to Terhune, but one of the men opposite answered it: an ugly man, taken all in all, for he had a red bulbous nose, a fat bulging chin, and protruding ears.

"It ain't only mornings that you likes a nip, Walter. And it ain't a nip in the air, neither."

A chuckle of laughter greeted this sally, from which Terhune gathered it was a matter of general knowledge at the *Load of Hay* that the prosperous-looking Walter was fond of his drink.

" 'Cording to my old girl, he's fresh enough as it is without needing nothing to make him more so," added an insignificant-looking man near the door.

More laughter. The big man remained apparently unperturbed. "But maybe there's no frost left by the time you gets up," he went on, still addressing Terhune. His voice was warm with joviality, but the chuckles died away—to give the rest a chance of hearing the reply, Terhune believed. The tense expression on one or two faces opposite warned him that, in spite of an affable manner, Walter was pumping him for information.

"Mostly," he admitted. "Seven-thirty is my time for getting up."

"You city people miss the best of the day. Down here on holiday, mister?"

Terhune grinned. "If you call a Bray a city—"

"You from Bray?" In spite of an attempt to remain impersonal, there was a note of disbelief in the farmer's voice.

A nod. "Ever since the war ended. I've seen you there on a Thursday morning." Terhune had not, but it was a safe statement to make: everyone for miles around who could spare the time visited Bray on market days: any Thursday morning was a social occasion, even among those who also visited Ashford market on Tuesdays.

"Most likely you have. I'm to be found there most Thursdays." He added, with sharp curiosity: "You've seen me? I disremember seeing you, mister."

"Through a plate-glass window. I run the book shop there."

"Ah!" A significant note underlined the exclamation. He laughed boisterously. "That's why I don't remember you. I'm no reading man. Now, if ever you were in the *Wheatsheaf* on a Thursday morning—"

"I don't have the time. Thursday is my busiest day."

"Is it now?" The farmer did not sound very interested in the fact. "I didn't know there was enough people about here what read books."

Again there was an enigmatic note in the farmer's voice which puzzled Terhune. The words were innocuous enough: nothing to cavil at in a man's thinking that there were scarcely sufficient readers in the district to give a bookseller a decent livelihood. In fact, there were not. The major part of Terhune's income was derived from his extensive dealings in antique books: he had clients in many parts of the world to whom he exported rare titles. But he was not prepared to explain this to his neighbour. More especially as he had another source of income which he did intend to mention. Though the farmer's words did not, in themselves, finish with a question mark, yet Terhune was sure he detected incredulity and suspicion in the otherwise impersonal remark.

"There aren't enough to keep me busy the rest of the week, so I write books during my spare time."

"You write books, eh?" The scornful inflection caused Terhune no surprise. He had long since learned that while townspeople for the most part showed visible respect for the artist or the creator, country people, on the other hand, were inclined to be somewhat intolerant of anyone whose living was not earned by physical sweat and toil. But the laughter which followed the remark was boisterous enough. "You wouldn't be one of them thriller-writers?"

"He would an' all," chimed in the ugly-faced man. "You're Mr. Terhune, aren't you, mister?"

Terhune nodded.

The ugly-faced man went on, "I read one of your books last year."

"Did you, George?" The big man did not trouble to turn his head. "Some people reads more than is good for them: they reads so much they don't have time for work. Meaning no offence to you, mister, but George Smiles's missus says she can't get him to take his head out of a book once he starts reading; and that ain't no ways for a countryman to be carrying on. It makes him think too much about other things, and it ain't good for any man to poke his nose into other people's business."

Terhune lit a cigarette. His thoughts were confused. He was glad to have George Smiles identified so soon. A slice of luck, that; the casual mention of the name of the ugly-looking man. That is, if the mention were casual! It had been introduced with apparent naturalness; even so, he felt that 'George' would have sufficed in normal circumstances. Or, perhaps, 'Smiles', if the farmer were an employer of farm labour. But the use of the full name was curious; even significant. As if the farmer had had the intention of 'accidentally' revealing George Smiles's name to Terhune.

He could not believe that this had been the case. Even on the assumption that the other man had had previous knowledge, both of his identity, and of his reason for visiting the *Load of Hay*, surely such knowledge would have caused the farmer to keep guard on his tongue; not to be overfree with it. Then, too, there was the rest of the remark to be considered. Had it been tossed off without an ulterior motive, or had it contained a subtle warning to someone not to do something? If the alternative were the case, at whom was the warning aimed? At himself? Or at George? If at George, on account of what? Did the farmer employ George as a farm hand; and was he, as an employer, warning George to work harder at his job? Or had the warning some reference to George's believed connections with the smugglers? Whatever the true answers to these questions, almost any of them indicated the possibility that the prosperous-looking farmer was mixed up with the smugglers.

In spite of possible alternatives, Terhune was sure that the warning was aimed at him, on the principle that 'if the cap fits, wear it'. In case his intuition was well founded, his immediate task was to persuade the present company, and the farmer in particular, that the cap did *not* fit.

He giggled, with convincing ingenuousness. "*I* make money out of poking my nose into other people's business."

An almost imperceptible threat passed across the weather-crimsoned face to his left. "You do, do you?"

An open invitation to explain; spoken in a jovial voice which would have made a career for a variety artist. Terhune quickly answered:

"Yes. That's why I'm here tonight."

He had never realized that mere silence could be quite so menacing. He could almost feel waves of mistrust and suspicion flowing about him. But when, at last, the hearty voice of the farmer boomed out, there was nothing unfriendly behind it to be distinguished.

"Going to write a book about farming?"

"Nothing so ambitious, Mr.——" He paused, and looked at the farmer with an enquiring glance.

"Matcham. Walter Matcham, mister."

"As I was saying, Mr. Matcham, I should not dare to write about farming. I couldn't hope to compete with A. G. Street, and others like him. No, I'm writing about pubs at the moment, which is more in my line."

"Pubs!" exclaimed the sour landlord. There was sharp suspicion in his voice.

"Well, inns, taverns and public houses. The derivation of their names, their history, if any—"

"You mean, like them adverts do in the papers?" The interrupter was George. "I saw one the other day what said the *Elephant and Castle* was named after the Infanta of Castile, or something like that."

Terhune nodded.

The landlord spoke again, still suspicion. "There ain't nothing funny about the name of the *Load of Hay*, is there?"

"I don't think so."

"Well, then—"

"But the inn itself might have a history even if its name hasn't."

"History! What do you mean? What kind of history? There ain't nothing known about this here inn—"

"Keep your wool on, Fred," Matcham broke in with a genial laugh. "There's no need to snap the gentleman's head off. Ain't there any stories of runaway marriages, or anything of that sort, you could tell him?"

In the light of his expression of surliness and aggression, the landlord's reaction to the mild reproof was remarkably sheep-like. He tried to grin; but the effort merely intensified his scowling suspicion.

"There was the girl Lucy what run away with the son of a belted earl, and slept the night with him here…"

This was the opportunity Terhune had been hoping for. "Lucy Brooks, you mean? You were telling me about her the last time I was here."

"You been here before, then?" Matcham demanded. His surprise was genuine, Terhune was ready to swear.

"Several times," he answered, with what he hoped was convincing casualness. "Though usually in daylight. I do a lot of cycling in the summer. I don't think there's an inn on the Marsh I've not had a drink at."

This was true enough, and his audience believed him. He could have chuckled, could he have dared do so, at the result of his explanation. Not that the reaction of the other people present was particularly visible, apart from a sheepish grin here and there. But he sensed a certain slackening of tension; a feeling of relief.

He pressed home his advantage. "I'm writing a book about the Marsh. One chapter is about its pubs, as I was saying."

Matcham roared with laughter. "Only a chapter, mister? I could write a whole ruddy book about pubs..."

2

On his way home Terhune considered that he had good reason to feel satisfied with his visit to the *Load of Hay*. Not, perhaps, for having achieved any positive success; which he had not. But his story had, he believed, been accepted. He might not be welcomed when next he went there for a drink; but he would at least be regarded as a nuisance that was to be endured with philosophical resignation.

At the same time, he realized that he had been lucky. By a fortunate chance none of the people in the inn, had, he believed, associated him with the Terhune who had been of assistance to the police on one or two occasions. Next time he might not be so lucky. Somebody might, in the meantime, put two and two together. Or there might be some other person there who would recognize him.

That there would be a next time he had already decided. For he had seen nothing, heard nothing, of consequence. Conversation had been practically monopolized by two subjects: farming and sport; the latter including many stories of prizes won or prizes just missed in the football pools. At any moment, had he closed his eyes, he could have imagined himself in any other inn in any other place. He had not expected a contrary result. He calculated on having to spend several evenings there before any of the regulars would dare to risk his over-hearing or seeing something. Even this chance was a most unlikely one, but still, it was a chance...

For the whole of the ride home a picture of the interior of the inn remained clear in his memory, and he was not too happy about it. The picture was much too true to type, as it were: it was too much a replica of a novelist's conception of the scene to be entirely credible; in its very reality it became a caricature of itself: a cartoon drawn by a jokester; a scene set by an unimaginative film producer. Everything had been there; from the scowling disagreeableness of the landlord to the weird leaping shadows on the lime-washed walls; from the sombre half-darkness to the furtive glances of the habitués. Nothing was missing. Only a person devoid of imagination could have remained entirely unaware of its atmosphere of brewing mischief, he felt.

All this worried him. He was afraid that he had found at the *Load of Hay* something which pre-knowledge had made him expect. The picture as he had seen it reminded him of statistics, from which one could draw whatever conclusion was most favourable to one's conviction. Commonsense warned him that an unprejudiced passer-by was unlikely to have sensed anything unusual about the inn other than extreme rusticity, perhaps, which many would have found romantic. Besides, argued commonsense, even if some of the men at the inn were members of a band of smugglers, it was unlikely that every one was similarly guilty.

Had there not been some evidence—namely the empty bottle of *Rhum Negrita*—to link the person of George Smiles (was any man ever less aptly named?) with the smugglers, Terhune would have felt inclined to distrust his own adverse reaction to the *Load of Hay* and its company. But there was the evidence to be considered; in the light of which he found it hard to dismiss the possibility of two other men being equally concerned: Walter Matcham, the farmer; and the landlord, whose name he had subsequently discovered to be Fred Link.

No two men could have been more dissimilar; both as regards physique and character. Where the farmer was large—beefy was the better word—Fred Link was sparse; where Matcham was red-faced, bull-necked, and hairy, Link was tall, round-shouldered, and thin of thatch; his pasty face was unhealthy in appearance and reminded one of a night-baker. Matcham was a jovial fellow; just as ready to tell a crude story as to listen to one; a regular 'hail-fellow-well-met'; a hearty, amusing, vulgar companion. But Link was unprepossessing, unlikable; his sullen, scowling expression warned one to take no liberties with him.

Two dangerous men; each in his own way. Terhune could not decide which would have to be the more feared in case of trouble. If there were a shade of difference—not admitted by most dictionaries—in the definition of cunning and crafty, he would have described Matcham as cunning; the other as crafty. Each in his own right a dangerous opponent in combination...

On the assumption that both were connected with smuggling, he believed that Matcham held the superior position—if there were such an anomaly among a band of law-breakers!—by right of a superior intelligence. Link did not look as if he could be easily browbeaten. Yet he had obeyed Matcham's order to keep quiet without hesitation; almost from habit, indeed.

Lastly, Terhune considered the ugly-faced George Smiles. Ugliness, when it is not caused by physical deformity, can be attractive. It was not so in the case of George Smiles. His face was repellent: and proclaimed him to be, not a vicious man, perhaps, but certainly a man without virtue. He had flabby lips, shifty eyes, and furtive mannerisms; a man whom one might justifiably judge to be either a petty crook or a shiftless scamp. If events should prove the man to have been the driver of the lorry which killed Kitchen, the discovery would be no great cause for surprise, Terhune thought.

3

Within a few minutes of his return to his flat he was reading the first of Kitchen's books. This was Shore's *Smuggling Days and Smuggling Ways*. He read slowly and with meticulous care: in spite of his dislike for Kitchen's widow, he believed her account of what had happened to put her husband on the track of the smugglers. For two reasons the effort to concentrate was not too easy. The first was an involuntary one which annoyed him exceedingly; his attention would keep wandering back to the room at the *Load of Hay*, so that he constantly found himself reviewing events there instead of reading the book in front of him. The second reason, paradoxically, lay in the book itself: every time he was able to forget the present in the past his interest in it was too enthusiastic; he became lost in the general at the expense of the particular. In consequence, he had to force himself to read page after page for a second time, just to make sure that he had not overlooked some item of significance.

This careful analysis took time. Before he had read through a third of the book he was disagreeably surprised to hear the clock at St. James's strike twelve. This was already some time past his usual hour for going to bed. He firmly but reluctantly closed the book and went along to the bedroom.

Early the next morning—long before Mrs. Mann came along to prepare his breakfast—he resumed his interrupted reading. Even during the meal, for he propped the book up against the milk jug and read on. But he found nothing whatever which, he felt, could have started Tom Kitchen off along the trail which led eventually to his death.

Ordinarily, he would have taken the book down with him into the shop, to read during slack periods. But, on a Thursday, there was no slack period, for Thursday was market day—the most important day in the week for Bray-in-the-Marsh: on that day the local world and his wife walked or rode or drove into the small town; some to buy, many to sell; but all to meet friends, have lunch, a drink at one of the three inns, hear the latest gossip, exchange books at his library.

And, as if to torment him, the day was even busier than usual. For hours there was a constant stream of people in and out of the shop; many with no other excuse than that of exchanging a few words with him on some subject as far removed from books as could be. For Terhune was well liked by all who knew him. All very flattering to him of course, but for once, unwelcome: being impatient to continue reading the smuggling books up in his den, he felt in no mood for trivialities.

For all that, the morning was not without interest. He was talking with young Jeffrey Pemberton, the youngest son of Mr. Justice Pemberton, when he grew uncomfortably aware of being stared at by a sturdily built man who, standing in a dark corner with his back to the window, had his face in shadow. It was only when he half turned his head that Terhune was able to recognize the florid features of Walter Matcham.

It required no great intelligence to deduce that a person who was 'no reading man' had not come to buy or borrow a book. A queer sensation disturbed Terhune's contentment. It was evident that his account of himself was being checked by the astute farmer.

He continued talking with Jeffrey, half expecting to see Matcham leave now that the purpose of the visit was presumably fulfilled. But Matcham remained where he was, picking up a book here and there, and looking through it with unconcealed disinterest. It soon became obvious that he was waiting for Jeffrey to leave.

He was by Terhune's side before Jeffrey had closed the door behind him.

"Good morning, Mr. Terhune," he boomed. "To think that I've been coming regular to the Market, and never noticed there was a book shop here. That's what comes of not being a reading man." He jerked his head towards the plate-glass door through which was to be seen a glimpse of the scene beyond. No more than a glimpse, though, for two stalls were set up opposite the door, and effectively concealed the rest of Market Square. "Pity them two stalls is there; they hide the view a bit, don't they? But there, folks keep you too busy to worry about a little thing like that."

The question was ingenuous: the smile which accompanied it, jovial as usual. All the same, Terhune sensed something significant about the artless enquiry. Quick reflection confirmed this impression when he recollected having claimed to have seen the farmer at the market on a Thursday morning through plate glass. Last night, he had felt sure that Matcham had accepted the answer: he realized now that he had deluded himself: Matcham had suspended judgment, as it were; he had come to judge for himself.

Terhune gazed at the restricted view of the outside world, and found nothing hopeful in it. No intelligent man seeing the circumstances for himself could believe his story. But to elaborate it, alter it, excuse it would do more harm than good; would warn Matcham that he, Terhune, suspected the other man of not believing the story.

"Yes," he admitted; "much too busy, generally speaking. I'm always glad when Thursday is over and done with."

"Shall you be coming to the *Load of Hay* tonight?"

Terhune was sure that a trap had been set for him. Uncertain as to what answer was expected of him, he decided to rely upon the truth.

"Not tonight. Too much work to do."

"You should come one night when the dart team's playing a match." The laughter which followed the suggestion was boisterous. "If you want a thick night—"

"When are they playing next?"

"Next Saturday, against *Toll Inn*."

"I'll be there."

The farmer laughed again—if one had not suspected him of being an arch dissembler one would have taken him to be a merry soul.

"So will I, mister, you can bet your sweet life. Well, I mustn't be keeping you…" He thundered out of the shop; his tread heavy, his laughter loud.

And perhaps jeering, too, Terhune reflected. He experienced an odd feeling that the prosperous-looking farmer was a very dangerous man.

Chapter Nine

Terhune had not exaggerated when describing any Thursday as a busy one. Thanks to a day too occupied to cope with routine jobs, he usually had to do these later after the shop was closed.

That night he rushed through the routine work, and settled down in front of the fire for another session of reading. He finished *Smuggling Days and Smuggling Ways*; but beyond reading of half-a-dozen or so unsuspected smuggling tricks which, though interesting, probably had no connection with the present circumstances, he came across nothing significant.

He turned to the next book, *The Smugglers*, by Lord Teignmouth and Charles G. Harper. He read through the first seventy-three pages of Volume II, finding plenty to interest him but nothing of significance. As he turned over the seventy-fourth a long, narrow slip of writing-paper fluttered out, and fell to the ground. Its purpose was obviously that of a makeshift book-marker—Terhune usually made used envelopes serve that particular purpose. Eagerly, he read the two pages thus marked, but, at first reading, they conveyed nothing to him. He read them a second time, with slow deliberation.

They referred to a particularly notorious run which had taken place on the night of November 8th, 1821, at a point about midway between the village of Sandgate and the Shorncliffe Battery. Here, at about 11.0 p.m., described the authors in previous pages:

"a large boat, laden with spirits, tobacco and salt, supposed to be
from Boulogne, came ashore and was immediately surrounded
by a party of between two and three hundred men, who had
been collected from twenty miles round, and formed into three
parties: the most numerous to work the goods; while the other
two, called 'fighting parties', carrying bludgeons and fire-arms,
were posted on each side of the boat, at a distance of about forty
yards, and extending from the sea right across the public road
towards the hills, so as to protect the men engaged in clearing
the boat."

This run was disturbed by one Lieutenant Peat, the stormy petrel
of the coast, an active, zealous officer, and a hard fighter of reckless
courage, who had previously distinguished himself at Lydd. When
Peat, accompanied by his orderly, John Green, attacked the smugglers,
shots were fired, which wounded the lieutenant in the leg. Other smugglers, meanwhile, fell upon Green, who was overpowered and bound.
Undaunted, Peat discharged his blunderbuss into the thick of the fray,
at close range, and then cut a way out, with his cutlass, to a house
called Ivy Cottage, or the Kettle-Net House. Later, he was joined by
Mr. Bolton and a seaman from Fort Twiss. These three men followed
up the smugglers, who were by then retreating with their contraband
into the wild country behind the coast. When the rear-guard of the
smugglers, numbering about sixty, perceived the blockade men, they
fired and wounded the seaman. This fire was returned—and here
began the first line—of page 74:

"by Lieutenant Peat, who discharged both blunderbuss and
pistol. Several shots were then exchanged, the smugglers meanwhile retreating in a compact body, followed by the blockade
party, and alternately halting, forming up, and exchanging fire,

and then retreating again, until they reached the top of the hill, whence they dispersed inland. It was now between half past eleven and twelve, and on returning to the boat Lieutenant Peat found the wounded seaman and two Midshipmen. By this time the wound in his thigh which had been received early in the affray was getting stiff, and two riding-officers coming up, they carried him and the two wounded seamen to the Sandgate watchhouse.

"Equally interesting was the evidence of James Walker, one of the wounded seamen quartered at the Tower near Sandgate, and who, on the night of the affray, was posted on the beach between Shorncliffe Battery and a house called the Squire's House. He stated that at about eleven o'clock five men armed with pistols came down the beach where he was and told him to keep off. He told them to keep off, whereupon he instantly found himself surrounded by a large party of smugglers, one of whom made a blow at him with a bludgeon, which he warded off with his pistol, and knocked another man down with the edge of his cutlass, upon which the rest called out, 'Shoot the b——', and a pistol was fired at him, wounding him in the thigh. He returned the shot and a man fell, upon which someone called out, 'A dead man!' and the body was picked up and carried off. The smugglers fired several shots at him, and he fired his pistol three times, and then dropped down, faint from loss of blood. Almost immediately after this, he saw a boat come in, and about 250 men come down to unload it. He then got up and walked towards the Tower, meeting Mr. Shallard and his party on the way. He further stated that he could see by the light of the pistol-shots that the smugglers had their faces blacked, or covered with black crêpe.

"Daniel Shehan, describing the treatment he received after being knocked down and badly beaten with bludgeons, said the smugglers talked of murdering him, and continued to kick and ill-treat him: his appeal to them, as Englishmen, to stop such cowardly treatment being unheeded.

"The only independent testimony obtainable was that of Joseph Arundel, servant to Mr. Magnaic, of Kensington, who was staying at Sandgate. He…"

As he laid the book down on his knees, Terhune realized that he was being unreasonably disappointed. The fluttering slip of paper had raised his hopes, for the late P.C. Kitchen had had a tidy, orderly nature which made unlikely the retention of the book-marker in the book except for some definite reason. But what that reason was he could not fathom.

Unless, he reflected, Kitchen had meant the book-marker to remind himself that, like the nineteenth-century smugglers, the twentieth-century contraband runners were likely to be dangerous men not to be trifled with, and were as likely to fight in self-protection. On the other hand, both volumes of *The Smugglers* were filled with similar incidents: there was no more reason for pages 74 and 75 to remind him of possible danger than, say, pages 112 and 113, which referred to the deaths, in like circumstances, of Lieutenant George Dyer, R.N., near Hythe, on April 5th, 1826, and Quartermaster Morgan, who was murdered by smugglers on the beach at Dover, on July 30th of that same year. Besides, any man of intelligence—and Kitchen had given proof of being a man of intelligence—would realize that risks would have to be taken in trying to effect an arrest, single-handed, of a band of desperate characters.

One other possibility, Terhune noted, was the brief mention of Sandgate. But he could not feel that this was the answer he wanted. If the risks and hazards of smuggling had not changed overmuch during the passage of a century and a half, the 'village' of Sandgate had. No sane smuggler was likely to try to land contraband on the beach at

Sandgate. The road across which the old-time smugglers had spread their 'fighting party' was now a busy main road along which it was usual to see not an occasional car pass, but a string of vehicles in both directions; a road that was lined on the far side with houses, many of which were certainly connected with the telephone. Reluctant to think that he was on the wrong tack, he doggedly read the two pages through for the third time.

They might just as well have been blank for all the good the third reading achieved. He was sure there was not a word on either page which could have given the late policeman even the vaguest hint. Why then had the two pages been especially marked? But had they, he presently asked himself? For, thinking back to the moment when he had first picked up the book to read, he had not seen the book-marker. Why not? Surely it was something that would have captured his attention at once?

On further reflection he realized that one of two answers could apply. He had not seen the book-marker because it had not been visible. That could have been so on account of the slip of paper being not a book-marker at all, but merely an odd piece which had been slipped into the book, between pages 74 and 75, by accident. Or, if it were, after all, what he had originally believed it to be, the probably the explanation lay in the possibility of its having been casually slipped into some other part of the book upon the policeman's taking it up to read, to be at hand whenever it should be necessary to mark a new place. But when that time had come, the book-marker—having slipped inside the edges of the pages—was not to be seen. So maybe the policeman had used a new book-marker. Or had finished the book.

He leaned over and picked up the narrow slip of paper. He had no definite purpose in doing so; indeed, he was not particularly conscious of having moved until his fingers were turning the slip over: it was an involuntary act induced by mental abstraction. But immediately he had done so his attention was captured by a few pencilled words that were to be read on the reverse side of the slip: Check H.P., page 105.

The policeman's handwriting? Impossible to say, for Terhune had never seen it; but he felt sure it was. Tomorrow he would show it to Mrs. Kitchen, for verification. Meanwhile, on the assumption that it was, he puzzled over the meaning of the tantalizingly cryptic note. The 'page 105' was easily interpretable, of course: less so 'Check H.P.' H.P.? Hire Purchase? A well-known sauce? Horse-power? He consulted a handy, one-volume encyclopaedia; turned up the section on abbreviations, and chuckled. He had not realized that H.P. could stand for such a variety of meanings, for the encyclopaedia contributed two more: Half pay, High priest.

Which of the five meanings? He quickly decided against High Priest, and H.P. Sauce. And, afterwards, Half pay. What of Hire Purchase? A possibility, this, to be investigated later. Horse-power seemed the most likely solution: but in what connection? Somebody's truck? Somebody's private car? Of the two he thought the truck the more likely. Perhaps Kitchen had been suspicious of one lorry in particular, and had made the note to remind him to find out whether its horse-power was sufficiently high to warrant its use by the smugglers.

Terhune turned to page 105 of the book he was reading, and carefully read it in the hope of finding some connection with the unknown H.P. He failed to learn any more from page 105 than he had from pages 74 and 75. He read it through the second time, with the same result. There was nothing on page 105 to call for a check-up of 'H.P.' of any description.

He frowned with disappointment: and began to suspect that 'hire purchase' was meant; and that page 105 referred not to *The Smugglers* but to a catalogue of sorts. Perhaps he had planned to buy a new bicycle on the 'never-never'; or a kitchen range; some new furniture—the list was unending.

'Check up H.P., page 105.' Check up hire-purchase terms of the kitchen range on page 105. It was a natural note for a tidy-minded man—or an absentminded man—to make. Much too natural to please Terhune, who would have preferred to believe it was a clue. If only he could have found something significant on page 105...

A sudden thought. Need the number 105 refer specifically to the book in which he had found the note? It was a commonsense assumption, of course; but there was an alternative theory. At the time of making the note, Kitchen might have been reading some other book, and later have transferred the home-made book-marker to still another book—to *The Smugglers*, for instance!

The theory was certainly one worth testing. He picked up *Smuggling Days and Smuggling Ways* again, and turned to page 105. Nothing. He substituted *The King's Customs*. Nothing. Then Chester's *Chronicles of the Customs Department*. Nothing. He turned to fiction. But neither *Doctor Syn* nor *The Man Within* was more fruitful.

Next, *The Smuggler*, by James. An old book, this; a double-volume book, for it contained not only *The Smuggler*, 447 pages of small print; but a 304-page story, of even smaller print, entitled *One in a Thousand*, or *The Days of Henri Quatre*.

Half-way down page 105 of the first story Terhune read a paragraph which seemed to have bearing on the cryptic note. Two men were, it seemed, discussing the prospect of a run.

"'... In the meantime, let us talk of the rest of the business. You say the night after tomorrow, or the night after that? I must know, however, for the men must be down. How are we to arrange that?'

"'Why, I'll see what the weather is like,' was Harding's reply. 'Then I can easily send up to let you know; or, what will be better still, if you can gather the men together the day after tomorrow, in the different villages not far off the coast, and I should find it the right sort of night, and get out to sea, they shall see a light on the top of Tolsford Hill, as soon as I am near in shore again. That will serve to guide them and puzzle the officers. Then let them gather, and come down towards Dimchurch, where they will find somebody from me to guide them'."

The light on the top of Tolsford Hill—the stack on Newdick's farm— was it too fantastic to deduce that the two events were, in a sense, synonymous? He did not think so. In fact, for the first time he realized the ramifications of the stack fire. Until that moment he had believed that the fire had had a purpose similar to the mischievous driving on to the road of Jim Davis's cattle. But not necessarily so. The stack might have been set alight for one of several reasons—to let the smugglers at sea know that everything was all clear for the run: contrariwise, to warn them of danger, or to advise them to postpone the run; as a signal of advice where to land (a fire at one place; a firework display another; an agreed arrangement of lights in a certain window, observable through a telescope, another; and so on).

The more thought he gave to this possibility, the more certainly he convinced himself that the pencilled note on the book-marker referred to the paragraphs which he had just read. He tried to put himself in the dead policeman's place on the night of first reading the book. As a newspaper reader he knows that, as a consequence of world conditions, smuggling into Great Britain had greatly increased. As a policeman he further knows that Romney Marsh is involved in that smuggling (even had he not been officially advised to keep a sharp look-out for unusual events, Terhune reflected, he must surely have picked up a hint from talking to fellow constables, the visiting sergeant, or the C.I.D. men with whom he had been in contact). One night, reading in an old novel of a method by which the smugglers of the past centuries signalled to their mates at sea, he realizes that Newdick's stack might have been set alight for the same reason. Perhaps the thought is, at first, more whimsical than serious; for, after all, stacks do catch alight, for a variety of reasons. But the thought is quickly followed by another. Cattle have been known to break out of their pasture, and stray along the highway; but in Davis's case it was strange... Suppose that the stack had been set alight as a signal—suppose that the cattle had been *driven* on to the highway for the purpose of impeding pursuit—and what about the car that had been slewed right across the road?...

Was the paragraph on page 105 Kitchen's first clue? Terhune reflected. The thought that it could have been appealed to his sense of drama; but he did not think that it was so. The words Check H.P.—if they referred to the paragraph, which he was sure they did—bore an implication that the clue was one of a series; hence the reason for checking 'H.P.'

H.P.! He failed to establish a satisfying connection between the light on the top of Tolsford Hill—or the burning of Newdick's stack—and horse-power, although he found it easy to think of several that did not stand up to analysis. For instance: speed in sending a message from one part of the Marsh to another, to give notice of a change of plans. But was speed necessary for that particular purpose in the second half of the twentieth century, when a 'phone call could be so much quicker, and even safer?

At length he concluded that the two letters referred to none of the accepted abbreviations, but to some cryptic combination known only to the policeman. He read the page through again, this time to see whether it did not offer a clue to the cipher. Could H.P. have something to do with distance, phases of the moon, the weather?

The next time of reading page 105 offered nothing new in information or suggestion. So far as he could judge, nothing in the action of the story needed checking; except, perhaps—he came back to it—the question of weather. Was Kitchen reminding himself to check up on what the night of the stack fire had been like regarding visibility, for instance? Likely enough, for if visibility had been too bad for the fire to have been seen at a distance, then the possibility of its having been started as a signal could be discounted.

H.P.! The letters had no likely connection with the weather. Fine—cloudy—fog—rain—visibility—starlight—new moon, full moon, old moon—calm—gale—stormy... It began to look as if every other letter in the alphabet could be used to represent some aspect of weather conditions save those two. With a feeling of exasperation he abandoned the problem for the time being, and returned to his reading of *The Smugglers*. He turned to page 76, and read what the Mr. Joseph Arundel, who had been staying at Sandgate, had to say.

"[He] said that, at about half-past eleven on the night in question, Thomas Byers came to the back door, opened the latch and wanted to come in, but he would not let him. Byers, who was dressed in a smock-frock, asked him if he heard the firing. Just before Byers came to the door a wounded man had come to the garden adjoining, and a servant from next door went to his assistance. Shortly before this he had heard a great deal of firing in the road. He further stated, that about a fortnight before Byers had come to the back door, dressed in the same manner, with the lower part of his face blacked, and asked for small beer.

"Incredible as it must seem, all efforts to discover the parties concerned in this daring outrage proved futile: the law agent having to return to headquarters not a wiser but a sadder man.

"It was never discovered who captained the smugglers on this occasion; though the excellence of the arrangements, by which so large a body of men were collected from a wide extent of country, at a pre-arranged time and place, without the knowledge of the revenue authorities; the masterly manner in which the parties were handled, and their retreat covered, to say nothing of the admirable arrangements for removal of the killed and wounded, not only gave evidence of a degree of discipline scarcely to be expected amongst a casual assemblage of rustics, but implied no mean powers of organization on the part of the captain. Everything, indeed, pointed to the redoubtable leader of the 'Blues' as the moving spirit in the business. It was subsequently ascertained that his right-hand man was actively engaged in the exploit.

"And what of the wounded? It was a point of honour amongst their confederates to convey wounded smugglers to some remote inland cottage, where they were well cared for, free of cost, until able to resume work. The surgeon called in to attend such a case could always be depended on to keep his own counsel: it was no business of his how the poor fellow came by a bullet in the leg: no questions were asked; and wise people minded their own business, and held their tongues. To have manifested too much curiosity would have spelt professional ruin in those wild, lawless days. As long as the fees were forthcoming, that was all a medical man need trouble about.

"Encouraged by the success of their first attempt the gang came down to the coast on the following night, November 8th, in even greater numbers, near Dymchurch, where, after surprising the blockade sentinels, and before a force could be assembled to oppose them, they succeeded in running the whole of their goods, consisting of 450 tubs and a number of packages, with the loss of only one tub and the boat. As for the latter, the smugglers attached no importance to it; boats of the description used could be built in France for about £40. And as the profit on a cargo of, say, 300 tubs amounted to from £450 to £500, an ample margin was available for contingencies of this sort.

"And here it may be well to explain that owing to a heavy bond being required from all owners of boats on this side of the Channel—which bond was forfeited, together with the boat, if found engaged in smuggling—a number of English boat-builders had started business on the French coast to meet the requirements of the trade: a circumstance so notorious as to form the subject of a report from Captain McCullock. These boats, built chiefly by men from Deal, Dover and Sandgate, were from 38 to 40 feet in length, and of the lightest framing and of the cheapest materials consistent with safety; and were navigated under licence from the French Government on condition that one-third of the crew were Frenchmen. No less than eighteen were under construction at this time at Boulogne."

2

Nothing further came to light that night. Nor the next; although, on both occasions, he read until his eyes were tired, and smarted from too much tobacco smoke, and the hour was past midnight. If the secret of the smugglers' movements were concealed somewhere in one of the books, it was too subtle for him to detect.

On the Saturday night he kept his promise to Matcham to visit the *Load of Hay* again. He arrived, as he had planned, ahead of the team from *Toll Inn*. The inn was much fuller than it had been the previous Wednesday night. So full, in fact, that he wondered just where it was hoped to play the match. At least, not where, for the darts-board was hung up in all its glory, but how: although no space had been cleared there was already scarcely enough room to hold up one's tankard of beer in safety. What room would be left for play when the opposing team arrived was anyone's guess.

In spite of the additional patrons present, and the consequent increase of geniality, he again felt that he had stepped back into an eerie and somewhat foreboding past. He was reminded of a cottage described in *The Smugglers*: the type once frequented by the Ransleys and the Questeds and other notorious smugglers of their day. At first he could not think why. The hut in the story—for, as the author said, 'it did not deserve the name of cottage'—had a floor of beaten clay; its two windows, containing no more than two complete panes of glass, were boarded up, or covered with coarse cloths, even filled up with paper; its only light came from one small tallow candle, stuck into a long-necked, square-sided Dutch bottle. The *Load of Hay* was not quite so primitive as that.

It took some time for him to understand the reason for his feeling: then he found the similarity to be more a trick of the imagination than an actual fact. The old smugglers' haunt had been kept by an old woman of nearly seventy whose skin was wrinkled and yellow, who wore on her head a 'cap, which had remained there night and day, for months; and thrust back from her forehead, which was low and heavy, appeared the dishevelled grey hair, while beneath the thick and beetling brows came the keen eyes, and a nose somewhat aquiline and depressed at the point'.

It seemed absurd to compare Fred Link to that vicious old crone, for Fred was tall and broad-shouldered, where the woman's shoulders were bowed with age. Fred's chin was blue-tinted with hair-roots, not 'wrinkled and yellow'. Above all, the sexes were different. Nevertheless, Terhune seemed to see in Link's hawk-nose the shape of the woman's nose, 'aquiline and depressed at the point'; in his beetling eyebrows, hers; in his gross lips, her thick, bloodless lips. It was almost as if he were looking at a double-exposure photograph, in which her figure had merged with the landlord's so that both were indistinguishable.

Link's expression, as he saw Terhune, was suspicious, unfriendly. But he had a good memory.

"Mild and bitter?" he enquired, in a voice that was a cross between a sullen growl and a shout to make himself understood.

"Please."

"We got a darts match on here tonight." He might just as well have added, 'Why the devil can't you keep out from where you ain't wanted?' for that was what the expression of his eyes and the tone of his voice said.

"I know. Mr. Matcham told me. He said he would meet me here."

"Ah!" The landlord looked astonished; but he said no more; he turned away to draw the drink.

"Mr. Matcham ain't here yet," explained George Smiles, who had unblushingly drawn near to join in the conversation. "I don't suppose he'll be long."

"Thanks," said Terhune, adding: "Have a drink?"

"Don't mind if I do," he answered, with a gratified leer. He raised his voice: "Another pint, Fred."

"Best respects, mister," he said, when Link brought the drinks. "You play darts?"

"Just about."

"I'm in the team." He pointed to a gilded vase which occupied a place of honour on Link's dresser-cum-bar. "See that there gold pot?"

"Yes."

"That's what we're playing for tonight. It's the Marsh Darts Cup. Any pub on the Marsh can challenge the 'older to a match, and the winner 'olds the cup until it loses. We've held it three months now, come next Tuesday."

Smiles was evidently in a mood for conversation. He rambled on, while Terhune listened—and occasionally answered—with half his attention. The other half he gave to the rest of the men present, and tried to listen to any coherent snatches of general conversation.

He studied the men about him. He thought that he recognized the majority from his previous visit; but among the new faces there was one in particular which attracted his interest. In build and size he was not unlike the landlord, but there the likeness ceased. To begin with, his clothes were different; more town than country. Not London, not one of the nearby seaside resorts, but one of the smaller provincial towns; a cut that was painstaking rather than smart. His hair-style was neat; he wore a tie with white shirt and collar; he wore shoes, and they shone. Easy to see that his shoes never came into contact with soil or dung.

His face was less conspicuous; at the same time it was vaguely familiar: Terhune was convinced that he had never met the man before, yet something about the face, some elusive quality, reminded him of someone he had once met. He studied the smooth-shaven, weak-chinned features, but the only other person they brought to mind was a film actor, a character star, whose name eluded him.

He would have claimed, in snap judgment, that the man was not of the company, but this appeared unlikely. He was too much at ease with the other people in the room, and they with him, not to be one of them by habit and in spirit. For this same reason Terhune decided that the other man was not the plain-clothes policeman of whom Murphy had spoken: it was too obvious that the man was no stranger to the district.

"Hey, George."

Smiles broke short his long dissertation on the merits of tractor ploughing in comparison with horse ploughing. He shouted back, "Yes?"

"Come here. Bob wants you."

He left without a word of apology, and Terhune was glad to be rid of the man. He could not decide which of three things about Smiles he disliked the most: the abnormally ugly face; the mumbling voice, and almost unintelligible dialect; or the nature of the man—obscene, narrow, sly.

This reflection caused him mental discomfort. It was not his habit to be over-analytical with other people, or to dislike them; he was much too tolerant, easy-going. But within the past week he had met several people whom he found himself disliking most heartily: Lil Kitchen, Smiles, Matcham, Link—and he felt sure that he would have little difficulty in adding the unknown man in the dark suit, white shirt and collar, to the list. He began to wonder whether his character was changing. For the worse. Perhaps he was allowing himself to be unduly prejudiced by the furtive atmosphere of the inn. Or perhaps his imagination was at fault; perhaps the atmosphere of the inn wasn't furtive at all; but just unprepossessing.

He did not have to turn round to know that Matcham had come in. "Good evening, Mr. Matcham." "You're late, Walter." "Where you been, Walt?" And Matcham's jovial, booming voice. "Give a man room, can't you? How the flaming hell do you think I'm going to get over to my usual place unless you make room for me?"

There was a general shuffling of feet, and a shifting of posteriors along the bench nearest the fire to make room for the broad behind and swelling stomach of the big farmer.

"So you come, mister, like you said?" Matcham laughed boisterously. "I would've bet on you coming." Why did the man so often create an impression that his words were underlined with secret meaning? Terhune testily reflected. On the surface, one of those trite remarks which modern laziness has made commonplace in everyday conversation: underneath, the hint of a positive certainty that Terhune would attend.

"Who is expected to win tonight?"

"The *Load of Hay*—s'long as Sam Plunkett does his stuff same as usual."

"Sam Plunkett?"

"Over there, next the man with the red scarf." Terhune glanced across. Plunkett was the man in the dark suit.

"Is he a good player?"

The best we have. If you want to find out how well, bet him a drop of Scotch he can't hit double top three times out of five. I've known him lose, but not often."

Glasses were circulating freely: Matcham had to speak loudly to make himself heard. Protracted conversation was a trial for Terhune, but his companion seemed used to it, and carried on talking. George Smiles forced his way back towards the bar. Link moved nearer to the fire. The two men drew close to each other. As they did so the general conversation died away with one of those unexpected pauses which usually make the superstitious look at a clock or a watch to see if the time is twenty past or twenty to the hour.

Smiles's low-pitched voice reached as far as Terhune in the quietness. "... says O.K. tomorrow, Fred, one-thirty..."

"Any sign of the *Toll* crowd?" Matcham bellowed.

The man sitting next to him almost dropped the tankard he was raising to his lips. "Gawd!" he muttered. "You nearly bust my ear-drum."

"A car's just pulled up outside, Walter," someone answered from near the door.

The noise started up again. But Terhune felt very, very cheerful. O.K... tomorrow... one-thirty... That was worth overhearing!

Chapter Ten

With the arrival of the *Toll Inn* team the atmosphere of the low-ceilinged room grew hotter, and more hilarious. Terhune found himself pushed into a corner near the fireplace, from which he would not have been able to move without using physical force. Between the heat of the fire and the warmth of the bodies pressing against him, he was soon sweating uncomfortably—worse still, his beer warmed up as a consequence of his having to keep the tankard on the shelf above the fire.

In spite of everything he felt as cheerful as any man in the room. With the enthusiasm and ingenuousness of a schoolboy, he looked forward to the moment when he would be able to tell Murphy that he had some news to pass on. Whether or no the sergeant would agree that the few words had reference to a proposed run was a question to which only time could give the answer; but he believed that the police would probably take precautionary action even if they were sceptical. He had no doubts himself—and chided himself, in consequence; for a more commonsense point of view was that there could be a dozen different explanations of the conversation between Smiles and the landlord, and none having any reference to smuggling. But his prejudice against the two men cavilled at the idea of giving them the benefit of the doubt.

The match took time to get started: the visitors needed to be warmed up, while the guests had no objection to keeping them company. Fifteen minutes or so after the *Toll* people had arrived, however, the players got together—somehow—in the middle of the room, and the match began.

Before the first leg was completed Terhune felt doubly pleased that he had chosen match night for his second visit to the *Load of Hay*. The prevailing interest and excitement communicated itself to him; and for no reason to which he could put a name, he experienced a partisan feeling for the home team. Which was ridiculous. As far as he was concerned there was nothing likable about either the *Load of Hay* or its team; whereas, regarding *Toll Inn*, precisely the opposite state of affairs existed. *Toll Inn* was a charming old place; its cream teas were famous for miles around; he very often dropped in there for tea, sometimes for a drink. He knew one of the *Toll Inn* players, too, a man named Jessop: the acquaintanceship was mainly a nodding one, but still…

Sam Plunkett was the key to the mystery. He was not, perhaps, at the top of his form—fortunately, for otherwise there would have been no contest, and the match would have been unexciting. But nearly every time he missed his objective, usually the treble twenty, the miss was accompanied by 'Ohs!' and 'Ahs!' of disappointment, so narrow was it; often no more than a wire's breadth.

The man's expression interested him. Hit or miss, it remained bland and suave. To Terhune it was full of self-conceit and superciliousness; but this opinion was not shared by the others present. As their conversation revealed, they thought him a good sport, a good loser. Not that he did lose in the true sense of the word; seven times out of ten when he missed treble twenty it was to get the twenty. All the same, the man's skill fascinated Terhune; he wanted the *Load of Hay* to win because he thought Plunkett's skill deserved its reward.

The home team did win, but only thanks to their star player. For the others in the team were not so good as their counterparts in the visiting team. After the match the two sides merged to drink one another's health. Jessop was pushed into the corner near Terhune.

"Hullo, sir, I didn't expect to see you here tonight."

"I drifted along."

Jessop chuckled. "Bet you're doing a spot of detective stuff—though I ain't heard of a murder hereabouts, come to think on it," he ruminated.

It was unfortunate that he had brought Smiles with him.

"What's that—detective work—what the 'ell you talking about?"

Jessop looked surprised, then eager. "Didn't you know?"

"Know what?"

With glistening eyes, and enthusiastic voice: "Mr. Terhune has quite a name for being one of these 'ere amateur detective blokes. Helped the police more'n once he has. And pretty successfully, let me tell you. I thought everybody had heard of him."

The ugly face turned uglier. "By Gawd!" it shouted. "A flaming 'tec—"

"Didn't you know that, George?" Matcham blandly interposed, as he stood up. "You should read the local papers more thoroughly. There was quite a good photograph of Mr. Terhune in the *Kent Messenger*—let me see, a year ago, was it? Underneath it said what Bill Jessop has just said."

So Matcham had been playing with him, Terhune reflected bitterly—like a cat with a mouse...

Meanwhile, a quietness spread through the room; an ominous, threatening quietness that was far more frightening than the quietness which had greeted his last visit to the inn. He felt abruptly glad that the *Toll* men were present—absurd, because whatever could have happened at the *Load of Hay* in 1780 was scarcely likely to happen in a century of civilian orderliness. Nevertheless, as he glanced quickly at the staring eyes of the *Load of Hay* men about him, he sensed such a feeling of hostility, he was convinced that a word from Matcham or Link would have set them about him, manhandling him in their rage.

He nodded in answer to Matcham's question. Matcham continued: "I met a police 'tec once who told me there ain't no such thing in this country as an amateur detective. He said the police would soon clap in gaol anyone who tried to do their work for them."

"That's true. I'm not really an amateur detective, Mr. Matcham. Just an expert on old books. Haven't you ever read in the newspapers of the police calling in the services of an expert?"

The farmer grinned. "I'm no reading man, like I told you on Thursday." A cunning remark deliberately intended, Terhune believed, to avoid giving a direct reply. The grin widened: soon his face was crinkling with laughter—all save the eyes, which were expressionless. "P'raps you're here on business tonight? Has someone done a murder what none of us know about yet?"

Terhune realized that he would have to be careful in giving his reply. A too-emphatic denial would probably not convince the astute farmer; on the contrary, it would probably increase his suspicions.

He pretended to chuckle. "I should like to hear of anything happening round about that wasn't known in the district within half an hour or so." This response produced an echoing chuckle from Jessop and another of the *Toll* men, also two local men whom Terhune instantly noted, believing them to have no connection with the smugglers. "But I'm here on business, if you call writing books a business. Most people call it a hobby. I'm talking about the book I mentioned the other night: the one about the pubs on the Marsh. I thought that something about this darts match ought to go down fairly well."

"It would an' all," Jessop chimed in. "I likes books about pubs and darts matches and that sort of thing."

A hint of indecision passed quickly across Matcham's face. "It would me, too, if I was a reading man."

"Would sort of make you feel at home, wouldn't it, Walt?" Sam Plunkett asked in a bland voice that was local and yet not local.

Either Plunkett's question, or a hidden signal from Matcham, relieved the tension. There was more general laughter, a shuffling, several calls for more pints of M. and B.s, browns, A.B.'s, the loud buzz of conversation. Terhune knew that the crisis had passed—for the time being...

2

He realized that it would not be politic to leave before it was necessary, so he stayed on until the party from *Toll Inn* left—which was not before closing hour! Before then he had reason to feel glad that he had stayed on; for he sensed from Matcham's behaviour and conversation that the farmer was in doubt about him, and trying to pump him for information. Matcham's questions were cunningly worded, and in themselves, betrayed an intelligence dangerously astute—and unexpected. This interrogation, concealed by a convivial joviality that might easily have hoodwinked anyone less suspicious of him, convinced Terhune that Matcham was either the leader of the smugglers, or the brains behind the titular leader. He tried, in his replies, to match astuteness with ingenuousness, and believed that he was successful.

As soon as he was back in his flat he rang up Murphy. The detective answered.

"I've just come back from the *Load of Hay*, Murphy. I believe a run is planned for tomorrow night, about one-thirty a.m."

"The divil it is! What makes you think so, sir?"

"I haven't much to go on, but it has something to do with George Smiles..."

"Ah!"

"I was talking with him when somebody called out to him that Bob wanted him. When he came back into the room again he went straight over to the landlord, Fred Link, and I overheard Smiles say, 'blank blank says O.K. tomorrow, Fred, one-thirty, blank blank'."

"What does the blank-blank business mean?"

"Words that I didn't hear because of the noise."

"I see. Then you didn't actually hear that everything was O.K. for one-thirty a.m.?"

"No."

"Then Smiles could have meant one-thirty p.m.?"

"Could have, Sergeant. Perhaps I've let my imagination run away with me—"

"Don't think I'm criticizing, Mr. Terhune," Murphy hastily interrupted. "I'm only thinking aloud."

"You're right, of course. But I'm sure he was referring to a run. There was something about his face..."

"I know what you mean. You're probably right, but I'm afraid we daren't take any action."

Terhune felt disappointed. And puzzled. It wasn't like Murphy to be quite so dampening.

"The hint's too vague?"

"That's not the reason, sir. If we were lucky enough to make an arrest tomorrow night the rest of the band would suspect that it was you who tipped us the wink, especially now that they know that you've helped the police now and again."

Terhune was surprised. "What makes you think they know?"

"I've just had a report from Gregory, the plain-clothes man from Maidstone whom we put on the job. He was there, too."

"I didn't see him there: I mean, anyone whom I suspected of being a detective."

"No?"

There was dry humour in the sergeant's voice which made Terhune realize the stupidity of his own remark: was it likely that a worthwhile man would allow his real job to be too easily guessed?

"He said that the situation looked ugly for you at one moment when a man from *Toll Inn* told everybody you were a private detective who had helped the police on several occasions."

"It didn't look pretty."

"He would have helped you if matters got worse, but as you managed to calm the men down he kept quiet... he seemed to think you handled the situation pretty smartly, if you don't mind me saying so. Anyway, he's satisfied that there must be something fishy going on at the *Load of Hay* for the men to be ready to start rough-housing you then and there."

"It certainly seems as if some of them have a guilty conscience, doesn't it? To get back to the question of tomorrow, Sergeant. Is it solely on my account that you don't propose to take action tomorrow?"

"Yes."

"That's damn' silly. Even if I should be suspected, it isn't likely that any of the men would do anything to me because of it."

"Maybe not, sir, but it wouldn't be fair to you for us to take the risk. I don't want to be melodramatic, but there's something about smuggling which makes men tougher than the ordinary run of criminals. I don't know why, but it does. Besides, the Commando training of the war hasn't helped the police a'-tall, a'-tall."

"I wonder if the Chief Constable would be quite so considerate about the consequences to me?"

Murphy chuckled. "I doubt it. The old Colonel is as tough—" He checked himself, as he grew anxious, suspicious. "What's in your mind, sir?"

"If the Colonel were to get wind of something, and get on to you—"

"You wouldn't go behind me back, sir?" Murphy reproached.

"I?" Nothing could have been more innocent. "I didn't say *I* would do anything."

"Begod! I have known yourself too long to be taken in by your soft answers whin you mean to have your own way."

"Sergeant! What a reputation to give a man!"

"You wouldn't really be doing that now, would you?" the sergeant wheedled. "Come, sir, tell me as man to man that you won't be up to any of your tricks? I've enough troubles on me shoulders as it is without having your death on me conscience."

"Death! Oh, come, Sergeant—"

"I said death, sir. That poor divil of a Kitchen is dead, and both yon and meself know that weren't the result of an accident."

"But that was in hot blood—in a sense..."

"Hot blood, begod! Kitchen's death was a coldblooded a murder as any I've ever come across. There's no evidence that the men in the lorry had any reason to believe that they were suspected: they just weren't taking chances. His life didn't mean a darn' thing to them, the blasted swine." There was a steely note in Murphy's voice to indicate the intensity of his feelings.

"All the more reason for not passing up a chance of arresting them," Terhune promptly pointed out. "You've finally convinced me, Sergeant—"

"To say nothing to the Colonel?"

"On the contrary."

Murphy sighed. "If you was Irish yourself you couldn't be spoiling for a fight more than ye are, sir. All right! It's meself what will get through to Maidstone this very minute. Will you be in tomorrow?"

"All day."

"I'll try to get along sometime in the afternoon. Thanks for ringing up. Good night, sir. And—"

"And what?"

"Just be taking care of yourself, sir, in the meanwhile."

3

Murphy appeared just before five o'clock. In time for tea, he frankly confessed.

"I was hoping you would offer me some. I could have had tea at home, but the wife has her sister there; when those two women get together, a poor male—that's me, at home—is best out of the way."

"Everything fixed for tonight?"

The sergeant nodded as he produced several maps from a dispatch-case which he had brought with him. Two of these he spread out on the table, side by side. He talked as he did so.

"It's not until one studies a map that one realizes how easy smuggling must have been in the old days. Look at this map first of all." He pointed to the right-hand map. "This is the Weald of Kent, scale one inch to the mile. Here's the Romney Marsh, taking up the entire right-hand corner. Roughly speaking, the Marsh is a triangle in shape, which lies on one side instead of standing up on its base. The coastline, from Littlestone-on-Sea to Hythe, represents the side it is lying on, with Hythe as its apex. Its base is the main road from Littlestone to Appledore; while the remaining side is represented by this road, which runs east from Appledore to Hythe. Do you see how many roads cross and lead out to the Marsh from the coast side to the Apple-dore-Hythe side? Including the base road itself—the Littlestone—New Romney—Appledore—Tenderden at the west end, and the Willingham-Ashford road at the east end, there are eight. Besides those eight, all of which proceed in a northerly direc-tion, we must take into reckoning at least twelve others which strike off the Littlestone-Appledore road in every direction ranging from west to south.

"Of course, not all these twelve are first-class roads. Far from it, indeed. Nor do I think they are roads which the smugglers would normally take, on the assumption that London is the Mecca of smugglers and that the quickest route there is the one they prefer to take. But all twelve are roads of a sort, and usable in case of necessity.

"The west-to-east road from Appledore to Hythe is another complication. This road"—Murphy traced it with his stubby forefinger—"as you know better than I, is on the high ground which skirts the Marsh, and is not, strictly speaking, on the Marsh. But once any vehicle gets on it the driver has a choice of taking any one of nearly twenty roads which either join or cross it—an average of one road running north for every three-quarters of a mile along the length of the west-east Appledore-Hythe road."

He pointed to the second map. "And I've been speaking only of Romney Marsh; and the coastline from Hythe to Littlestone. There is still the coast between Littlestone and Rye, and the flat country behind, to be considered, all of which isn't properly part of Romney Marsh, though many people think it is. But if we were to try and throw a cordon round the entire district we should have to ask the co-operation of the Sussex police, which the Chief Constable is not willing to do on this particular occasion."

"In case it's a mare's-nest?"

"Yes."

"So you are going to concentrate on your own area?"

Murphy frowned—a little uneasily, Terhune thought. "Concentrate isn't the word I'd care to use, sir," he answered slowly. "You see, to make reasonably sure of catching anyone making a run across the Marsh we should have to cordon off nearly thirty roads, which would need a considerable force of men. If the Chief Constable could be sure of two things: one, that a run is being attempted tonight; and two, that it would be attempted within this triangle "—he pointed to the Romney Marsh—"he would take a chance and make a thorough job of it. But as he isn't sure he's not ready to take the risk."

"Does that mean you're doing nothing—" Terhune began.

"Oh no! A cordon is being set—but more as a dress rehearsal than a main performance."

Terhune did not follow, and said so.

"Every road is to be watched from midnight to four a.m.," Murphy explained. "Anything and everything entering or leaving the Marsh will be noted down. That will give us some idea of the smugglers' methods—if there is a run tonight, of course. For instance, whether they take the shortest route, or the longest; whether they take a direct route or a roundabout one; and so on. With that and other information in our possession, if we should be lucky enough to have another tip-off—"

"If!"

Murphy's grin was wry. "Of course! But if we do, then we shall be able to throw a cordon which even the most daring drivers won't get through."

Terhune was disappointed. It was asking rather much of Fate, he thought, to hope that another tip-off would be forthcoming quite so fortuitously. On the other hand, he had to admit to himself that the Chief Constable's plan was a sensible one. If, during the next few hours, further evidence was found to show that a run was being made, that at least would be reasonable proof that George Smiles was one of the smugglers. Once that fact had been established, thereafter the police might find it easier to get on the track of the smugglers by keeping a close watch on both Smiles and Link. The police had unlimited time and unlimited patience. A starting-point might well be all that was needed to bring about the eventual arrest of the entire band.

The sergeant went on: "We haven't enough radio apparatus to keep in touch with every watcher, so those without will have to use the telephone. We've arranged to use the house of P.C. Tankerton as a temporary headquarters. The old boy told me to ask you whether you would care to be there."

Would he care to be there? What a question to ask a man!

Chapter Eleven

M urphy presently remarked: "One of the smugglers must be a pretty good weather-forecaster. On my way here I noticed that a mist was beginning to rise from the Marsh."

"There was a warning of fog tonight in the forecast broadcast this morning,"

"But there wasn't last night. I checked back with the B.B.C."

"You can't teach country people much about weather-forecasting." Terhune was thinking of Matcham. "In fact, for local weather conditions some of them are better than the meteorological blokes."

"So are some fishermen."

"You are thinking of the sea trip?"

"Yes." The sergeant went on, musingly: "The simplest way of stopping the run tonight would be to have a revenue cutter handy on the job. Radar would probably help it to pick up the craft even in fog."

Terhune laughed wryly. "I hadn't remembered radar. Shouldn't that mean that running an illegal shipment into the country is next door to impossible?"

"If the revenue cutter is on the spot. But it can't always be at the right place at the right time; and to keep enough cutters continually afloat to cover the whole of the vulnerable coastline would cost more than the revenue lost through smuggling."

"What about land-stationed radar equipment?"

"I don't know. I have an idea it isn't advanced enough, for that. It will be one of these days, I don't doubt. But I'd rather catch the people on this side than the chaps who make the run across the Channel: ten to one they're foreigners, anyway."

"And good luck to them if they make it?"

"Well, no; I didn't mean quite that, but—generally speaking—the sea breeds men, not ruddy murderers."

Terhune served tea; the two men began to discuss other subjects. Soon after six the sergeant left, after promising to return about eleven. Presently, Terhune settled himself before the fire, to await that hour, and took up another of the smuggling books close at hand. There were still four more to be read, and he was convinced that in one of them was to be found the clue which had enabled Kitchen not only to guess the time the run was to be made, but the route also.

Eleven o'clock—and Murphy—arrived without his having found anything of interest in the book he was reading. They left at once and went in Murphy's car to Police Constable Tankerton's house. By that time the mist had increased, but there was just enough visibility for the sergeant to keep the engine in top gear. There they found Superintendent Drake of the Ashford Division, together with Superintendent Boil and Detective-Sergeant Raines of the Hythe Division, and Detective-Inspector Collins of the C.I.D. headquarters at Maidstone. Introductions were quickly effected, though Collins's greeting was far from friendly. Terhune was not long left in doubt of the reason for the inspector's manner.

"It is unusual for a civilian to be present at a police operation of this nature, Mr. Terhune," he said shortly. "Of course, we are grateful to you for the information you passed on via D.-S. Murphy, but you are a writer as well as a bookseller, I understand. I trust that there is to be no question of your writing this operation up for a newspaper."

"I think I can speak for Mr. Terhune's discretion, Collins," Drake drily interposed.

"Quite, sir," Collins did not seem unduly abashed at the subtle reprimand of his superior officer. "I understood the same from the Chief Constable, but it's always as well to know where one stands, I think, and Mr. Terhune might not have realized that police procedure is confidential."

"Collins's bark is worse than his bite," Murphy later commented in a low voice to Terhune. "He's a smart man: one of the smartest in the county. Got a hope of being the Chief Constable himself one of these days. So some of the Maidstone people say. He's the man who arrested Marsh. Remember the case?"

Terhune did. The case had caused a local sensation at the time, for Marsh, like Murphy, had been a detective-sergeant attached to the Ashford Division. Directed to help solve the death of Jack Evans, Marsh had discovered that he had himself committed the crime while delirious. He had maintained silence, and planned escape to Canada; but only to be arrested, by Collins, aboard ship within a few minutes of sailing.

"It was a smart piece of work on Collins's part," Murphy generously admitted. "Ever since then he's been the old Colonel's pet. Poor old Marsh. I'm glad he got off on a manslaughter charge. Last I heard of him he was farming in Canada, and doing fairly well."

While the small party awaited zero hour, midnight, a check was made, with the map, of the points at which police had been posted to record the movements of all traffic. Even Collins appeared satisfied with the arrangements. He stood by the side of Superintendent Drake and stared down, with flinty eyes, at the large-scale map which was spread out on Tankerton's sitting-room table.

"Looks watertight, sir," he admitted. "As long as the men keep alert I don't think there is much chance of anything slipping through."

Boil, who stood on the other side of Drake, shrugged his shoulders. "Unfortunately, there will be no way of checking up on the guilty one if that happens." He looked at his watch. "What do you make the time, Drake?"

"Four minutes to."

"One of us is a minute out: I make it three minutes."

"I checked mine by nine o'clock, Big Ben."

"Good enough. Cigarette?"

It was an unlucky round for Boil: every man took a cigarette; perhaps, like Terhune, they were all affected by varying degrees of tension. Terhune felt like a general on the eve of battle.

Ten minutes after midnight the telephone bell rang. Both bell and instrument were in the tiny hall; and the sound was muffled because Tankerton had stuffed the bell with paper to prevent its waking his children, who were asleep upstairs. Even so, it made the men inside the sitting-room start, though they had been waiting for it.

The police constable, who had been stationed by the 'phone to take the calls, opened the door.

"Two private cars, FRN 616 and GOR 25, passed point two at midnight plus two; believed making for Burmarsh from Hythe, sir."

"Right."

As Tankerton closed the door behind him the bell rang again. He was soon back.

"A private car, BUQ 991, proceeded south past point eleven, at midnight plus nine."

"Right."

During the next fifteen minutes only private cars were reported entering or leaving the watched area. Nobody was surprised, or disappointed: it had not been expected that vehicles other than private cars would be seen before one-thirty a.m., and probably not for some time after that.

Just before the half hour after midnight Tankerton had a different message.

"Green-covered three-ton lorry, CFT 137, passed point six at midnight plus twenty-three, proceeding southwards."

"Southwards?" Drake sharply queried.

"Yes, sir."

The superintendent turned to the others as the constable left. "Sounds interesting."

"Why?" Boil was the questioner. "It's travelling southwards. Probably somebody returning from a long-distance trip—a load of potatoes, maybe."

"Maybe," Drake agreed. "Maybe it is proceeding to a rendezvous with the craft making the run."

"Ah! Pity we can't follow its progress through the Marsh. We might find out the exact location where the stuff is being landed."

Drake shook his head. "I don't think the information would help us much. It's unlikely they would use the same spot twice."

"Why not, as long as it's convenient and safe?"

The Ashford man frowned his doubt. "If these runs are organized by a man of intelligence, as we believe they are, he must realize that the police are not blind to the fact that a hell of a lot of contraband is coming into the country. What do you think, Collins?"

"I agree with you, sir," the inspector replied in his clipped manner of speaking. "After all, we've laid enough traps for them, at different points, but haven't had a sniff of them."

For a long time the telephone was silent. The men present did not talk much; Boil read a magazine which he had found on one of the chairs; Drake did *The Times* crossword puzzle, which he had brought with him; Collins wandered about within the very limited area of space, Murphy and Terhune played cribbage, the sergeant having spotted the board and a pack of cards, well-used and sticky, on top of the upright piano, which occupied more space than the tiny room could spare. As they all smoked, the room was soon hazy.

"How came this place to be chosen as the headquarters tonight?" Terhune asked, as Murphy shuffled the cards for a new game. The sergeant was looking pleased with himself at having snatched the last game from Terhune when only one point was needed. "I should have thought the Ashford or Hythe police-station would have been more convenient."

"We're handy here in case of trouble, that's why."

"I thought you were not anticipating any."

"Nor are we, but everyone agreed that we would be better here." The sergeant grinned, and lowered his voice. "I think the Super wants to create a precedent, so next time they can be near at hand if any arrest is made—one never knows; there might be a bottle or so to be sampled so as to make sure it was contraband."

Terhune chuckled; he knew that the slanderous remark was not intended to be taken seriously. He saw Drake looking their way. "Fifteen two, fifteen four, a pair for six, and one for his nob," he hastily counted.

Another twelve minutes passed before Tankerton entered again. "The lorry, CFT 137, has just passed out of the area, sir, at point twenty-two at one o'clock plus four, proceeding south-west." The constable vanished again as the five men glanced significantly at one another—point twenty-two was situated midway between Littlestone-on-Sea and Greatstone-on-Sea.

"This looks like it," Drake said quietly.

Collins nodded. Murphy, with an apologetic glance at Terhune, placed his cards face downwards on the table and glanced at his watch. For his part Terhune was not sorry to stop playing; he, too, was feeling too interested to concentrate on the game.

The succeeding minutes passed slowly; cigarette after cigarette was lighted; the fug in the small room grew steadily worse, but nobody thought of opening the door to let the smoke out. Terhune stared down at the faded plush tablecloth; and, remembering accounts he had been reading of some of the nineteenth-century runs, compared them with those of modern times.

In particular, he thought of the runs made by the Aldington Gang, or the 'Blues' as they were more popularly known by the residents of that area. The Aldington Gang, like their modern counterparts, had been cleverly organized by a farm labourer of the name of George Ransley. But, apart from that fact, there was very little resemblance between the operations of the nineteenth century and those of the twentieth. The smugglers of the nineteenth century had worked hard for a mere handful of shillings: a reward which seemed ridiculously inadequate for the hard physical labour involved in carrying tubs of contraband on their shoulders—to say nothing of the risks involved of being killed in a brush with the blockade party, or transportation to Botany Bay in the event of arrest. Not for them a furtive slinking along side roads in fast-travelling motor-vehicles; but hours of patient plodding across fields and ditches, through woods and hedges, up hills and down; beasts of burden in all but name.

Compared with the mean creatures who had not given P.C. Kitchen a sporting chance to defend his life, those old smugglers had been men for all their faults. More especially the members of the 'working parties', for they had been unarmed, and would have refused—as many did refuse—to take up arms against representatives of His Majesty. They smuggled, many of them, as a gesture of sullen defiance against what they genuinely believed to be repressive customs duties, rather than from a desire to lead a criminal life. In fact, the majority of the non-armed smugglers were normally hard-working, respectable members of village communities with regular jobs who would already have done a day's work before answering the call to make a run, and who would, the next day, do another day's work.

Desperate they may have been; and bold and daring, for many a run had they made in daylight, or in bright moonlight: many a time had they attacked a blockade fort to obtain goods captured earlier on by the preventive officers, or to release arrested comrades. But certainly not mean; nor cowardly; nor murderous.

Terhune thought of the seven shillings or so for a run which the old unarmed smuggler had earned—a guinea for the fighting men— and wondered whether the modern smuggler was content with the twentieth-century equivalent of that sum. He thought not; doubted not but what they demanded their full pound of flesh for a minimum of work and risk. He could not imagine George Smiles or Fred Link, or Walter Matcham, risking their precious skins for adventure, for excitement, for a gesture, for a few pounds. For those at least, he was sure, the be-all and end-all of smuggling was greed.

He saw Collins glance at a watch with a quick, impatient gesture; so he looked at his own watch and saw that time had passed quickly while he had mused: at any moment Tankerton might be entering to report that CFT 137 was passing into the area again. Tankerton did enter that very moment.

"Private car, AKS 352, travelling south-east, passed point six at one plus thirty-two, sir."

"That's Doctor Hardcastle's car, sir," Murphy announced.

Drake nodded. "I thought the registration sounded familiar. Been called out on a case, I suppose."

Collins was not interested in Doctor Hardcastle and his cases. "I wonder where the stuff is being landed," he muttered.

Boil shrugged, and lit another cigarette.

More time passed. Terhune wished that Tankerton would come in with further messages if only to help the time pass more quickly. Meanwhile, he tried to visualize the actual landing: he saw the slow rise and fall of the landing-craft ramp (was a landing-craft being used?—or an open motor-boat?—or a fishing-craft?), its bulk practically hidden by the damp salty mist which swirled about it; he saw shadowy figures descending the ramp, staggering somewhat with the weight of the bulky cases they carried in their arms; he saw the same cases being passed to men who stood inside a lorry, ready to stack the contraband; saw the cases mounting up behind the driving-seat one by one... Then he chuckled.quietly as he realized that his vivid imagination was probably seeing much more than his eyes would have done were he on the spot; for he did not doubt that there was not a gleam of anything to be seen; not even the comforting glow of a cigarette; everything, he was sure, was being done by feel rather than sight.

Half the night seemed to have passed before Tankerton interrupted again. "The lorry, CFT 137, has entered the area again, sir"—Tankerton sounded almost excited—"travelling east. Reported at two plus eleven—"

"Point twenty-two again?"

"No, sir; twenty-one."

"Ah! Taking a different road back." Drake nodded. "All right, Tankerton. Keep on the alert."

"Yes, sir." The constable quickly vanished.

Even the blasé police officers were not entirely unaffected by a feeling of satisfaction that the careful plans that had been made were not, as far as could be judged, being wasted.

"That lorry wouldn't be running to and fro unless it were up to some mischief," Collins said with a snap. "You don't think, sir, that it might be as well to take the chance of stopping it as it comes out of the area again?—it's possible that it may even pass outside."

The Ashford superintendent shook his head. "The Chief Constable's instructions were explicit: whatever happens we are not to let the smugglers suspect that we are on the watch."

"I agree," snapped Boil. "If we wait for the right opportunity we might be lucky enough to nab more than a lorry-load of contraband."

"You mean, sir, the man who's supposed to be organizing this racket?"

"I do, Mr. Collins."

The inspector continued to look doubtful. "Personally, I don't like passing up an opportunity. We may not get another tip-off quite so easily." He glanced at Terhune.

"That's a chance we must take. I suppose you realize that if we were to make an arrest tonight it's more than likely that the rest of the gang—if any, of course—would link it up with Mr. Terhune here?"

Collins said nothing, but the expression on his thin face hinted that the unpleasant possibility did not vastly disturb him. In fact, Terhune was fairly certain that the inspector was thinking, If a civilian chooses to mix himself up with police affairs he must take the consequences.

"How long did it take the lorry to pass through the area on its way south?" Boil asked.

"Forty-one minutes," Collins snapped out before anyone else could do so.

"The return journey may take longer. Cigarette?" Boil handed his case round.

Although the previous minutes had been interminable, the next forty dragged on still more slowly: each one of the five men present looked at his watch at least twice; Boil, three times: each time he did so his irritation increased. After the fourth time of looking he announced more cheerfully, "Any moment now."

Instinctively, the others checked the remark by looking at their own watches. Drake said, "Another four minutes."

"I wonder what's been brought in this time."

Boil was the questioner. The Ashford superintendent answered, "Drink again, probably."

"Why, sir?"

Collins's question surprised Drake. "Drink's about the only thing France has to spare—"

"How do we know the stuff hasn't been transhipped from a foreigner outward bound from the States? That's how the rum-runners used to work in Prohibition days. I reckon a cargo of nylons and tobacco would be worth more than drink."

Drake whistled. "Right enough. By old Harry! If we should allow this racket to get the upper hand of us there's no end to the stuff that would be worth bringing in at the present time."

"Including currency."

The superintendent looked grave. "Including currency," he agreed. "A few currency runs could affect the national economy." He glanced at his watch again. "Zero hour."

Amid silence and a mounting impatience the men waited for Tankerton to enter. But the minutes passed—five ten, fifteen—and there was no news from the constable. With unexpected abruptness Collins strode to the door and opened it.

"You awake?"

"Yes, sir."

"Been so the whole time?"

"Yes, sir."

"The lorry should have passed through by now."

"I know, sir. There's been no call."

The inspector closed the door and turned round. His face was angry. "I don't suppose they are sitting by the roadside having their supper."

Twenty minutes passed, twenty-five, thirty. By this time the police inspector was fuming with impatience.

"Do you know what, sir?" Murphy asked suddenly.

"I'm damned if I do."

"Maybe the stuff's been taken to a hide."

"B—!" exclaimed Boil with feeling.

Chapter Twelve

When another thirty minutes went by without news there was no doubting Murphy's presumption.

"We'll hang on as arranged," Drake announced in a tired but snapping voice. "But I don't think anything will come of doing so. The stuff has been planted somewhere in the area, probably to be collected in small lots, during daylight. I wonder how many of the loads of hay or straw we see on the roads have a few cases of contraband hidden underneath." His voice was bitter.

"Don't you think it might be as well to institute a search, to begin at daybreak?"

"For the contraband?"

Boil shook his head. "For the lorry. That's something which it shouldn't be too easy to hide."

"There must be dozens of lorries between here and the coast. Almost every village has its local carrier."

"All known to our local men. Besides, there's only one CFT 137."

Drake hesitated. Inspector Collins stubbed out his cigarette with a decisive movement.

"I think Superintendent Boil is right, sir. The local men would know where to look. All they would have to do would be to keep their eyes skinned. They wouldn't have to raise suspicions by questioning anyone. It would help a lot to know what particular parish to concentrate on."

Presently Drake nodded. "There shouldn't be any harm in trying to locate the vehicle. I'll get through to the Chief Constable—"

Boil grimaced. "He will be pleased!"

The Ashford superintendent chuckled. "I shouldn't be surprised, but he told me to keep in touch with him." He moved towards the door. "I hope to God we're not on the trail of a mare's-nest. Lorry-drivers have been known to leave their usual routes to visit a girl friend."

Drake was not long in returning. "The old boy agreed right away. Beginning at dawn every local constable in the area is to patrol his beat, and report back to his own headquarters when he's finished."

"Even if he has no news?"

"Yes."

Nothing of further consequence happened during the rest of the night. Doctor Hardcastle's car moved northwards again, heading for Ashford. Some time after that Tankerton reported the movement of two motor lorries—neither of them the missing one—a horse and tug, and two cyclists—it was evident that the work of the day was beginning.

"I think we can go. Don't you think so, Boil?" Drake smothered a yawn.

Boil agreed. He was too tired to smother his yawn. "To think we are due to begin a day's work in a few hours' time. 'A policeman's lot is not a happy one—happy one'," he hummed tunelessly.

Murphy turned to Terhune. "Coming, sir?" As the two men left the cottage he added, "I'll keep you in touch with the result of the search, sir."

"Thanks," Terhune was too sleepy to add more than that.

2

Murphy did better than telephone Terhune the next day: he conveyed the news in person.

"No good news of that lorry, sir," as he sat heavily down on the chair beside Terhune's desk in the shop. "Damned if I can understand it a-tall, a-tall."

"Why not? If it's hidden—"

"Look, Mr. Terhune, if you were the one wanting to hide a ruddy five-ton lorry, where would you hide it?"

"If I were a farmer, in my barn."

"And if you were a policeman looking for that lorry, where is the first place you would take care to look?"

"In the barn—ah! I see what you mean. It would almost certainly have been spotted."

"I think you can take it from me that, if the lorry had been put away for the night in any normal place—a garage, barn, or any other outbuilding—one of our chaps would most likely have spotted it. For all his slow ways, the village bobby isn't a fool, especially when the matter has something to do with the type of crime connected with country life—poaching, chicken-stealing, and so on. I'm willing to bet a week's pay that that lorry is—was—in some place where our chaps wouldn't normally look."

"Was!"

"It passed through Ashford just after midday."

"I'll be damned! Wasn't it seen *en route*?"

"No. What is more, when it was seen in Ashford it was empty."

"Perhaps it wasn't..."

Murphy guessed what Terhune was about to say. "Yes, it was. That is, if a false registration plate counts for anything. The number was false, by the way. No, sir, I don't think there's any doubt but what that lorry picked up a load of contraband from some place beyond Greatstone, and dumped it somewhere within a few miles of here." He recognized Terhune's doubt. "You don't agree?"

"How do you know that the lorry was empty when it passed through Ashford?"

"The policeman who spotted it was able to see into it from behind: its flaps were open."

"Then what was the object of bringing a lorry all the way from somewhere north of Ashford, to collect the stuff from the beach and dump it somewhere in the Marsh? Wouldn't it have been simpler to have used a local lorry? Don't forget that the lorry that killed Kitchen didn't dump the goods in the Marsh."

"As far as you know!"

"You mean the goods might already have been taken to a hide before we started to follow it? I don't think so, Sergeant. If there had been no contraband in the lorry, the men inside wouldn't have had to worry about its being searched by the police."

"Exactly! So we can take it for certain that it was not empty. And there's the reason for using a lorry which had a hide somewhere closer to London to go in to the event of possible trouble nearer the coast. Besides, local lorries get to be so well known, not only to the police but to everyone else in the neighbourhood, that no amount of false registration plates would stop it being recognized if seen."

Terhune admitted the truth of this reasoning. "Then why didn't the lorry take the stuff to that other home right away? I can't imagine the smugglers taking the trouble, and the risk, of trans-shipping the stuff if the road ahead were clear." He saw a worried expression pass across the detective's face. "Or do you think that they had reason to suspect that the road ahead wasn't clear?"

Murphy shrugged. "If I were a smuggler I think I should work on the principle that a number of short journeys with small consignments were likely to be safer than one long journey with the whole load aboard."

"You wouldn't put all your eggs in one basket, as it were, in case of an arrest?"

"Quite! With the proviso already mentioned: that, in the event of danger, a lorry-load of stuff could be taken right through to the next hide." The sergeant leaned forward. "You have a pretty good knowledge of the Marsh, haven't you, sir?"

"I've cycled there quite a lot."

"Do you know of any place where that lorry could have remained hidden from sight? I don't mean buildings."

"Woods, for instance?"

"Yes. A fairly extensive stretch, thick enough to hide the lorry well and truly."

"But what about Windmill Woods. Which side of them did you station your men?"

"Above the rise." Murphy scratched his chin. "And the woods are part of the rise. It could have been hidden there, I suppose."

"Easily. As a matter of fact, in the olden days smugglers often used Windmill Woods as a hide. The excise people had a very strong suspicion that the owner of the woods was in league with the smugglers, as many of the magistrates and the gentry were at that time, but they were never able to find enough evidence to take action in the matter."

"Who is the present owner?"

"Godfrey Hutton. A descendant of the owner I've just mentioned."

"I wonder—" the sergeant began reflectively.

"I doubt it. I meet him occasionally. I don't think he's the type to take any risks. He's the playboy type. Not a bad sort, but not what one might call the adventurous type."

"And well enough off not to want to make some money on the side?"

"Definitely—at least, as far as I can judge."

"The lorry might have been parked in the woods for the night without his knowledge."

"Might have, but I doubt it."

"Why?"

"In the first case, he's fond of getting up at daybreak and having a shoot; in the second, he has a keeper who is rumoured to be down on poachers."

"But possibly well in with the smugglers?"

"Possibly."

"Anywhere else you know of, sir?"

"There are a couple of farms alongside the canal which are well away from any road, and only connected with the nearest by a cart track. One of them has ample outbuildings. I don't see how the local bobby could have looked into them without being seen from the house."

Murphy began to look disconsolate. "It looks like we wasted the men's time this morning. Any other places?"

"I can't remember off-hand. I'm sorry I didn't think of the other two last night; I could have mentioned them. I was too tired, I guess. Of course, if you wanted the names of any places skirting the Marsh I could tell you plenty."

Murphy nodded. "So could I. Lady Kylstone's woods, for instance. And the woods round Willingham Manor. And Mr. Justice Pemberton's place. Whatever place they are using the smugglers must be well satisfied with it to use it in preference to one above the Marsh."

"The countryside isn't so deserted up here."

"I suppose not. Well, I suppose I mustn't keep you, Mr. Terhune." The detective made a move to rise.

"What happens next?"

"If we're lucky enough to get another hot tip—the real thing... The old boy was on the 'phone to the Super early this morning. He says he will call on every police constable in the county, if necessary, so as to cordon off the Marsh from end to end. And he'll issue fire-arms."

"I've an idea they might be needed."

"What good could it do for the smugglers to fight it out with the police?"

"As much good as in the old days. A fight gives the majority a chance to scatter, and as I don't doubt that the men know the countryside like the backs of their hands, I don't think they would find it difficult to escape. Have you ever tried chasing anyone across ploughed fields and dykes in the dark?"

"No."

"I have. During the war, when we were training for D-Day. And believe me, Sergeant, I'd back the man who knows the country every time. Once the men have a chance of getting clear of the roads, they leave the twentieth century behind, with its ninety m.p.h. M.G.s, its radio cars, its headlights, and all the rest of the modern paraphernalia. Once in the fields they would be no worse off than the nineteenth-century smugglers, and as more than ninety per cent of them were never arrested..." Terhune gave an eloquent shrug.

"Give us one man in our hands, and we'll nab the rest."

"You mean, if you could persuade him to turn King's Evidence?"

"Yes. Besides, our men would probably identify some of the smugglers."

"I doubt it."

Murphy looked astonished. "Why?"

"Look, Sergeant; maybe I'm making a mountain out of a molehill, but I've an idea that the man who is organizing this present racket has been studying last century's methods, and has improved on them. Do you know why so many of the old-time smugglers were never arrested? In the first case, because the men took precautions not to be recognized, either by other smugglers or by the preventive officers, by blacking their faces and wearing smocks. I don't suggest they still wear smocks, but it wouldn't surprise me to hear that, if a larger number of men than usual should be used, to deal with an extra big run, all their faces would be blacked. After all, it is what the Commandos did in the war, to avoid being seen in the dark. What would be the value of your King's Evidence if you could not produce other evidence of identification to substantiate the evidence of the informers?"

Murphy did not commit himself. "Go on."

"There's still another leaf which I believe has been torn from the old books."

"What is that?"

"Back in the early part of last century it was almost impossible to obtain evidence against any smuggler who wasn't taken red-handed. One reason for this immunity was the fact that the majority of the inhabitants of the Marsh wouldn't do anything to help convict a smuggler because they were sympathetic to the idea of buying drink on which no customs dues had been paid."

"What about the minority?"

"They were just as silent, but for a different reason. They wouldn't give evidence against smugglers because they were too afraid of the consequences. Even the local magistrates were too nervous to be of any help to the Government men. When Law officers wanted warrants they applied to magistrates living right away from the district."

Poor Murphy! He tried his best not to look too incredulous. He was not very successful.

"You are not trying to make out that the modern Marsh inhabitant is frightened of the smugglers?"

"I am."

The sergeant's eyes began to twinkle. "The trouble with you, sir, is that you can keep a serious face while making a joke."

"Why should you think I am joking? It takes a brave man to peach on a New York or Chicago gangster."

The twinkle vanished. "True enough. And what can be done there could be done here, I suppose. Especially in a scattered community." Murphy's voice sharpened. "Are you guessing, sir, or—"

"'Or' is the answer, Sergeant, but I'm pledged to secrecy."

"Why?"

"For that very reason: the person concerned is too frightened of what the smugglers might do to risk getting in direct touch with the police. That is why that person got in touch with me, because I could make a visit to the house without raising the suspicions of the gang."

"Begod! If anyone but you had told me—"

"It takes some believing, doesn't it, that a little corner of rural England should be afraid of a band of smugglers? But it's happened before, and it's happening again. Reminds one of the old tag about history always repeating itself."

"May I pass on what you say to the Chief Constable?"

"I leave that to your discretion."

The detective laughed dismally. "Thank you for nothing. What's the betting he'll think we are both crazy?"

Terhune grinned. "Perhaps we are at that. But since I've been reading about what happened in the old days of smuggling—"

"Ah! So that's why you know so much about the past! I wonder—"

What the sergeant wondered never came to light. The telephone bell interrupted him.

"Mr. Theodore Terhune?" asked the earpiece.

"Yes."

"Is Detective-Sergeant Murphy with you?"

"He is."

"The Superintendent would like a word with him if that is convenient."

"Quite. Hold the line, please." Terhune covered the mouthpiece with his hand. "The Super, Sergeant."

"The divil! Can't the old so-and-so ever leave me in peace?" But his voice was bland the next moment. "Hullo—yes, sir—begod!—at once, sir—yes, sir, the moment I return."

Murphy replaced the instrument on its stand, and regarded Terhune with a quizzical stare.

"I suppose Mrs. Kitchen wasn't the person you mentioned just now, about being nervous of the smugglers?"

Terhune temporized. "If it were?"

"Then she had good reason. Her cottage has just been gutted by fire. I wonder if it was an accident…"

3

Sometime later that day Murphy again called on Terhune. His expression was grave and worried.

"It was arson, right enough."

"The swine!"

"Ay, sir. The swine!"

"Anything left?"

"Only the walls. Of course, it's not her cottage, but now she has nowhere to live, and no furniture. She's leaving this afternoon for Yorkshire, to live with a sister for a time. She seemed in a divil of a hurry to catch the first train." He stared at Terhune with challenging eyes. "Any ideas on the matter, sir?"

"Yes. It was Mrs. Kitchen I was referring to. She came to me one day with some information—"

"And she a policeman's wife!"

"I know. That's what I told her. She said that she dared not get in touch with the police because something would happen to her if she did."

"How did she know that something might?"

"She didn't say. But she was certainly frightened. Which makes me think that fear of the smugglers is widespread."

"And the information…"

Realizing that he was being asked to betray the widow's confidence, Terhune hesitated at first to answer the implied question. But in view of the fire—he felt fairly certain that the smugglers were guilty of setting the cottage alight—and of the fact that she was leaving soon for the North of England, he felt that he should be absolved from the promise. He nodded, and told the inspector of all that had happened to date.

"Begod! The Chief Constable will have to be told of this, sir. We shall have to set a guard over this shop right away."

"That might be a fatal move, Sergeant."

"Why?"

"I believe that the cottage would not have been set alight if the smugglers had known about my having bought the books. You remember the diary that was stolen from the cottage? What I think happened is that the men found some reference in the diary to Kitchen's having found a clue to the smugglers' movements in the books. Not knowing that I had bought them, they set alight to the cottage more for the purpose of destroying the books than the cottage."

"You may be right. The point is"—the sergeant leaned forward, his face eager, hopeful—"have *you* found a clue in any of 'em?"

"Only this." Terhune passed over the book-marker.

Chapter Thirteen

That evening, soon after nine, Terhune took his bicycle from the tiny hallway downstairs and set off for a ride. In contrast to the cloud and patchy fog of the night before, the evening was fine. Cold for the time of year, but ethereal; bracing. The sky above sparkled with star-dust, and was silvered with the radiance of a moon only one night short of full. He was vaguely surprised to see its fullness; the fog of the previous night must have been thick overhead, he reflected, for the night had been quite dark—very dark in comparison.

He automatically turned south for the Marsh. He had no particular route in mind—or, for that matter, any destination. He had a twofold object in riding off into the night, and neither was that of going anywhere. What he wanted was fresh air in the first case and the opportunity for quiet, undisturbed meditation in the second. So he rode on, unheeding the steely beauty of the night but immersed in the problem of how P.C. Kitchen came to know where and when the smugglers intended to be on the night of his death.

By this time Terhune had read every one of the smuggling books he had bought from the police constable's widow. He had found them both fascinating and instructive but—apart from the book-marker, and the faintly pencilled note '? H.P.' in one of the books, which looked as if someone had partially rubbed it out—not one of them had supplied him with even the remotest clue to help answer that question, 'How?' He had read each book through with scrupulous care; many chapters or pages he had read several times; but all to no purpose.

How? How? How? The question tormented him. Nature herself flung the word back at him in the sough of the breeze, in the hum of his tyres on freshly tarred roads, in the dismal lowing of a cow robbed of its calf. Where in the name of old Harry had Kitchen found the one vital clue which had led him to a tragic death? In the hope of elucidating that point he tried to put himself in the constable's place, and to see the problem from the moment of its becoming a problem.

I am a police constable, he thought. I have proved that I have a flair for detective work; I have worked with C.I.D. men and like that side of police duties; I am ambitious, and am prepared to be a slave to hard, wearying labour for the sake of achieving a better living than I am likely to finish up with if I remain in the uniformed branch. With luck I might, before I become pensionable, become a sergeant; but I dare not hope for quicker or better promotion than that. But as a plain-clothes man...

I know that a certain amount of smuggling is going on in England. I have been warned to keep an eye open for anything happening of a suspicious nature. But that my particular beat is likely to be involved, or even that the warning is anything more than one of those periodic shake-ups—well...

One day I am told that one of Ted Newdick's ricks had recently caught fire. I think nothing of that: ricks do catch fire now and again from various causes. Another time I come across a car slewed right across the road, blocking the way in both directions. I think it a stupid thing for a motorist to do, even if it is at a time when nothing might normally be expected to pass in either direction. But the matter passes out of my memory. And then I hear about Jim Davis's cattle. That strikes me as a strange business; but there you are! the world is made up of many types of people; not all of whom are entirely normal—no doubt somebody had a spite against Jim—

Then, one night, while I am reading a history of the old smuggling days, I come across an account of the tricks and stratagems of the smugglers to protect their 'working parties' and avoid pursuit: carts drawn across roads to delay horsemen; armed men to keep off blockade parties; signal fires for their comrades at sea.

Unexpectedly, I am impressed by the similarity between the events I am reading of and several unexplainable local incidents. 'Good lord!' I exclaim. 'Twentieth-century smugglers?' The more I consider the theory, the less fantastic, the more feasible, it appears. Feasible enough, at any rate, to warrant investigation. But by whom? The C.I.D.? The proper course for me, as a police constable, is obvious: to pass on my suspicions to the sergeant, for transmission to the Divisional C.I.D. But will the C.I.D. give attention to an admittedly far-fetched theory submitted by a rural copper? Well, yes: it is their duty to do so. But will they do so in all seriousness, believing in it? Maybe yes; maybe no. How much better if I could submit evidence in support which would force them to give the theory really serious attention!

The idea appeals to my ambition. No time will be lost by spending a few weeks in making investigations on my own in the hope of obtaining supporting evidence. And if eventually my report should lead to the arrest of the smugglers, it is almost certain that I should be invited to join the C.I.D. as soon as possible. Exalted by hope and excitement, I go up to my wife, and impulsively blurt out: 'Lil, old girl, I've just had an idea that makes me think I'm on to something big. Something that may get me into the C.I.D. quicker than you can say "Jack, Robinson".'

The next few weeks I spend in making my preliminary enquiries. In the first case I establish, at any rate to my own satisfaction, that Jim Davis's cattle were driven on to the road to prevent pursuit of the smugglers. I next satisfy myself that Newdick's rick was deliberately set alight. The more enquiries I make, the more I convince myself that somebody connected with the smugglers has a more extensive knowledge of the Marsh, as a whole, than I have myself. That probably means that local people are involved—another link with the old-time smugglers, who were mostly local. How am I to identify them?

So far, so good—but at this point Terhune's imagination grew less helpful. Mrs. Kitchen had said that her husband had spent all his spare time off duty away from home, even to being away at all hours of the night. Some of that time was probably spent in making discreet enquiries of farmers and cottagers living in different parts of the Marsh. It was easy to imagine him jumping off his bicycle upon seeing a man digging his own bit of garden after work hours. 'Hullo, chum,' he would have begun, as an opening gambit, 'how are your spuds this year?' Once gardening talk begins it is like a flood, of course—hard to dam. But no doubt Kitchen had eventually been able to direct the conversation along the course he wanted. 'Speaking of cabbages, was that lorry full of veg—the one that went by here during the night? Or was it a night or so before that when it went by?'

As likely as not this question, or something like it, could have been asked ninety-nine times without obtaining the desired reply. But the hundredth answer may have made up one piece of the jig-saw puzzle the constable had been trying to construct. 'Ay, the beggaring thing! Woke the kid up at three o'clock. They things oughtn't to be allowed on the road at that time o' night.' Or: ' 'Tweren't last night, Tom. It were last Tuesday. Came by here at a fair lick, but I doan't know as how I could see what were inside.'

Perhaps none of the items had been important in itself, but it could have helped in the gradual building up of a composite picture of nocturnal movements for which there was no local explanation. But between possessing knowledge of general smuggling activities, and the apparent certainty that one particular run would be made along one particular road on one particular night, was a wide gap that ordinary routine enquiries would seem unlikely to have bridged.

There was another aspect about Kitchen's action that night for which Terhune found himself unable to supply a convincing explanation. If, as seemed almost certain, Kitchen had had foreknowledge of the run, why had he not passed on the information to the Divisional C.I.D.? It was understandable that he should have made all the preliminary investigations without sharing his secret; but not that he should have hoped, single-handed, to arrest the smugglers and break up what he must have known was a strong organization. There was evidence to prove that he was no fool: he must have realized that, at that point, a slip on his part would have done him more harm than good; for, with the smugglers warned that the police were very close on their track, gone would be the immediate opportunity of rounding up the entire gang.

Until he had read the last of Kitchen's books Terhune had been hopeful that something in one of them would have bridged the gap. Now he knew better. The books had undoubtedly served Kitchen as the initial clue; but it was evident that some other element had intervened between the books and the tragedy of the constable's death. Was that element the elusive H.P.?

He pedalled slowly on through the silvered darkness, and wondered if the *Load of Hay* had played any part in the constable's investigations. In the light of his own suspicions—his positive certainty, indeed, so far as Smiles and Link—yes, and Matcham, too—were concerned (Matcham had been too quick to bellow out his piece not to have a guilty knowledge of the information that Smiles had been passing on to the sullen landlord)—it was tempting to assume that it had. Yet, he felt doubtful that this had been so. Kitchen would have been known there, if not as *the* village copper—for his beat did not embrace the *Load of Hay*—at any rate, as a local copper; so the habitués of the inn would certainly have been doubly cautious whenever he was around.

I'm Kitchen, Terhune reflected. (He picked up the thread from the point at which he had dropped it.) I have a suspicion that some of the locals are part and parcel of this smuggling organization. How am I to find out who is, and who is not, innocent? I've got to get people talking about their neighbours. But suppose, by a piece of bad luck, I happen to interrogate one of the smugglers! Then the fat would be properly in the fire! And the end of any hope of yours truly making a sensational arrest.

Terhune's lips parted in a dry sort of a grin; judging by his complete lack of success in seeing himself in the role of police constable, he would not have been of much use as the real thing, he reflected with amused exasperation. For the life of him he could not imagine how, in Kitchen's place, he would have set about the job of trying to find evidence that some of the local inhabitants were smugglers in their spare time. What did one do in such circumstances? Station oneself in hiding alongside each of the Marsh roads in turn, and there make a note of everyone who passed; and particularly of the registration marks of all passing vehicles? This course might, with luck, eventually result in revealing the existence in the district of a lorry with a false registration—which would be something to work on, especially if it were to be in the habit of visiting a local farm for no good reason.

But surely one man working on his own could not hope to collect enough evidence to justify the time spent in doing piecemeal a check-up of this sort. Assuming that there was such a lorry to be spotted, it might easily happen—probably would happen, in fact—that when the watcher was on the spot, the lorry was not; or, when the lorry was about the solitary watcher would be elsewhere. To make sure of the lorry's being seen, every road in the Marsh would need to be watched. And, even then, there would still have to be done the work of checking up and identifying the various numbers, which would mean applying to the police of perhaps a dozen counties for their assistance in turning up their records.

He frowned. Every minute spent in trying to discover how Kitchen had proceeded in his self-appointed task of getting on the trail of the smugglers made it more certain that he could not have succeeded on his own unless he had had more information than that supplied by the books. For, on the face of it, he had had less to work on then Terhune himself. For he, Terhune, had the benefit of the information which Murphy had passed on about George Smiles and the empty bottle of French *rhum*, which clue in turn had led to the *Load of Hay*, with its saturnine landlord, Link; and the bucolic, prosperous-looking Matcham—and others. Whereas, as far as was known, the police constable had had no suspicions of Smiles and company.

Or had he had vague suspicions that the old inn was up to its bad tricks again? Had he, perhaps, watched the *Load of Hay* night after night, until at last something had happened to crystallize his suspicions? Suppose, for instance, a lorry—or maybe a private car, or a shooting brake—had stopped outside the inn at some early hour in the morning; suppose the watcher had seen cases carried in; suppose, later, after the lorry had driven off, men had come out of the inn and walked and ridden off for their homes; suppose Kitchen had followed one of those men to his home. That would have been more than enough for a determined, ambitious man to work on.

Once set upon this line of reasoning, Terhune's thoughts raced along it with enthusiasm. Kitchen may not, at first, have had definite suspicions of the *Load of Hay*. He may have agreed to himself that, if contraband were being smuggled through the Marsh, some of it, more particularly anything of an alcoholic nature, would inevitably find its way to one or several of the Marsh inns. With this thought in mind he may have watched each of the inns in turn; and so, by good luck, have witnessed one night some suspicious circumstance which had at last put him on the track of the smugglers.

2

"But that still does not explain how Kitchen came to know when and where that run was planned for," Murphy moodily commented, when he was given the gist of what had passed through Terhune's thoughts during the course of the bicycle-ride across the Marsh the evening before. "Nor, as you yourself pointed out, why he didn't let the C.I.D. know so that the whole damn' shoot of the smugglers could have been roped in.

"Look, Mr. Terhune," he earnestly continued; "we know, or think we know, that George Smiles is one of the gang. But does that mean that we have definite knowledge that another run is being planned by two-thirty a.m. next Friday, and that the lorry with the goods will take the Dymchurch-Willingham road, for instance? It does not. Not by a long chalk. To my way of thinking there is only one explanation to account for the accuracy of his knowledge. One of the gang squealed. Smiles, perhaps. Or Link. Who knows?

Terhune shook his head. "I don't believe that is the whole explanation."

"Why don't you?"

"It is agreed, isn't it, that the smugglers are a pretty desperate crowd—no, I don't mean desperate, exactly, but—well, tough?"

Murphy grinned good-humouredly. "That's your idea, sir."

"Not yours?"

"No, Mr. Terhune; frankly, it is not. It's all right for you writers to make your crooks tough guys; they go down well in books. As a reader I can enjoy Lemmy Caution and The Saint, and all the others like 'em; but in real life your average British crook doesn't say boo to a goose."

"British—"

"Yes. There have been some tough customers about since the end of the war, but most of 'em are foreigners. But you're asking me to accept—and I do—that the majority of the smugglers at work round here are local born."

"They were local born at the beginning of the last century; most of them being farm labourers. But they were quite ready to shoot it out with the preventive officers—the military, too."

"You persist in linking the past with the present?"

"Why not? Surely men haven't changed so much even if machines have?"

Murphy pursed his lips in disagreement; and in silence puffed away at his pipe for a full minute. Then he nodded his head.

"Perhaps you're right, sir. A man's life wasn't less precious to him then than it is now. I can't find any good reason for denying that what the Marsh people did in those days they wouldn't do now. Except, of course, the odds on their being arrested are greater than they were then."

"But the reward is greater."

"Granted. Well, sir, let's agree that the smugglers are as tough as you believe. What had that to do with Kitchen?"

"Just this. It would have taken more than just a threat of Kitchen's to have made a man like Link, or Matcham or Smiles, squeal. Kitchen must have had something pretty damning to have made one of the smugglers squeal and a chance of what the other members of the gang would do to him if the news of it ever leaked out."

Murphy took the pipe out of his mouth and pointed the stem at Terhune. "They burned down Mrs. Kitchen's cottage. They would do at least as much to a squealer. Go on, sir."

"The point I am trying to make is this, Sergeant. Kitchen must have known that the tip-off was reliable. The very chance, one would think, that he had been working and planning for: an opportunity of a lifetime to make the powers-that-be conscious of his existence. Why then didn't he pass the information on to the C.I.D.?"

"You tell me, sir," the sergeant muttered in a grim voice.

"I can't, and that is what's worrying me. There's something fishy about Kitchen's revealing his hand so soon. That is why I think your idea that one of the gang squealed is too straightforward, too simple, an explanation to be wholly correct."

Murphy grunted. "The worst of you people with imagination is that you won't be satisfied with the simple: you always have to look for the complicated. If us coppers know for certain that a certain man cracked a certain crib, we nab him, shove him up before the beak and let it rest at that. Now, if you were to be given the same job I suppose you'd start wondering why the devil the man cracked that particular crib, and not some other."

Terhune chuckled as he recognized how much truth there was in the sergeant's criticism. After all, Kitchen might have been blinded by his own ambition; he may have taken what he hoped would be a short cut to promotion by effecting single-handed the arrest of the gang. But, in spite of all arguments, Terhune was sure that, for once, the simple explanation was not the true one.

3

On Wednesday evening Terhune settled down to do a spot of writing for his new book. It did not take him long to find out that original work was off for that night; he felt far too restless to settle down to the serious business of literary creation. After thirty minutes or so of struggling against the inevitable, he gave up the attempt to finish Chapter Five. He put the work aside, and dressed for a bicycle ride. A few minutes later he was pedalling along the Bray-Farthing Toll road.

The weather had changed overnight. Heavy cloud formation concealed the rising moon; pockets of mist created conditions which called for a certain amount of care. The night, in spite of the moon behind the clouds, was fairly dark. He was reminded, vaguely, of the night when Julia and he had chased a speeding lorry across the Marsh.

This made him think of Julia with guilty conscience. He had neither seen her nor contacted her for many days: a fact which was not likely to please her. He felt remorseful for his neglect even to 'phone her, for he knew, without embarrassment, that she liked to go out with him at least once a week—oftener, whenever the circumstances were propitious. Sometimes they merely went for a drive, sometimes they went dancing, sometimes for a meal, sometimes for a swim. He must 'phone her soon, he decided, and fix up a meeting.

From thinking of Julia, his thoughts wandered, via the episode of the chase, to Mrs. Kitchen. She puzzled him; set him an enigma which he strongly desired to solve. The enigma was a simple one. How much more did she know about her husband's death which she had failed to divulge? That she had concealed an important item of fact he was still certain; though he had not a shred of evidence to support this view, but only an intuitive feeling. From the first he had believed that her fears had not been justified by the circumstances she had revealed—and that view of justification had not been changed by, first, the theft of her husband's diary, and, second, the burning of her home. He was convinced that she had been influenced in all her acts by a fear that had anticipated the possibility of something worse than either theft or fire. He was very sorry that she had already left the neighbourhood: he had hoped to question her more thoroughly, and had only delayed doing so in the hope of gaining her confidence.

He was still thinking of her as he neared *Toll Inn*. Suddenly the road before him was lit up for yards ahead by the dancing, powerful headlights of a car behind him. He moved well into the side of the road and would have thought no more of the incident, which is common enough to all cyclists, but for the fact that the furthermost limit of the lights lit up the rear of a stationary lorry outside the inn. Then the car flashed past him, with a roaring exhaust and a draught which all but made him swerve into the ditch, and disappeared round a curve.

But during those few seconds when the white headlights of the car had penetrated the mist and played upon the rear of the lorry, Terhune had recognized the commercial vehicle as the one which had killed P.C. Kitchen.

Chapter Fourteen

D oubts, of course, followed immediately. Doubts prompted by
sober commonsense. The lorry which stood outside the inn was
no different from many like it which were always to be seen going in
and out of Ashford on market day; or, on other days, transporting
livestock to and from farm sales, or a load of timber, or logs, or hay or
straw. The lorry was a mass-produced one: there was probably nothing to distinguish it from the thousands which had come off the line
before it, or those which came after it. It was unreasonable, he argued
with himself, to identify it with the one which, allegedly, had killed
the police constable; there was not one distinguishing feature about
it at which he could point and say, with conviction, 'That proves my
contention'. Not a scratch on the woodwork; not a dent in one of the
rear mudguards, not a mark on the closed flaps. Literally nothing—yet
he remained convinced that it *was* the same lorry.

Why was he so sure? He did not try to answer the question; for
who could explain what intuition is, or how it works, he told himself.
On the other hand, he knew of a very convincing and logical argument
to explain why the possibility should have suggested itself to him so
unexpectedly. Association of ideas! Thy psychological result of having
the lorry constantly in his thoughts, in conjunction with a similarity of
circumstances: the dark night, the mist, the headlights lighting up the
rear of the lorry. The probability was, he reflected, that had the lorry
been illuminated by any form of lighting other than headlights, the
possibility of the lorry's being the one Julia and he had chased would

not have occurred to him: he would have taken it to be just one of the many dozens of similar lorries garaged in the vicinity.

He arrived opposite *Toll Inn*, alighted, and leaned his bicycle against the wall as if having the intention of joining the cheerful crowd inside. In fact, this had been his intention until he realized that there was nobody else about. So he paused outside the door of the saloon bar, ostensibly to light a cigarette, but in reality to inspect the lorry in the light which escaped from the bar through a gap in the chintz curtains. In doing so he discovered one important difference between it and the majority of the vehicles owned by local carriers: it nowhere openly advertised its owner's name, address, or telephone number.

This was an interesting fact, though one not to be considered too significant; not all carriers advertised themselves. But it made Terhune snap his fingers in self-criticism—the registration number! What more evidence did he need?

He moved back towards the rear of the lorry so that he could read the registration. He grew despondent on reading EKQ 721. He could still remember the number of the lorry they had chased—SKK 16 something or other—SKK 164—yes, that was it: SKK 164. So intuition had misled him: the two lorries were not one and the same.

After that disappointment a drink seemed called for. He gave what he intended to be a last baleful glare at the registration plate and turned back towards the door of the saloon bar. But still not to enter it; for one more reflection brought him to a quick halt. Murphy had reported SKK 164 as being a false registration. Maybe that plate was kept exclusively for runs: the EKQ 721 plate for normal purposes.

He stared into the night to see if anyone was about or approaching. He saw nobody; but, to make sure, he listened for the sound of footsteps. There was plenty of noise from inside the inn, but not a sound from without. Deciding to take the risk of being surprised, he examined the registration plate with the aid of a lighted match, then chuckled with boyish glee—the plate itself was thinly caked with dirt, but the heads of the two bolts which secured the plate to the lorry were as clean as new pins!

He was now fully satisfied that his intuition had justified itself: without a doubt the plates had recently been changed. This fact, taken in conjunction with the absence of any visible owner's name and address, was all the evidence he needed. And all the evidence Murphy would need, he felt. What better clue could the police ask for than the name and address of the owner, which they would obtain as soon as they had checked up on the new registration?

The moment of jubilation soon passed, for this sobering thought intruded: what proof had he that EKQ 721 was not as false as SKK 164? The short answer was: none. And if it were—and he could see no reason why it should not be—the police would be no better off for his fortunate discovery. He leaned up against the wall of the inn and tried to think of what could be done to make certain that the opportunity of learning something more about the lorry and its owner should not be wasted.

The obvious course was to telephone Murphy so that mobile police patrols might be sent out to pick up the lorry, and trail it to its presumed home. This he was tempted to do until further consideration exposed possible flaws. If the driver should become aware of being tailed—an all-too-likely contingency: for what driver does not soon get to know that another vehicle is sticking close behind?—he would not only take precautions to lead the police a wild-goose chase, but the very fact of being tailed would be warning enough to him, and thereby to the rest of the smugglers, no doubt, that the police suspected him. A tactical error, that, which could mean all the difference between the gang's being arrested and their escaping scot-free.

A second course was this: that he should enter the inn and make discreet enquiries about the driver of the lorry, and where he came from. Like his first idea, this, too, was open to objections. If the driver were a stranger in the district, nobody would know anything about him. If he were not, then it was inevitable, sooner or later, that he would hear that 'that there Mr. Terhune—him what sells books in the shop in Market Square and helps the police to solve murder mysteries', was making enquiries about him—a consequence that would have the same result as the first course.

A pity he couldn't follow the lorry with his bicycle! At that, he reflected, this passing fancy might not be quite so fantastic as it seemed at first examination—if the lorry were a local one, and did not have too far to go! But as there was no method of checking up on this fact in advance he grinned wryly, and discarded the idea as wasting precious time. For time was precious: the driver might emerge at any moment.

His thoughts grew desperate, chaotic. He hated to think that a clue which might lead to the arrest of Kitchen's murderer was there to be had for the asking, as it were, and yet lay beyond his grasp. But beyond taking a note of the registration in the faint hope that it might prove to be the real one for a change, he could not think of any scheme whereby the lorry might be traced to its home without raising the suspicion of its driver.

One thing that he could do presently occurred to him. He could, if the opportunity remained favourable, take a quick look in the lorry to see what it contained—there might be a parcel or two inside, if the gods were kind, with names and addresses on them. A delivery note, a label, an identification tag—who could say what treasure might not be unearthed for the want of daring?

He listened, heard the sound of approaching footsteps and voices coming from the direction of Farthing Toll. Two more people coming for a drink, no doubt. Not wishing to be caught by them outside the inn, nor desiring to be forced to go inside, he wondered what he should do to avoid suspicion. The crisis spurred his memory: he recollected the existence of a small shed behind the inn where bicycles could be stored on a wet night. Thither he wheeled his machine, and waited there until he heard the newcomers reach and enter their destination. Then, without his bicycle, he returned to the lorry.

Nobody was about. He parted the flaps at the rear of the lorry, sprang inside with a quick vaulting leap, and closed the flaps again. He waited a few seconds to make sure that his action had not caused any alarm, then struck a match. One glance was enough to warn him that he was unlucky: the floor was littered with straw which had been freshly dunged: evidently the lorry had been used that afternoon for the transport of cattle.

With a sigh of disappointment he parted the flaps again with the intention of jumping out. Before he could do so a broad beam of light shot across the road as the inn door opened; the sound of voices rose to a crescendo. He quickly dropped the flap back into position, with the intention of waiting until the road should be quiet again.

He had waited too long. Instead of moving off along the road, two men who had come out of the inn climbed into the front of the lorry and started the engine. The next moment the lorry was jolting along the road, south-bound.

2

Terhune's first reaction to the unexpected was to grin with sardonic amusement. If that wasn't life all over! Just plain cussed! He hadn't been inside the damned lorry more than five seconds or so—just long enough for a match to burn nearly out—yet the driver of the lorry had had to choose that same, almost infinitesimal, period of time for his departure from the inn. The coincidence of the timing was almost too fantastic to be true—five seconds one way or the other would have prevented what was promising to be an embarrassing *contretemps*. If that didn't mean that life was downright mischievous—well...

The ever-ready grin turned into something more grim when he began to foresee the possible consequences of his involuntary ride, the least of which would be his having to find his way back, either to *Toll Inn* or to his flat at Bray. That could easily mean a many miles walk, if not to one or the other, then to the nearest railway-station or bus route. Well, he didn't object to walking: liked that form of exercise, in fact... at the right time and place!

What was more disturbing was the possibility of discovery. The chances of that were even, he considered. The driver might, on reaching his destination, make a point of looking inside to make sure that everything was in order, or even for the purpose of cleaning out the fouled straw. But, from the little he knew of lorry-drivers, he did not believe that he would be discovered on account of that particular reason.

No, there was a fifty-fifty chance of his remaining in the lorry undetected, but—suppose that the driver and his companion, having garaged the lorry for the night, were to lock or padlock the garage doors; and suppose that there were no other way out!

He lost his balance, and was flung against the side of the vehicle as it swung round a left-hand corner; his head suffered a nasty crack in consequence. If that were to happen every time the lorry rounded a corner he would be a mass of bruises before long, he reflected. The speed of the vehicle, paradoxically, suggested a simple solution to his present difficulty: all he had to do to escape from the lorry was to drop off from the back as soon as the speed dropped below ten miles per hour. He chuckled at his own slow-wittedness for not having thought of this act before. Meanwhile, the driver was giving no sign of slackening speed: in fact, the hum of the engine seemed steadily to rise.

He took a firm grip of one of the uprights as the vehicle lurched round another left-hand corner, and realized that, in the absence of traffic or other hold-ups—a more than likely absence at that time of night—the lorry might easily keep up its present rate of speed. In which case he must at least face the possibility of being carried to the lorry's home garage.

He must be prepared for all eventualities, he grimly decided. For discovery, for instance. And, if so, for quick action. That, and the element of surprise, might enable him to get clear away before it was too late. At the same time, he should also be ready, in case of his not being able to get away, with a good excuse for being in the lorry. Such as...

After rather desperate thought the best reason he could think of was that he had mistaken the lorry. For Jock Fraser's, for instance. Fraser's lorry was the sister of the one he was in, and was garaged at Fraser's home at Willingham. He was as pleased with this answer as he could be, in the circumstances, for anyone recognizing him, or knowing the neighbourhood well enough, would, at the same time, recognize the feasibility of the excuse. On the other hand, if he were not recognized, then the story would sound as good as any other.

The whine of the engine dropped to a lower note as the speed of the lorry slackened. In the hope that an opportunity of a quick escape was imminent, he put one hand on the tail-board and parted the flaps with the other. But the vital moment passed: the speed increased again before it had dropped sufficiently for him to take the risk of leaping out.

A few moments later he felt glad that the opportunity to escape had not offered. Not many minutes previously he had been trying to evolve some way of tracing the lorry's destination. By remaining where he was, that way was his.

Dispassionately, he weighed up the possible advantages of remaining where he was against the possible risks. The chief advantage was the possibility of learning, without further trouble or delay, the name and address of the lorry's owner; and perhaps, in consequence, the name of Kitchen's murderer. The risks were twofold: the first, that his intuition had played a mean trick upon him, and that he was chasing unnecessary details. The second, that if he were on the right trail, he would find himself confronted by some of the smugglers before he had a chance of escape.

What then might happen to him? They might, by beating him up, and threatening worse, try to frighten him from passing any information on to the police. They might even kill him—but this alternative he found hard to accept: it lent itself far too much to melodrama to be true to life. But accept it he had to: Kitchen's murder had been cold-blooded and deliberate enough; the burning of Mrs. Kitchen's home likewise; the smugglers were ready to commit crime upon crime to protect their liberty.

As if to mock him—or maybe tempt him!—the lorry presently slowed down to a walking pace: a god-sent opportunity for an effortless escape. For a moment he was tempted—damn it! he reflected, he was no ruddy hero; never had been one; was never likely to be one—but, grim-eyed, grim-lipped, he pictured the crushed body of the policeman sprawled in the dust of a countryside road, and resisted the impulse.

3

The lorry swirled round a right-hand corner, and began jolting along a road which Terhune was ready to swear had never had a roller on it. Then it stopped with a jerk which nearly flung him off his feet; the sound of the engine first throbbed with a hollow echo, then abruptly stopped. One of the two men in front yawned loudly. It required no special intelligence to comprehend that the vehicle had probably turned off the public road on to a rough farm road, and so into a shed of sorts: in short, that it had probably reached its destination. Now for it, Terhune thought, as he tensed his muscles for action.

"Fag, Ernie?"

"Don't mind if I do."

A match was struck; the fragrant smell of tobacco flowed back into the interior of the lorry.

"Don't mind a spot of bed, neither."

"Nor me."

Terhune heard first one door being opened, then the other: the sound of feet scraping on a hard floor, the tinny bang of doors being slammed. Voices drifted towards the rear as both men walked that way, one on either side.

"Who's on tomorrow?"

"Wally."

"Blast 'im! He can clear the muck out for hisself."

The other man chuckled—Ernie, Terhune believed. "You know what Wally is. It won't take us long."

"He ruddy well left his mess for me to clear up, didn't he, last time I was on the early run?"

"Yus, but he's a couple of stone heavier nor you, ain't he?"

By now the two voices were stationary at the end of the lorry.

"Look here, Ernie, if you think I'm flaming well afraid of that gorilla, I ain't; and one day I'll show you."

Ernie laughed good-naturedly. "It's that last beer, old man, what's making you cock-a-hoop. Don't forget it'll be gone by tomorrow. C'mon, it won't take us long." A hand moved one of the flaps aside. Terhune saw the glowing ends of two cigarettes, and tensed himself for a sudden spring and dash.

"Mr. Flipping Wally can do the job hisself," the second man, the driver, maintained with alcoholic obstinacy. "I ain't doing it, and that's straight."

"Have it your own way." The cigarette ends were blotted out as the flap was dropped again. "Only don't blame me if he gives you a shiner tomorrow night. Coming?"

"I ruddy well am."

Terhune relaxed as he heard footsteps again, and knew that the two men were moving away from the lorry. But the next moment there was a rumble, a squeal and a heavy thump, followed by a second rumble—squeal-thump, as the doors of the shed, or garage, or whatever the place was, were slammed shut. If those doors are bolted or locked... he thought.

He waited for what he judged to be more than ten minutes before venturing out of the lorry. The shed was as dark as the inside of the lorry had been; not a thing was visible. He struck a match, and saw three yards or so before him two fairly massive double doors, in neither of which was a handle of any sort visible. They looked ominously shut—and were, as he found when he tried to push them open.

In darkness he moved back to the lorry, and along its off-side. Half-way along it, as far as he could judge, he struck another match in the hope of seeing a window. There was none; but what was visible at the far end of the shed—it was a farm shed—was a small door. When the match went out he felt his way round to the other side of the lorry, and struck another. No window there, either. Apparently his only hope of escape was by way of the small door, and that might be locked, too; or, if it was not, might lead into some other windowless *impasse*.

The door was locked, though on the other side, which meant that there must be a way out on the far side. But when, rather despairingly, he gave it a firm thrust with his shoulder to see if there was any possibility of bursting the lock, he was delighted to hear a significant crack. He risked striking one more of his few remaining matches: by its light he saw that the upper panel of the door was rotten, and would take little more than a hard blow to knock a hole in it. He raised a foot and kicked hard with his heel: something gave way. When he rubbed his hand near the spot it was to find a jagged hole big enough to admit his arm. He inserted his arm in it; and, after a lot of fumbling, succeeded in grasping a key and turning it. The door opened: he found himself in the open air.

Not being a hero, he wasted no time. There was just enough moonlight reflected through the dark clouds to show him a road about one hundred yards away. So he ran in that direction as quickly as he could—and ran straight into trouble. As he gained the road a massive hand gripped his arm, and a bucolic voice said, "Now then, what's all this 'ere going on?"

He turned, ready to battle; but to relax when he recognized the welcome uniform.

"Good evening, Constable," he greeted in a gay voice.

"Hey, no funny business." The grip tightened until it hurt. "What have you been up to?"

"Where are we?"

"C'mon, what you been up to? I seen you running away from that shed. Up to no good, by the looks of you."

"You tell me where I am, and I'll answer you."

The policeman hesitated, but apparently decided that no harm could come of his answering that simple question.

"Springham."

Terhune had never heard of the place. "Is it in the Ashford Police Division?"

"No, it ain't. It's part of Maidstone—" The constable stopped short as he recollected whom he was answering.

"Look here, young fellow-me-lad, you'd better come along o' me to meet the Sergeant."

"Ever heard of Detective-Sergeant Murphy, of the Ashford Division?"

"No, I ain't."

"Will you let me telephone him? I'm a friend of his, and have something of importance to pass on to him. You can keep hold of me—"

The other man laughed. "Don't you fret, mister. I'm going to. You don't pull no wool over my eyes with that sort of yarn."

"Is there a telephone near?"

"A hundred yards off." The answer was very reluctant.

"I'll come quietly."

"You bet you will." A long pause. "All right, but if you're trying some funny business…"

"Just one more thing, Constable. That shed you saw me coming out of—who does it belong to?"

"Well, I'm jiggered!" The constable sounded it, too. "What's all this 'ere about?"

"I want to let Detective-Sergeant Murphy know."

"You does, does you!" Another pause, although the grip tightened more than ever. "The Springham Fruit Farm," the constable said at last. "And that's all I'm going to tell you. Come along, you. And no tricks."

He began to walk down the road, easily pulling his prisoner with him. Presently, through a gap in the hedge, Terhune saw the black outline of a large house of Tudor design.

"Is that the farmhouse?"

"Yes."

"Who lives there?"

"I ain't telling you no more."

"I only want to tell Murphy. It's a police matter."

"Police matter be damned! C'mon." A few yards, then, hesitatingly, "Plunkett's the name," he muttered with extreme reluctance. "Albert Plunkett."

Plunkett! The name was of the *Load of Hay's* star darts-player.

"Good lord!" Terhune exclaimed with jubilation.

Chapter Fifteen

By a lucky chance Murphy was at home, and answered the call.

"This is Terhune speaking, Murphy. I wonder if you would do me a slight favour—"

"Of course, sir," the detective interrupted briskly. "What can I do for you?"

"It's this way. I've just been arrested—"

"Begod!" Murphy's first reaction was astonishment. This was quickly followed by hilarity; his laughter made the earphone crackle at Terhune's end. "To be sure, an' niver have I come across such a man for finding trouble, sir, if you don't mind me saying so. If it's not finding corpses, it's getting ye'self smashed up in a car, it is; and now, begod! if it's not getting ye'self arrested. What's the charge, sir? Drunk and disorderly?" He began spluttering again.

"I think it's loitering with intent to commit a felony, or something of that sort. If you would have a word with the constable who's hanging on to my arm like grim death."

"Where are you?"

"Springham."

"Springham! Where the divil's that?"

"Somewhere in the Maidstone area, he tells me. I've been taken for a ride—"

"What!" The note of anxiety in Murphy's voice made the exclamation sharp, discordant. "You're not hurt?"

"Far from it, Sergeant. The men in the lorry didn't know I was in it."

"Lorry!"

"Possibly the one in which we're both interested."

"Begod!" Besides astonishment there was a note almost of veneration expressed in that one word. "Let me speak to that constable."

"Hold the line." Terhune turned to the policeman. "Detective-Sergeant Murphy wants to speak to you."

The constable showed that he meant to take no chances of his prisoner's snatching liberty. The hand which pinched Terhune's arm did not relax its grip: he took the earpiece with the other.

"Hullo," he bellowed, in the voice of one who regards the telephone as something contagious.

The conversation was not a long one, but Terhune could make little of it from the constable's staccato bellows.

"Yes… is he?… no… yes… I reckon I will… you will… yes… no… yes… left at the Snelling crossroads, about two miles along it on the right… yes… about that, I reckon… yes…" He slammed the receiver down upon its hook with the air of a man disposing of something distasteful to him. "He says he'll be here within the half-hour."

"Good lord! He need not have troubled to do that. I could have got home easily—I suppose!…"

"I daresay you could an' all," the constable drily muttered. "But I'm not that much of a mug—to let you go that easily."

"But, surely, now that you've spoken to D.-S. Murphy—" Terhune protested.

"How do I know he is a D.-S., and not a pal of yourn?" the constable asked shrewdly.

"Look up the name in the telephone book and compare the number with the one I asked for."

"And do the telephone book say as how the man at that number is a D.-S.? Now, if you'd spoken to him at the police-station…"

In spite of his annoyance, Terhune's sense of justice had to agree that there were grounds for the constable's canny reasoning. The man had said, from the first, that he had never heard of Detective-Sergeant Murphy, which was likely enough considering that they were in different Divisions, and therefore unlikely to meet on normal occasions. And if the name of Murphy were unknown, still less the voice! Anyone could pretend to be a detective-sergeant of the Ashford Division over the telephone, and there was no way for the constable to check back: a pretty fool he would look if he allowed a real criminal to escape from him merely on account of a voice over the telephone. The more Terhune reflected upon the constable's caution, the more he appreciated its justification.

Nevertheless, he was more than pleased when, in less than the promised thirty minutes, a car drew up alongside the telephone box, and the thick-set figure of Murphy stepped out and stood in front of him.

"All right, you can free Mr. Terhune," the sergeant began, in a breezy, confident voice. "I told you that over the telephone. Surely you haven't been hanging on to him all this time?"

The constable still did not relax his grip on Terhune's arm. "I s'pose you have your warrant card on you?"

"Warrant card! What the divil… What's that to do with you?" Murphy snapped.

"I want to see it before I lets go this man."

"Begod!" There was a snap in the sergeant's voice. "You'll let him go right now—"

Terhune chuckled. "Hold hard, Sergeant. You wouldn't want him to let go of a real crook, would you—just because some pal came along and pretended to be a detective-sergeant?"

Murphy was no fool. A moment's reflection convinced him of the reasonableness of the constable's precautions. He pulled a wallet from his breast pocket, and showed his warrant card to the uniformed man.

"Satisfied?"

The constable nodded. For the first time in more than thirty minutes he relaxed his grip of Terhune's arm. "I am sorry, sir, but there's been two or three thefts just lately round about these parts: it was my dooty not to take any chances."

Terhune's grin was rueful; he rubbed his arm, which the constable's fingers had left numbed.

"Fair enough," he agreed. "But I don't mind saying that any crook that tries to get away from you will have my sympathy."

A pleased chuckle greeted this remark. "I ain't a amateur heavy boxer for nothing."

"Shall we go, sir?" the impatient sergeant urged.

"Not if you've a moment to spare. I think you might find it worth while asking the constable a few questions about the Springham Fruit Farm just down the road."

"You do?" Murphy swung round to face the constable. "Well?"

"What do you want to know about it?"

"Ask Mr. Terhune here."

"Do you know much about the place?" Terhune asked.

"Enough, sir. I shouldn't mind owning it."

"It's a big farm, then?"

"Not so big as farms go, but big enough for Mr. Plunkett to send lorry-loads of fruit up to Covent Garden every weekday of the year."

"Plunkett?" Murphy queried sharply. "I've heard that name lately."

"Same name as the *Load of Hay's* star darts player," Terhune supplied.

"Ah!" There was something almost beatific in the sergeant's exclamation; Terhune knew that the detective was beginning to add two and two together. He added, "Even in the winter months?"

"Oh ah! He has gas chambers what the fruit is stored in."

"How many lorries go up each day?"

"Sometimes two, sometimes more."

Murphy seemed to forget that he had suggested that Terhune should do the questioning. "Many men working for him?"

"Enough."

"By which you mean more than enough?"

"I ain't a farmer. I don't know. But he pays 'em well. Leastwise, some of 'em seem to spend enough. Gives 'em a bonus, he does, whenever the fruit sells well."

"How many lorries has he got?"

"Five."

Terhune broke in: "Where does he keep them?"

"In a garage at the back of the house."

"What about the shed you caught me coming out of? There was only one lorry in it."

"That's for bringing the fruit to the gas chambers; and for a spare, in case one of the others breaks down."

"What about the house? It looks a pretty big place."

"It is. It used to belong to the Earl of Springham until the old Earl died twenty years ago."

"And then?" snapped Murphy.

"The young Earl sold it to pay death duties. Leastwise, that's what everybody hereabout says. Some of the old people of the village cried when the family moved away."

"Did Plunkett buy it from the young Earl?"

"No. Plunkett's only had it these last two years. It was a man named Rookwood what turned the property into a fruit farm. They say Plunkett gave enough for it."

"Who built the gas chambers? Plunkett or the other man, Rookwood?"

"Plunkett. He says fruit farming needs to be done scientific, like."

There was a slight pause. "Anything more, Mr. Terhune?" Murphy asked.

"Not at the moment."

"Then we'll be going." He turned back to the constable. "What's your name, by the way?"

"Evans."

"You can report what's happened to the sergeant, but not a word of it in the village, you understand?"

"Yes."

"Good night."

"Good night, Sergeant. Good night, sir. I'm sorry if I were a bit cautious, like."

"There's no need to apologize," Murphy snapped. "You can't be too cautious in these days."

He followed Terhune into the car, and pressed the self-starter. "Now, sir…" he chuckled as they began to move.

Terhune was not long in relating what had happened earlier on. He continued, "I hope I haven't dragged you out here on a wild-goose chase, Sergeant."

"Do you still think you might have, sir?"

"You once accused me of being too ready to make facts agree with my theories, instead of the other way about. All the same…"

"As you say, sir: all the same! Everything fits like a glove. The stuff is brought here from the coast, and warehoused; maybe, in one of the gas chambers. From here it is taken to London, probably disguised as a case of fruit; one case each day. Begod! The scheme is almost foolproof. Every morning a lorry-load of fruit—apples, for the most part, I suppose—is seen leaving here for Covent Garden. I don't know how many cases of fruit make up a lorry-load. But say twenty-five, for the sake of argument. Who's to suspect that one of 'em contains contraband instead of fruit? Then, as soon as the real stuff has been unloaded, the lorry goes on to leave the contraband somewhere else—"

"Or even at the same address as the fruit, Sergeant."

"That's it!" Murphy waxed enthusiastic. "The case of contraband is unloaded with the fruit, put on one side, and transported elsewhere at some other time. That plan would prevent any chance of other people in Covent Garden becoming curious to know why one case was often being taken elsewhere. Begod! sir, this man, Plunkett, if it was he who organized the racket, must have brains; as far as I can see there are only two weaknesses to be guarded against."

"The chances of the stuff's being stopped by the police on the way to and from the farm?"

"Yes, and that's been guarded against, as we know, as far as anyone could possibly work out a scheme to allow for all eventualities."

"And the other weakness?"

"The chance of one of the gang splitting on the rest—but that's not too likely as long as the men are paid well."

"Especially if they know what else would be likely to happen to them if they do! Where does the *Load of Hay* crowd fit in?"

"Helping to unload from the ship, I'd say. And possibly in shifting the stuff on from the local hide to the fruit farm." After rather a long pause Murphy continued, "Don't you agree, sir?"

"Oh yes! But at least a couple of points about that theory puzzle me. We are assuming that the fruit farm is the main warehouse, aren't we, and that the hide in Romney Marsh is probably only an emergency one?"

The sergeant did not commit himself by a direct answer. Instead, "Well, sir?"

"Why didn't the gang take the stuff direct to Springham the other night if the Marsh hide is only an emergency one?"

"I see what you mean," Murphy said presently in a reflective voice. "The fact that the stuff was taken to an emergency, instead of the main base, could have meant they were suspicious that something was brewing?"

"Yes."

"Maybe." The admission was lingering, doubtful. "Our men were given strictest instructions to remain well under cover. There may be an alternative answer. Did you know that the mist that was hanging about the other night was only local? The other side of Ashford was as clear as a bell. The smugglers may have decided that it was too risky to run the stuff right through to Springham."

The explanation, for want of a better, satisfied Terhune. Murphy went on:

"And the other point, sir?"

"I don't believe that the Plunkett of the fruit farm is the real brains behind the gang."

"Why not?"

"We know that there's big money involved, don't we? Evans let that out when he said that Plunkett paid enough for the farm, which means, in the local dialect, that he paid too much. If the farm Plunkett had that much money to play about with I can't understand how Sam Plunkett comes to be one of the *Load of Hay* crowd—that is, assuming that they are related: brothers or cousins, probably."

"They may not be."

"Quite! But the name is too unusual, for this part of Kent at any rate, for them not to be related."

"You think the fruit farmer is a figurehead?"

"I think it very likely. You've said yourself that there are brains behind this smuggling racket. Surely a man with brains wouldn't lay himself quite so openly to arrest in the event of the racket's being blown sky-high?"

"True enough," Murphy grunted, then lapsed into a long reflective silence; which Terhune, beginning to feel rather sleepy, was more than ready to share.

2

As was usual on a Thursday morning, Terhune awakened to the cheerful hubbub of market day from the Square below the south windows of his flat—the windows of his dining-room. Predominant above all other sounds was the unceasing chatter of voices; and the echo of dull thuds as exhibitors erected the stalls from which they would soon be selling their wares.

As soon as he was dressed he went into the front room, and surveyed the scene below. He often did this, and never tired of doing so. A man of simple tastes, there was, for him, something particularly soothing in the sight of a quiet English market town preparing for the invasion of the inhabitants of the surrounding countryside: there was a suggestion of timelessness about market day which especially appealed to his reactionary temperament—for hundreds of years the ancestors of these same people had weekly flocked into the small town, ostensibly with the idea of buying or selling produce; in reality, using this excuse as a cloak for gregarious instincts, and the love of gossip. For hundreds of years in the future their descendants would, given the opportunity, do the same.

What usually impressed him above aught else, however, was the sublime peacefulness of the picture. It epitomized the spirit of peace, and mankind at its best; in a changing, restless world market day was changeless and substantial; in a period of distorted political idealism the people of the market, citizens and sellers alike, stood for the only sound and truly practical political ideal: the well-being and contentment of the inner man, an earthy, materialistic outlook, perhaps, but a sane one!

For once, Terhune's thoughts dwelled less upon this personal conception of Utopia, but more upon the chastening reflection that everything which glitters is not necessarily gold. It was all very well to look down upon the slowly perambulating crowd and tell oneself smugly that these people were the salt of the earth—but who could say that this one, or that one, or t'other one, so innocent-looking in the early-morning sunshine, had not, but a few hours before, been hurriedly unloading contraband from some foreign-owned landing-craft, or furtively transporting the illegally landed goods along deserted highways, and quiet lanes? It was useless to pretend that the smugglers of last night would have been out of place in today's picture; for that would have been to pursue idealism at the expense of reality. Walter Matcham was proof to the contrary, with his jovial guffaws, his hearty manner, and his bucolic innocence. As like as not he would be turning up soon, to play his conventional role of prosperous farmer; no doubt he would later be found in the private bar at the *Wheatsheaf*, discussing one of the many invariable farming topics: to outward appearances as genuine a farmer as one could ever hope to find—as indeed he was, during daylight hours!

And there were others like him: for sure, he was not the only one. That young chap with a puppy in his arms for instance, with cap pushed well back off his forehead, to reveal a mass of unruly hair and a twinkling face. Heaven knows! one could reasonably judge him to be a pleasant enough young fellow, who wouldn't do anyone a bad turn. Yet Terhune had a shrewd suspicion that the pleasant enough young fellow had been one of the men at the *Load of Hay*, whose angry glance had, at one moment, threatened extremely unpleasant consequences.

In this mood he went in to breakfast. He propped his morning paper up against the marmalade, and began to read. The effort soon petered out: the world news was exciting enough, but in comparison with his experience of the past few weeks impersonal. No doubt to the inhabitants of Florida the hurricane which had wrecked half-a-dozen villages and killed nine souls was a catastrophe not easily to be forgotten; to him it was an incident which neither quickened his pulse nor chilled his spine. Florida was many thousands of miles distant; the unfortunate victims, unknown strangers. But Romney Marsh was no more than a few minutes' cycle ride away.

Instead of reading, he thought of the smugglers; of the fruit farm at Springham; of the *Load of Hay*; of the lorry Julia and he had chased through the fog, and of the lorry which had involuntarily transported him well on the way to Maidstone just about one week and twelve hours previously; of what steps the police were taking to investigate the activities, known and unknown, of the fruit farm.

Presently he went down to the book store below, and was just in time to open the door for Anne Quilter, his assistant, before the telephone rang. He hurried over to his desk to answer it, thinking that only Julia MacMunn would ring him quite so early in the morning.

"Hullo," he cheerfully welcomed the caller.

But the voice which answered him was male. "Mr. Theodore Terhune?" it asked in precise tones which were vaguely familiar to him.

"Speaking."

"This is Stallybrass speaking. Please forgive my 'phoning you up so early—not too early, I trust?"

"No. I live here. I am always available."

"I am glad to hear that. Concerning the offer which you made for my books some weeks ago, shall I be taking too much of a liberty if I ask you to do a favour for an elderly man?"

For some time past Terhune had been wondering why he had heard nothing in response to the genuine and reasonable offer he had made for Stallybrass's library, especially in view of the fact that Stallybrass had expressed anxiety to complete the transaction. He frowned with annoyance. Apparently the offer had not, even so, been good enough. But he was not prepared to increase it. At the best of times he loathed bargaining…

"I'm sorry, Mr. Stallybrass, but my offer represents the limit I can afford to pay—"

"Young man, you mistake me," came the stern correction. "The offer is quite satisfactory as regards price. I was about to ask you whether you would do me the kindness once more of calling upon me: there is a matter I should like the opportunity of discussing with you."

"Of course. When?"

"Tonight?"

"Thursday night is my busiest night, Mr. Stallybrass."

"Oh dear! Oh dear!" The voice sounded distressed. "I am afraid that no other night is really convenient for me."

"I am here every day until five o'clock."

"Yes, yes, of course, but I rarely leave my home here. Are you really quite sure you cannot manage tonight? The matter is quite urgent, for reasons which I should prefer not to discuss over the telephone."

Terhune hesitated. If the matter was really urgent—and if the old boy couldn't, or didn't—choose to leave his own home, well… for once…

"I might be able to manage tonight if it's really important."

"My dear Mr. Terhune! How very kind of you!" Stallybrass sounded genuinely grateful. "At eight o'clock?"

"Eight o'clock," Terhune agreed.

"Good-bye, Mr. Terhune," said the dry, precise voice. "I shall express my thanks to you when I see you."

There was a click as Stallybrass disconnected. Terhune did the same, and looked up as the door opened. Murphy entered.

"Have you a few minutes to spare, Mr. Terhune?"

What a question to ask a man whose patience to learn the latest news had been exhausted days ago!

Chapter Sixteen

"I suppose you've been wondering what has been happening this past week?" Murphy questioned, as he sat down beside the desk.

"Not really. I've learned enough from you at different times to realize that police investigations sometimes take a devil of a time to achieve results."

Murphy nodded. "The present investigations have proved no exception to that rule. I've been on the point of ringing you up once or twice, but—"

"No news is—bad news?"

"In this case, yes. I'm only here now because I have to visit Doctor Edwards about the car smash on the Folkestone road on the night of Kitchen's death, so I thought I'd take advantage of being here to drop in and see you. The progress we've made since your ride to Springham is precisely—nil! The Chief Constable is damned furious, I'm telling you."

"You've been keeping watch on the farm, I suppose."

"Of course. Day and night. And the Metropolitan Police have been co-operating with us by doing the same at Covent Garden. The facts of that fruit farming business are much as P.C. Evans indicated. At least one lorry, and very often two or three, all loaded with fruit and vegetables in cases, leave the farm every weekday for Covent Garden. There they are delivered to a firm by the name of Messrs. T. X. Larroque and Company."

"What's the X stand for? Xavier?"

"The divil only knows! Is Xavier a French name?"

"Spanish, I believe."

"Then that is probably what it stands for. The firm was founded by a man from the Basque country—so he might have been one or the other—with the object of importing oranges. When the war put an end to imports, they turned to native produce, which they have dealt with ever since. Larroque himself died in nineteen-forty; killed by a bomb, as a matter of fact. The business was then sold to a man named Wittering, who re-sold it, two years ago, to a William Black."

"Two years ago!"

Murphy smiled grimly. "Yes. About the same time that Rookwood sold the fruit farm to Plunkett."

"Is there a tie-up of some sort between Plunkett and Black?"

The sergeant shrugged. "Your guess is as good as mine, sir. What is an interesting fact is this: that both the wholesale business and the fruit farm were sold on a basis of one-eighth cash and seven-eighths mortgage, the whole of which has already been redeemed."

"Good going for less than two years working."

"Too good! It makes me wonder if the proceeds from the sale of contraband helped to redeem the two mortgages. But here the police are up against snag number one. The fruit farm is a first-class concern, and efficiently run; the wholesale house is doing well. It is barely possible that the money which redeemed the mortgages could have come from current profits."

"An audit would soon show whether it did or not."

"Of course, but we can't put auditors in until we've charged them. There are, as Evans said, more than enough men working on the farm, and most of 'em have money to fling about—much to the envy and annoyance of men employed on other farms round about. But as Plunkett has often said in public that he is willing to pay bonuses for good work, here again it is possible that the money is legitimately earned.

"I've told you that the fruit is unloaded at Larroque and Company's warehouse at Covent Garden. The Scotland Yard man who has been keeping the place under observation reports that each lorry is completely unloaded, and subsequently refilled with returned cases. So it looks as if you were right about the contraband being unloaded at the same time. As soon as the lorry has been reloaded with the empty cases it returns to Springham, always by the same route.

"In short, Mr. Terhune, nothing could be apparently more open and above-board. I doubt whether we are likely to find any evidence of smuggling activities without searching the farm and the warehouse. And it is not much use our applying for search warrants without some evidence of criminal activities—which we haven't got at the moment. It looks like we're in a bottleneck which will take some getting out of."

"Has Plunkett a clean record?"

Murphy nodded. "He was farm bailiff to some sort of relative before he bought Springham Fruit Farm."

"He must have earned good money to be able to buy it."

"Don't forget that he bought it on mortgage."

"I had forgotten," Terhune admitted. "What about the other chap, Black?"

"A commercial traveller for a rival Covent Garden firm before the war. He was called up, and finished up as a colonel in the R.A.S.C. He is supposed to have used his war gratuity to help buy Larroque and Co."

Terhune whistled. "Everything seems sewn up neat and pretty. What's the next move?"

The sergeant looked grim. "The next move will have to come from the smugglers. We shall continue to keep the farm and the Covent Garden firm under observation, of course; but without further evidence it will be no use our applying for a search warrant, and without a warrant we shall be lucky to get that evidence—unless we nab some of the fruit farm workers while on a run, or one of the farm lorries." He paused, then added hopefully, "You've no further news for us, I suppose?"

"Yes and no, Sergeant. Nothing material. I visited the *Load of Hay* again last Monday, but there was no trouble. Much the same crowd was there that I had seen before, but they were more or less friendly in comparison. Smiles wasn't there, but Matcham was, as jovial as usual. Link hadn't changed much, either. He looked at me as if he would do me in for a couple of bob, but Matcham seems to have him tamed."

"Was Plunkett there?"

"No."

"You haven't found out where he works yet?"

"I haven't dared ask."

"Quite right. Nor has our man there. All we know is that he works in the district, but not on a farm."

"What I have learned..." Terhune swivelled round in his chair and reached for a large, dusty volume, which he put on the desk before the sergeant. Murphy opened the book and glanced at the title-page. *Little Known Kent*, it was titled, with a sub-title, *Gleanings from History and Romance*. And underneath: By an Antiquarian. Illustrated from the Pen of Josiah Allardyce.

"Look up pages fifty-three and-four."

Murphy did so. In the middle of page 5 3 was a reproduction of a pen-and-ink drawing of 'Sir Michael Rivers' Stately Home, Springham Manor, as it was in the Year Anno Domini 1603'.

"The Fruit Farm?" he barked.

"Yes. Sir Michael's son became the first Earl of Springham, for services rendered to Charles II. The only item of importance that matters to us is that the old Manor House had extensive cellars attached to it in which several important Royalists are supposed to have remained successfully hidden from the Roundheads."

"Cellars, eh! And possibly secret ones at that, if they weren't discovered by the Roundheads—bad cess to them. Begod!" the sergeant exclaimed in sudden exasperation, "if that fruit farm isn't being run by smugglers then me name isn't Tim Murphy. And it's not a damn' thing we can be doing about it, not a-tall, a-tall."

2

The rest of the day passed quickly for Terhune. In the evening he set off for *Pennyfields* to keep his appointment with Stallybrass. The sky above was overcast; otherwise the night was clear enough for him to see the lights of a ship passing along the horizon, also twinkling pinpoints of light scattered here and there across the black-enveloped Marsh, and the white glow above Dymchurch.

Willy-nilly, his thoughts reverted to the one subject which he seemed unable to forget. He excused himself on the grounds that he had a double reason for thinking of the smugglers on this night in particular. First of all there was Murphy's visit to him, which he had not yet had time to null over; more important, his present journey reminded him of his previous visit to *Pennyfields*, and the subsequent phase along the road he was travelling at that moment.

During the intervening weeks little progress of real value had been made either towards arresting the murderer of P.C. Kitchen or identifying the smugglers. True, the potentialities were good; certain evidence had come to ought which seemed to incriminate the *Load of Hay* and the springham Fruit Farm as being directly or indirectly connected with the activities of the smugglers; also the persons of Link, Smiles, Matcham at the one place, and Plunkett and his employees at the second. But what lawyers sometimes called 'best'—or real—evidence, in contrast to hypothetical deductions, was still lacking. Without it no further progress by the police was likely to be made: without it the death of the constable would continue to go unavenged; and the smugglers would doubtless make more runs, to the detriment of the country's moral and financial exchequer.

Somewhere, he reflected, there had to be a link to connect the bottle of *Rhum Negrita* which George Smiles had emptied, to his subsequent detriment, and the smugglers. That link, it seemed fairly safe to assume, was the sullen landlord of the *Load of Hay*. The next link in the invisible chain, which joined the ports of Calais or Boulogne with the clubs, the hotels and the cellars of London, was probably the still unknown 'hide'. There were next in sequence the link between the hide and the fruit farm, and the one between the farm and the warehouse in Covent Garden. These two were not unknown, and could be exposed when the occasion arose.

In short, the only unknown link was somewhere on the Marsh—for aught one knew to the contrary, one of the tiny pin-pricks of light which he could see twinkling below him. Once that link were discovered the police would, in time, probably be given the opportunity of hauling in the whole length of chain.

Having decided this to his own satisfaction, he was immediately conscious of having overlooked the most important link of all: the leader of the smugglers—the man who was running the organization on the lines of the old-time 'Blues', and who had possibly financed the purchase of the Springham Fruit Farm, and the firm of Messrs. T. X. Larroque and Company. No doubt, once the hide was discovered, the police would proceed to destroy the organization without necessarily waiting to learn the identity of this man—assuming that he existed, which was by no means certain!—but, it would be a pity, he thought, if this were to happen: he had a particularly strong sense of justice which always made him regret to hear of ringleaders going unpunished.

The physical effort of cycling grew steadily less as his machine began to descend the road to the Marsh. The distant lights vanished as the horizon closed in upon him; before long his vision was restricted to his immediate surroundings. A consequence of this was a psychological reaction in himself: his mood grew despondent as he dwelt—just as if the matter were one personal to himself—upon the difficulties which were certain to stand in the way of identifying the organizer of the smugglers' gang. It was certain that any man with a wit, the ingenuity and the courage to adopt legitimate business as a cloak for the import and distribution of contraband would have been equally cunning to devise safeguards to protect himself from possible police investigation.

With his thoughts thus preoccupied, the journey to *Pennyfields* passed quickly: he reached the entrance gates before he was consciously aware of being anywhere near his destination. He cycled up the long curving drive, and so into the bowl-like depression which sheltered the ugly Georgian building.

He rested his machine against one of the columns of the portico, then lifted the massive knocker. He rat-a-tat-tatted with good will, and waited. When the door was opened he saw Stallybrass standing in the hall, and not the solitary male servant he had expected.

"You are punctual, Mr. Terhune," the tiny-figured man remarked in his dry, formal voice. "That clock there"—he nodded his head—"struck as you knocked. Will you come in?"

Stallybrass stepped aside; Terhune entered, and automatically glanced towards the library. The little man chuckled drily.

"Yes, the same room," he went on, answering the unspoken question. "The drawing-room is more comfortable, but we'll be talking about books. Would you go there while I fetch the coffee, which is all ready? You do take coffee?"

"I do, but please do not trouble—"

"It is no trouble. I drink coffee at all times of the day."

Terhune walked across the square hall, his footsteps echoing on the polished boards although his shoes were rubber soled. He did not hear his host move; but when he glanced back while he opened the library door he saw that the hall was empty. He could not think how anyone could move quite so silently.

The library seemed unchanged: a fact which vaguely surprised him, for he had anticipated signs of the removal which had been Stallybrass's reason for offering the books for sale. He sat down; and, gazing at the surrounding walls, wondered why his reaction to the room was so negative. Such was his love of books that, as a general rule, he instantly felt at ease in any room which housed books in quantity.

Not so in the present room. He could name no reason: everything was as it should be. So much so that, presently, he decided that everything was too much as it should be: in fact, that the library was more of a museum piece, as it were, than a room away from the rest of the world, a place where one could browse among old and tried friends, in which one could relax in a mood of sublime contentment.

There was nothing about this room at *Pennyfields* to induce so pleasing a sensation, he decided. There was no smell of ageing leather, no suspicion of the dust which books so easily collect, no atmosphere of drowsy unworldliness. On the contrary, the shelves of books were ostentatiously worldly. They seemed to be saying: 'Consult us. We are here for that purpose. Take us down, but be sure to put us back exactly where we are now.' As if any self-respecting book ever expected to be immediately replaced! As if a library could be a real honest-to-goodness library without there being a few books lying about, here and there, higgledy-piggledy!

"Black or white, Mr. Terhune? Cream, not milk."

Terhune started. He had not heard a sound, but there was Stallybrass by his side offering him coffee.

"With cream, please," he admitted with a rueful feeling of guilt—he was quite sure that his host would privately deride anyone who chose to desecrate good coffee by adding cream to it; he repressed a grin when he observed the other man drinking his black.

"Please accept my apologies for bringing you out here instead of visiting you at Bray," the little man presently began. "But I do not go about much: I abominate automobiles, and do not go about in one if I can avoid doing so."

Terhune remembered having seen horse-dung on the drive. "You ride?"

Pale, thin lips parted in a watery smile. "You are observant, sir. You saw visual evidence of a horse's presence, perhaps? No, I do not ride. I drive a pony and trap. It is much the most pleasant way of travelling short distances. Slow, perhaps, but restful."

Terhune felt at a loss for words. "I mostly cycle," he muttered.

"Ah yes! Of course! I saw your bicycle outside, did I not? Bicycling, although more strenuous, is almost as enjoyable. But you are a young man, sir, while I—well, I am not. More coffee?"

"Thank you."

Stallybrass poured out two more cups, offered cigarettes. At last, "You are, I believe, Mr. Terhune, aware of my reason for disposing— very regretfully, I might add—of my books?"

"You told me that you were leaving the neighbourhood."

"That is so. I also asked you to be kind enough not to tell anyone of this fact."

There was a vague question mark behind the clipped words which disturbed Terhune. He had told Julia—but that was as good as telling nobody; there wasn't a more trustworthy person in the world—but nobody else, of course. Believing that the other man wanted an assurance, he settled on a white lie: he nodded his head in an indeterminate way. "I told my assistant, Miss Quilter, that

I was trying to sell you some books." Which was true: he had told Anne that.

"Good! Good! As a matter of fact there has been a slight change in my plans. I had intended to leave before now, but circumstances prevented my doing so. Now I am no longer sure that I shall leave here."

"Then you will not be wanting to sell the library?"

"Ah! I did not say so, sir." There was reproof in the sharp voice. "May I take you into my confidence?"

"I shall consider it a privilege."

"In that case, to speak baldly—I am not as wealthy as I am sure you believe me to be." Once again the question mark.

Terhune felt somewhat embarrassed. "I did think you were—well—settled."

"Of course! Why not? Everyone else thinks so, too. But I have an income large enough only to keep this place going as it is. No more. Not enough to indulge in some of those pleasures of life which make old age more bearable, unless—"

It was obvious that Terhune was supposed to say something. "Unless, Mr. Stallybrass?"

"Unless I sell my library. You see, now that you have made your offer I have less compunction about letting you know my secret."

Terhune grinned. Wily old bird! Not that the fact would have made a pennyworth of difference to the offer, which was based on the worth of the books, not on the least amount for which they might be bought.

Stallybrass went on: "One of the pleasures of life I have mentioned is that of wintering abroad, sir. That I can indulge in this winter, by selling you the books. As for next winter"—he shrugged his narrow, stooping shoulders—"much can happen in twelve months to an elderly man."

A cheerful conversation, Terhune thought. "Then you accept my offer?"

"Upon conditions," Stallybrass sharply retorted.

Terhune looked blank.

The older man went on, in a more conciliatory tone: "I should have said one condition, Mr. Terhune. A simple one. That is, that the transaction is one of mutual trust."

"I do not understand."

"I did not expect you to. You are, I understand, a book-lover as well as a book-buyer?"

This was a question which could be answered without prevarication. "I am."

"Then you will appreciate how I should feel at seeing my precious books taken off their shelves and carried away from this house."

Terhune could. "Yes."

"I wish to avoid that pain by asking you if you would do me the favour of waiting to collect the books until after I have left the country."

"Of course—"

Stallybrass raised a warning hand. "Wait, sir. I mentioned mutual trust. I want you to pay me for the books *before* I leave, by means of a post-dated cheque which I could cash in Paris on the due date. Would that course be an agreeable one to you?"

Terhune could think of no reason why it should not be: in the event of his being refused the books he could always request his bankers to dishonour the cheque.

"Why, certainly—" he began.

"Wait!" Stallybrass cocked his head sideways. "Did you hear a noise?"

"Only a door slamming—your servant—"

"Is out for the night," the little man snapped. He rose swiftly; before he could move across the room the door opened.

"Did you ring, sir?" respectfully asked Sam Plunkett.

Chapter Seventeen

"What are you doing here?"

"I came home early for once, sir. I felt one of me heads coming on, so I thought bed would do me more good than playing darts at the *Load of Hay*. When I came in I heard voices; I thought you might have rung." He glanced pointedly at the tray. "If I'd known you was expecting a visitor I needn't have gone out this evening."

The explanation was too specious to ring true in Terhune's ears. He had an idea that his host thought along the same lines.

"Mr. Terhune rang me up after you had gone to say that he wants to sell me some books," Stallybrass snapped. "There is no need for you to wait up if you are not feeling well."

"Very good, sir. Good night, sir."

"Good night."

The door closed behind Plunkett: the two men heard his footsteps receding—once more Terhune wondered how his host always managed to move about so silently.

"A conscientious man," Stallybrass murmured, a little too casually. His keen eyes sharpened. "Forgive the untruth about your ringing me up, Mr. Terhune. I see no reason why my servant should learn too much about my affairs. At least, not before I am ready that he should do so."

"Of course. I quite understand." Which was not true: there were several aspects of his visit to *Pennyfields* which he was unable to understand.

Stallybrass's voice sank to confidential pitch. "Then our transaction is agreed, Mr. Terhune?"

"I think so. When do you propose going?"

"Shortly. If I give you two or three days' notice, by telephone, would that be satisfactory? You could send me the cheque by post, on the understanding that you would come here to collect the books, say, three days thereafter, the cheque to be post-dated four days after that."

Terhune agreed, whereupon his host grew suddenly anxious for him to leave. Desiring an early opportunity to think over the latest developments, he quickly took the hint and left. He was not out of sight of the house before he began to puzzle over the surprising fact that Sam Plunkett was Stallybrass's servant. The first question he asked himself was: Is the fact so surprising?

From the first it had been obvious that Plunkett was not a farm labourer; everything about him had contradicted that likelihood—his clothes, his deportment, his speech. Indeed, he had looked so precisely what he was that Terhune chided himself for not having guessed the man's occupation right away. Not that the man's occupation had any bearing upon the points that were at issue in his thoughts—was Plunkett one of the smugglers?

If so, was *Pennyfields* also involved? For, with mounting excitement, he began to realize its possibilities as an ideal 'hide' for contraband. Built in a shallow depression which would, in any case, have effectively concealed the ground floor from the road; and further protected from sight by the thick belt of trees which surrounded it, and the tall hedges each side of the drive which encircled it, the building was completely hidden from the road. Anything happening in the immediate vicinity of the house would be as private as anything could be.

This thought was quickly followed by another. He recollected the range of outbuildings which had particularly attracted his attention on the occasion of his first visit to the place. As he remembered them they were large enough to have sheltered at least two three-ton lorries besides, probably, a couple or so private cars—to say nothing of the room still left that should be available for the storage of the contraband itself.

Memory succeeded memory. He recalled the moment when, later that same night, he had sat in Julia's car and waited for an approaching vehicle to pass by so that they could follow its tail-light. He recollected particularly that, as the white glow of headlights had rounded the nearby corner, the hum of the engine had dropped to such a low pitch that Julia had said something about, "Don't tell me that he is expecting me to lead *him*". In short, as he now began to appreciate, the sound of the engine had given every indication that the driver intended to slow down—but he had accelerated madly the moment the glow of the lorry's headlights had enveloped Julia's car.

The solution of the mystery was beginning to look plain enough. The lorry had evidently slowed down in order to turn off the road into *Pennyfields'* drive; but, observing by the gates a car that looked suspiciously like a police-car, the driver had jumped to the conclusion that the police had discovered the hide and were lying in wait for him and his mates. Whereupon he had decided to make a run for it.

He was a little worried at the ease with which the pieces fitted into his mental jig-saw puzzle. That particular reasoning was just a little too slick; it fitted in with the other facts just a little too easily to be true—he had a healthy distrust of the pranks which real life could play with a man; when life ran too smoothly he looked for, and often found, hidden snags. A pessimistic outlook, maybe, but one which had paid him in the past and helped to prevent his making facts fit in with theories, instead of the reverse.

How wise the precaution was he appreciated a moment later, when he realized that there was one fact which did not fit in with that last theory. If it were a fact that P.C. Kitchen had had good reason for waiting for the smugglers north of *Pennyfields*, then the assumption that the lorry had been slowing down preparatory to turning into the drive and parking contraband there was a wrong one. On the contrary, if *Pennyfields* had been the original destination, then the constable had not been waiting for the lorry—in which case a fresh theory to account for his death would have to be worked out.

So much for *Pennyfields*. What of Plunkett? And Stallybrass? Whether or no *Pennyfields* was involved, there was little doubt that Plunkett was. If he were a relation of the Albert Plunkett who owned the fruit farm, then it would be absurd to assume his innocence. On the contrary, the fact, allied to his friendship with other regulars at the *Load of Hay*, was fairly convincing proof that he was the link between the people on the Marsh and those further inland.

And Stallybrass? On this point he was uncertain. It was easy to assume that if *Pennyfields* was being used as a hide it must be with the owner's connivance and knowledge. But it was difficult to imagine anyone who looked less like a smuggler, and acted less like one, than the tiny-figured, stooping-shouldered, dry-mannered owner of *Pennyfields*. He looked what he undoubtedly was: a scholar, not a man ready to take risks for the sake of financial gain. Besides—a small point!—Stallybrass was hard up for money, and desirous of wintering abroad. Such a description scarcely suited a bold, bad smuggler!

2

As soon as he was back in his rooms Terhune telephoned Murphy to give him news of the latest development. But the sergeant was out on a case; and, according to his wife, there was no knowing when he would be returning. Probably not before midnight. Should he 'phone when he returned?

Terhune thought that tomorrow would be time enough for Murphy to telephone, and said so. After a few politenesses he said good night and disconnected. Then he turned to his work, arrears of which had been steadily mounting up as a consequence of the time he had spent trying to aid the police in their hunt for Kitchen's murderer.

Part of his uncompleted work consisted of pricing for resale purchases which he had made in the past few weeks. Because the stacks of these books were beginning to get in his way he decided to spend what time was left before eleven p.m.—his normal bedtime—in pricing them so that Anne could get them up on the shelves the following morning.

He gathered together all the necessary impedimenta, then squatted down on a stool beside the piles of books. He picked up the first: *The Human Boy*, one of Eden Phillpotts's earlier novels. It was in fair condition, so he priced it, in his private code on the fly-leaf, at 3/6, and put it on one side. The next two volumes were the 1st Edition of A'Beckett's *The Comic History of England*. These two volumes, because they were rubbed, he priced at £3 3s., the average price for the same in good condition being £4. As this title would be suitable for his next mailing list he started a different pile with the two volumes.

So the work continued: slowly on the whole, for he was both a conscientious and an efficient bookseller. To make sure of not selling a damaged book on the one hand, while getting the best possible price for a good copy on the other, meant examining each volume for missing, torn, or thumbed pages (particularly for missing illustrations), mould spots, and other blemishes; for date of edition; for autographs or author's annotations, and so on. Even so, the pile for Anne to deal with in the morning had grown considerably by the time he picked up a copy of Edith Nesbit's *House of Arden*.

Unfortunately, the covers were rubbed. Even so, provided that the pages were moderately clean and intact it should sell, for since the broadcast there had been a steady demand for the old title. He opened it: there was writing on the fly-leaf:

> *To Lily Plunkett*
> *Wishing her Many Happy Returns*
> *On her Tenth birthday.*
> *Aunt Sue. (Great Hinton—16th July.)*

Plunkett! The name seemed to be haunting him. First Sam Plunkett, then Albert Plunkett, and now Lily Plunkett. Were all three related? He felt that they must be: the coincidence of his coming across the three names in so short a time was already strange enough; it would pass beyond the bounds of credulity if they were unrelated.

He wondered how he came by the book. He grabbed for his records of purchases made; glad that he had made a rule of keeping a detailed note of purchases as well as sales. It took him no more than a minute to run his glance down the latest pages until he reached the title. Having done so, he whistled with astonishment. The book had been among those purchased from P.C. Kitchen.

Coincidence? Perhaps! But he did not believe that it was. It was not just by chance that the book came to be among those others: there was a reason for its being there. Perhaps this book was the key to the solution of the mystery which had led to the constable's death.

Work was put aside. He was no longer in a mood for any more. He went upstairs to his study, settled himself in the armchair and began to read.

3

The *House of Arden* yielded nothing. He liked the story well enough to wish that he had read it as a young boy. But from first page to last there was not one significant word which he could construe as having any bearing on smugglers. He went to bed, disappointed.

The next morning he left the book store in Anne's charge and cycled to Great Hinton in time to be there when the doors of the *Dusty Miller* opened. Ted Shore, the landlord, greeted him with a friendly but surprised nod.

"Good morning, Mr. Terhune. Don't often see you about at this time o' the day."

Terhune had anticipated the landlord's curiosity. "I feel a bit muzzy after working late last night. Friday is a slack day with me and I thought a breath of fresh air would soon put me right. So here I am."

"Glad to see you, sir." The sharp face wore an enquiring expression.

"A bitter I think. What about yourself?"

"The same, thanking you kindly." Shore filled two pint tankards, one of which he pushed across the bar: the other he raised to his mouth. "My best respects." With one effortless swallow he disposed of fully half the contents of the tankard. "A little colder today, but fine."

The usual opening gambit. The two men talked of the weather for the best part of a minute. Then on a variety of subjects, ranging from Arsenal's chances of winning the Cup to the dastardly plans of the Government to stop people drinking beer. At last a pause.

"Do you know who Aunt Sue is, Mr. Shore?" Terhune casually asked.

The landlord looked puzzled. "Aunt Sue?"

Terhune chuckled. "I came across a book in the shop the other day which I had bought from somebody; it was a birthday present from Aunt Sue of Great Hinton."

"Oh!" The sharp-featured face relaxed. A chuckle echoed Terhune's. "I sees what you mean. Aunt Sue, now..." A frown of concentration. "Would it be an old book?"

"Say about twenty years old, or thereabouts."

"Twenty years. I mind Susan Talbot, but I never heard tell of her having any brothers or sisters, so she can't have been no real aunt. She died four year ago come Christmas Eve."

"Many 'Aunts' and 'Uncles' aren't relations at all."

"Oh ah! I'm 'Uncle Ted' to half-a-dozen young rips. Then there was Susan Ames, Bob Ames's widder, but she's been gone these last ten years or more."

"Dead?"

"No, moved away, up North somewheres. She had a brother living down Rye way somewheres. Let's see—what was the name—Peters—Potts—"

"Plunkett?"

"That's it. Plunkett. When he died his kids went to live with relations. Mrs. Ames had one of 'em. A girl."

"Lily?"

"That's the girl. Lily Plunkett. Not a bad looker, but a bit on the sly side if you knows what I mean."

Terhune nodded. "It's a small world. Funny to think of a book which her Aunt Sue gave her on her tenth birthday should come into my possession. I wonder if she'd like it back, for old times' sake. Did she go up North with her aunt?"

"Lord love you, no! She married when she were nineteen, and went to live on the Marsh. Her husband's bin in the news lately. Went and got hisself killed one night by a flicking lorry. You know the man I mean, sir. Tom Kitchen."

4

So *House of Arden* was not, after all, a link with the mystery surrounding Kitchen's death. Evidently it had been in the constable's library simply on account of its being one of his wife's books. But indirectly it represented an important piece of evidence which might have far-reaching results. Terhune cycled back to Bray in a mood of exultation. He reached there to find that Anne had news for him.

"Detective-Sergeant Murphy telephoned about half an hour ago, Mr. Terhune."

"Damn! Did he leave a message?"

"He asked whether you would be back, for lunch. When I told him that I was expecting you back before then he said that he would be calling upon you."

"Good! Thank you, Anne. Anything else?"

"No, Mr. Terhune."

Twenty minutes later Murphy showed up. His face was drawn; there were dark pouches under his eyes which seemed to suggest that he was suffering from lack of sleep.

"Sorry I wasn't in when you 'phoned last night. I was out on the Hothfield rape case." His tired eyes brightened with hope. "Anything happened?"

"Plenty."

"Thank God for some good news! And for Mr. Theodore I. Terhune! If you weren't doing so well both as writer and bookseller I'd suggest your joining the police force." The grin faded. "Well, sir?" he snapped with unexpected impatience.

"In the first place, I believe I've discovered the whereabouts of the Marsh hide—"

"You have, begod!"

"In the second, I've just learned, not one hour ago, that Kitchen's wife is sister to the *two* Plunketts."

The sergeant's expression hardened. "You mean that the copper was in with the smugglers all the time?"

"No, I don't. Nor his wife. But I think that the relationship probably had something to do with Kitchen's finding out what the smugglers' plans were on the night he was killed."

"You've said it, sir." His mouth set in grim lines. "Begod! If I weren't so busy it's meself that would be asking the Chief Constable to let me go up to Yorkshire to have another talk with that woman. As it is, he'll probably send someone else."

"Could I go, Sergeant? Unofficially, of course. I could think up some excuse about the books I bought from her. Besides, knowing the state of her mind, I think she would be more frank with me than with an official policeman. If I fail you could still fall back upon one of your own people."

The detective's expression indicated that he was sorely tempted to accept this offer: but he shook his head.

"You have your own work to do, sir. We can't be expecting you to be giving up your time whiniver the police haven't a man to spare. To be sure now, you'll have been doing enough already. D'you know for certain that Mrs. Kitchen was own sister to the owner of the fruit farm?"

"Ted Shore told me the whole family history. When the father died—he was a widower, by the way—the family was split up. Lily was sent to Great Hinton to live with her Aunt Sue; the two boys, Albert and Sam, being packed off to another uncle, a farmer by the same name living near Lympne. When Sam was fourteen he ran away to London, and became a page-boy at one of the smaller hotels there. Albert continued to work for his uncle until the uncle died."

"Leaving his property to Albert, I suppose?"

"No, to a son. Albert only received a sum of money, which the people of Great Hinton varyingly estimate—upon second-hand information, I'd say—at one hundred to three hundred pounds. Anyway, on the strength of this money he bought Springham Fruit Farm."

"He did, did he? Tell that to the Marines! What about Sam?"

"Apparently he met Stallybrass in London some years ago, and became the other man's personal servant when Stallybrass bought a property in Kent."

"About two years ago, I suppose?"

"A little longer than that, I think."

"What about this Stallybrass? What is he? Who is he? What property did he buy? D'you think it's himself that could be having anything to do with the smugglers through Sam Plunkett?" The series of questions was rattled off with machine-gun speed: Murphy's eyes flamed with eagerness.

"That's the point, Sergeant. I can't make up my mind about Stallybrass. But if *Pennyfields* isn't being used by the smugglers as a hide I'll—I'll—"

Murphy's eyes twinkled. "Eat your hat, sir?"

"Not in these days of austerity," Terhune answered promptly.

Chapter Eighteen

A s Terhune sped north on his way to see Mrs. Kitchen—for he had not had much difficulty in persuading Murphy to consent to the journey—he had an intuitive feeling that the tempo of the case was rapidly increasing, and moving towards its climax. There were still loose pieces to be fitted into the picture to complete it, but the framework seemed there, in its entirety.

He had not dared to advise the widow of his coming, for he believed that she might try to avoid him. But he was fortunate. He found her at home—and was not over-surprised to learn from the child who opened the door that the house belonged to her Aunt Sue, now an aged, half-deaf, half-blind invalid.

"Please accept my apologies for worrying you, Mrs. Kitchen, but I want to ask you a few questions."

Her weak lips trembled slightly. "About Tom's death?"

"Yes."

"The police ain't got the man what killed him yet?"

"Not yet, but—they have hopes."

For a moment she looked glad; diabolically glad. He realized for certain how much she had loved her husband, and with what pleasure she longed to hear of the execution of his killer. The next second she was trembling with fear, her mouth was setting in obstinate lines, and an expression of cunning. The change did not perplex or worry him now that he knew the cause: fears for the security of her brothers.

He thrust the copy of *House of Arden* before her.

"This was among the books I bought from you."

She nodded. "Yes."

"It was yours, wasn't it?"

"There was two or three books of mine among Tom's. I used to be fond of reading when I was a girl. That was before I got married and had kids of me own. Since then I ain't had no time for books." She glanced down at her swollen body, and he knew that she was thinking of the future when she would have still less time. He also believed that she had forgotten the writing on the fly-leaf.

"Open it," he urged, "at the beginning."

Puzzled, she took the book from his hand. He carefully watched her as she opened the book. A stricken expression passed across her face as she read what was written therein.

"Oh!" she gasped.

"That was your name, wasn't it?" he demanded. He thought she was going to deny the fact. "And you are again living with Aunt Sue, aren't you? Your little boy told me so," he quickly added.

"Yes," she gasped.

"You are sister to Albert Plunkett of Springham Fruit Farm, and Sam Plunkett of *Pennyfields*?"

She nodded.

"Do you still want the man who killed your husband arrested?"

"Yes." The one word carried conviction in its fierce undertones. "Yes, I do. I loved my Tom. God damn the man what run him over!" she continued with vicious spite.

"I suppose you have no suspicions who he is?"

She started. Her hands began trembling again. He knew that she was horribly afraid of something, or someone. But her expression turned sullen. "No," she muttered. "How should I have?"

"Of course not," he soothed. "I was only asking the question in case you could be of more help."

"I've told you everything I know."

"Yes, yes." He paused. "I suppose you had visitors at your home sometimes?"

"Not when Tom was out on dooty."

"Naturally. But when he wasn't?"

"Sometimes."

"Neighbours?"

"Yes." The answer was prompt.

"Friends from other villages?"

"Now and again."

"Your brothers?"

She hesitated. "Not Albert. 'Bout two or three times a year."

"And the other brother?"

"Harry?" She shrugged. "We saw him now and again."

"Harry? Is that another brother?"

"That's Sam's other name. Samuel Henry was his full name. Me and Tom didn't like the name of Sam so we always called him Harry."

Harry Plunkett! H.P.! Terhune sighed for the hours he had wasted by overlooking the simple in his hunt for the complicated.

2

The sergeant was waiting in his car at Ashford station. "Don't tell me, sir," he began, "I can see by your face that you have had a successful trip. Step in. I'm running you home."

Terhune protested. "I can easily catch the bus, Sergeant."

"After you giving up a couple of days' work for nothing!" Murphy seized hold of Terhune's bag and threw it into the back seat, so Terhune obediently stepped into the car. Murphy pressed the starter. "Well, sir?" he asked eagerly, as they slid out of the station yard.

"I've discovered what H.P. stands for. Harry Plunkett."

"Harry! Who's he? Another brother?"

"Another name for Sam. His family always called him Harry, including the two Kitchens."

The sergeant nodded thoughtfully. "So that is how he got his information?"

"That's my bet."

"Didn't Mrs. K. confirm it?"

"I don't think she knows anything for certain. She just suspects. That's why she wouldn't give me a hint in the first place. She wants to see her husband's murder avenged, but either she didn't want to get her brothers into trouble, or else was afraid of them—which I think was the more likely explanation. I think she had an idea that she would be blamed by them if the police were to find out about the smugglers."

"Very likely. Any ideas on how Kitchen came to link up his brother-in-law with the smugglers?"

"Several; none with any evidence to support it. Harry used to visit the Kitchens every now and again. Perhaps he was a little under the wind on one occasion, and was indiscreet in his conversation. Or perhaps he made some reference to Jim Davis's cattle, or the firing of Newdick's stack—a reference which he wouldn't have made if he had not had some inside knowledge. Or he may have taken along a bottle of unusual French cognac, or a bottle of *Rhum Negrita*. We know that Tom Kitchen was on the look-out for some clue to the smugglers, and that he had a nose for detective work: he might have pounced upon the clue and started to add two and two."

"Yes," Murphy agreed slowly. "What about his finding out the exact time and place of the run?" Conscious of a hesitation on the part of his companion, he glanced sideways, then grinned. "If I know anything of you, sir, you've worked out that one, too."

"I have," Terhune confessed. "That's the worst of being a novelist: especially a writer of detective stories. One can always work out a theory even if it's a thousand miles away from the truth."

"Some of your theories have been a deal closer than that," the sergeant drily remarked.

Terhune chuckled. "You've asked for it: here it is. My idea is that Kitchen accused his brother-in-law of being one of the smugglers and then, for the sake of his wife, struck a bargain with Plunkett."

"Information about the next run in consideration of keeping his mouth shut about Mr. Harry?"

"Something like that."

A long silence followed, which Murphy was the first to break. "I think that may be half the truth, sir, but not the whole truth."

"Quite likely. Why?"

"I think that if the bargain between the two men had been as simple as that Kitchen would not have tried to arrest the lorry single-handed, as I said once before. As a sensible man he would have passed the information on to the C.I.D. so that the job could have been done efficiently."

With this conjecture Terhune was forced to agree. "Anyway, you'll probably find out the full facts after you have arrested the men. One way and another you have enough information now, haven't you, to apply for a search warrant?"

"Yes, but I don't think the Chief Constable wants to do that. Not yet, at any rate."

"Why not?"

"In spite of all the work you've put in, we are not much more advanced than we were to building up a case against the smugglers. Unless we should be lucky enough to find contraband on the premises we've still not enough real evidence to justify a prosecution. And by this time they've probably disposed of everything they brought in on their last run."

"The last run we know of, Sergeant."

"Of course, but I don't believe they would risk more than one run a month at the most. Or even as many as that, for how often does the weather favour them?"

"What is the Chief Constable's idea, then?"

"He's hoping to catch them red-handed on their next run, which may be any night now. There's a new moon Tuesday, so anything is likely to happen between now and next week-end."

"He's hoping for a miracle, isn't he, if he anticipates another tip-off like the last one?"

Murphy chuckled. "He's no believer in fairy stories, sir. Extra C.I.D. and uniformed men have been drafted into the Marsh since yesterday. Every night this coming week watch will be kept on the coast, on some of the roads, and also on the men we suspect to be members of the gang. At the first suspicious happening a general alarm will be given and both the Marsh and the roads surrounding Springham will be cordoned off on the lines of the rehearsal at the end of last month."

"A pity one couldn't get to know the exact date," Terhune murmured.

The sergeant stiffened. "I'm beginning to know that particular voice, sir. You've another of your ideas?"

"I was just thinking that a man who, we believe, had been willing once before to save his own skin at the expense of his fellow-smugglers might be willing to do so again."

"Begod! Harry Plunkett!"

Terhune nodded.

3

Two nights later Terhune dressed in his warmest clothes, and left No. 1 Market Square by way of the side door which opened on to Three Hundreds Lane. In the faint white glow spread by the near-side wing lights of the car which stood outside he saw long fingers of fog eddying round about, agitated by the warmth of the soft, humming engine. The air was damp and cold to his face; but, warm with excitement, he was barely aware of the unpleasant chill.

"Jump in, sir." Murphy's voice came from the rear, and sounded eerily hollow.

Terhune entered the car by the near-side rear door. He could not see anyone else in it, but the warm glow of three lighted cigarettes indicated the presence of three other people.

Murphy's voice came from beside him as he sat down. "The shadow beside me is D.-S. Raines, sir."

"Good evening, sir."

"Good evening, Sergeant."

"If tonight isn't the night, then I'm a Dutchman," Murphy went on, as the car rolled slowly forward. "Did you hear the fog warning on the radio?"

"I just switched on in time. When did the Meteorological Office give you notice that they were going to broadcast a fog warning?"

"Half an hour before I telephoned through to you at midday. Are you prepared for an all-night session, sir?"

"If I'm allowed to."

"The old boy said that if anyone deserved to, it was you. Besides, we still want your help, as I said on the 'phone."

"What's the programme?"

"It depends. We propose dropping you first at the *Load of Hay*. If Plunkett is there then we'll wait for him to come out and nab him then. If he isn't, we'll move on to *Pennyfields*, where he should be if he's not at the pub. If he is, he'll open the door to you."

"Suppose Stallybrass answers the knock—he's done so each time I've been there."

"We'll think up what to say either to him or to Plunkett, when we know for certain that our Harry isn't at the pub."

"How do you want me to let you know whether he is or isn't?"

Between them Murphy and Raines had worked out a simple system for Terhune to communicate by signals to the car which would be waiting behind the hedge of a nearby farm. This system the sergeant proceeded to explain. A long silence followed.

The driver was the next to speak.

"Fog's getting worse, sir."

"Is it, begod! I hope it doesn't get too thick even for the smugglers."

"It was thicker than this on the night Kitchen was killed," Terhune told the sergeant.

"Was it? That's all right then. This much won't stop 'em."

"I hope it doesn't," said Raines. "I'm damned if I want to stop up for nothing on a night like this."

A few yards short of the *Load of Hay* the police-car stopped, then reversed into a field and round behind a hedge which concealed it from the road. Terhune and Raines alighted, regained the road and walked as far as the door of the inn. Here they parted company; Terhune to enter, Raines to remain outside.

There was fog inside as well as outside the inn; it mingled with the tobacco smoke and made the atmosphere so thick that the faces of the men at the far side of the room were barely visible. But it was a warm fog; it flowed about Terhune, caressing his cold face, and made him feel cheerfully relaxed.

One quick glance round the low-ceilinged room was enough to cause disappointment: Sam Plunkett was not one of those present, although Smiles and Matcham were. He sneezed loudly, then again. Having thus passed on the message to Raines that their man was not in the inn, he moved nearer to the fire.

"Don't you bring that cold in here, Mr. Terhune," Matcham greeted with a loud, boisterous laugh. "Us countryfolk want none of you townspeople's leavings." As usual, this sally was applauded with sycophantic laughter from some of the other men present.

"Don't worry. I've left it outside. Same as usual, Fred, please." He had to shout to make himself heard; although only a handful of men were in the bar their conversation was loud; their laughter louder. In fact, he sensed a quality of tension in the atmosphere; an excitement verging on something that would have been called hysteria if it had applied to women instead of men.

He paid for his drink, and carried the tankard over to one of the tables. As he did so a hush came over the room, and he realized that he had become, for no explainable reason, the centre of attention. Unexplainable because, until that moment, he had not been particularly in any man's thoughts.

Smiles leered at him from across the room. "Not much of a night *tonight* for a bicycle ride round the country, mister."

"You've said it," Terhune agreed—and hoped that the slight tremble he felt inside him wasn't noticeable in his voice. "I shall be glad to be home."

"You wouldn't think anyone with any ruddy sense would've come out in the first case." There was a challenge in the unpleasant voice, and a slight alcoholic unsteadiness. Terhune knew that Smiles was spoiling for a fight, and provoking him to make the first move.

"I agree. You wouldn't have found me out in this fog it if hadn't been for business."

"Business my foot!" The taunt was deliberately insulting, and was followed by one still more so: Smiles turned and spat into the fire; his spittle sizzled as it fell on the hot ashes. Another man on the same side of the room laughed. "What kind of business, eh?"

"Buying books," Terhune answered mildly. "Somebody in Dymchurch has some books to sell, and asked me to go there and make an offer for them. On my way back I thought I might as well drop in for a quick one and a warm." He wondered if he were being too conciliatory. "Any objections?" he added pointedly.

The reasonableness of the explanation apparently impressed Smiles, whose only retort was to glower across the room with hate-filled eyes.

But Matcham's booming voice picked up from where Smiles left off. "You took a risk, didn't you, coming out on a night like this?"

"Risk!"

"Of fog, of course."

"There was no fog about when I left Bray."

"There was a broadcast warning of it, wasn't there?"

"Was there? When?"

"Just before the one o'clock news. And again before the six o'clock news."

"I was on my way to Dymchurch at one o'clock. Besides," he added, in the realization that he would have to be more aggressive if he were to make the men believe in his story, "I should still have gone there even if I had heard the warning."

"You would?"

"Of course. I have my work to do the same as the rest of you. What do you think I am? One of the landed gentry?"

The counter-attack was successful. One of the other men shouted out, "I'll bet you won't stop farming tomorrow neither, if it's still foggy, Walt." Two others laughed at this. So did Walter Matcham himself. His jovial bellow filled the small room.

"Right you are, Mr. Terhune! Us workers can't let the weather interfere with our business, can we?"

Smiles was less amenable to reason. "I still think it's ruddy funny him coming here tonight," he shouted. "Let's show the b—what!" He rose unsteadily to his feet. So, with a grunt of approval, did two of his companions.

This is it! Terhune thought, and felt a little sick. But he turned to the sullen-faced Link. "Is this a public house or isn't it?" he demanded.

The landlord glared at him, but rounded upon Smiles. "Shut yer bloody mouth, George, and keep it shut." He turned back to Terhune. "Don't take no notice of 'im: he's always like that when he's had a drop too much."

"Look 'ere, Fred——" Smiles began.

Link interrupted: "You heard what I said. Shut yer bloody trap. I ain't having the police coming round here on account of the likes of you."

"Sit down, George," Matcham added with a snap. Smiles sat down.

The crisis was over for the moment, but Terhune believed that another could soon arise. Some of the men were drinking heavily; among them Smiles and Matcham. The next time Matcham might not choose to exert the authority which he seemed to possess, or Link might fail to control his clients. In the circumstances an early departure seemed indicated.

For the sake of appearances, Terhune decided to wait five more minutes. It took all his courage to do so, for even in that short period tension increased. By the time he was ready to leave there was no doubt in his mind but that there was to be a run that night.

He rose, and said "Good night". Smiles half rose, as if to stop him leaving, but there was a fortunate interruption. A newcomer entered the inn—Harry Plunkett of all people! Smiles saw him.

"About ruddy time, Sam," the half-drunken man began. Link dropped a trayful of tankards on the floor. Matcham bellowed with laughter. Somebody dug Smiles in the ribs. And in the hubbub Terhune left the inn. Very gladly.

Chapter Nineteen

The men in the police-car did not have so long to wait for Plunkett as they had feared. Half an hour after he had entered the inn he came out again, this time accompanied. Fortunately the companion went the other way after a few bellowed words which Terhune, had he heard them, would have recognized as coming from Matcham's mouth. From where he was hidden Raines gave the signal. The police-car was driven out on to the road, where it waited for Plunkett to draw level with it. As he did so Murphy called out:

"Sam Plunkett?"

The man stopped, and peered at the car through the foggy darkness. "What do you want?"

"Step inside. We want to speak to you."

"No damn' fear—" Plunkett began.

A pair of firm hands seized him, propelled him into the car. "Inside, you," muttered Raines, who was not being too gentle with his victim.

Clutched by Murphy and the uniformed driver in front, and Raines behind, Plunkett had no option but to enter the car and subside on the rear seat, with a detective-sergeant on either side of him, whereupon the car started forward.

"What's this mean—"

"All right, Plunkett. We are police officers. We've a few questions to ask you. If you want to see our warrant cards—"

Apparently Plunkett was satisfied that they spoke the truth. "What do you want? You've nothing on me. You let me out, or I'll tell the newspapers. I know my rights. Where you talking me?"

"We are taking you nowhere special. Perhaps to *Pennyfields* if you're a good boy. See, we may be saving you a walk home."

"Like hell! What do you want?"

"Just to know whether there's a run planned for tonight."

After a long silence: "What the hell you coppers talking about?"

"You heard, Sam. We know more than's good for you and some of your friends, and suspect a lot more which you'll confirm if you've any sense."

"You're barmy."

"You think so? Listen, Sam. Suppose we tell you that we've proof that you're a smuggler; enough to put you inside for a few years. You and your brother at Springham."

"I can tell fairy stories, too. Once upon a time there was a dear old lady who lived in a shoe—"

"Cut that out, Sam," Murphy snapped. "We're not bluffing. We're offering you a choice between standing trial with the rest of the gang, or—"

"Or what?"

"What your brother-in-law, Tom Kitchen, offered you."

"God!" The exclamation was barely audible, but it was enough to assure the other four men in the car that Murphy's last remark had shaken Plunkett's self-assurance. The two sergeants knew better than to fluster him, and perhaps spoil their advantage. They maintained a discreet silence. At last he spoke.

"I don't know what you're talking about," he muttered, but it was obvious to his audience that he was, to all intents and purposes, defeated.

Murphy sighed. "All right, Thompson, you can drive to the station; he doesn't mean to talk, so we may as well book him and get back to the others."

"What's the charge?" There was apprehension in the anxious question.

"Suspicion of being concerned, with divers others, with importing excisable goods into this country contrary to the Customs Consolidation Act, 1876."

"Suppose I tell you what you want to know?"

"We promise nothing. But—"

"But what?"

"You're a man of intelligence, Sam. Just put two and two together. Of course, I don't say you'll go to penal servitude for life, unless you've shot at a naval or revenue ship, or wounded a preventive officer. But if you want to be helpful..."

Terhune chuckled to himself. That 'but' of Murphy's was a clever piece of diplomacy. Without laying the sergeant open to the charge of uttering either threats of promises as an inducement to give evidence, to a person with a guilty conscience there was a wealth of significance underlying it which made it quite an effective weapon.

"Will you give me a chance of clearing out of the country if I talk—I can tell you more than you'll find out in a month of Sundays—"

"Don't make any mistake, Sam. We know plenty. If you don't talk, George Smiles will, so take your chance."

"George!" the name apparently shook Plunkett. "All right; what do you want to know?" he asked quickly.

"Is a run planned for tonight?"

"Yes."

"What time?"

"The stuff is supposed to be landed about two-fifteen."

"Where?"

"St. Mary's Bay."

"The nearest telephone, Thompson," Murphy snapped.

"Right, Serge."

To Plunkett again: "Where's the stuff destined this time? Springham Fruit Farm or *Pennyfields*?"

"God! So you do know—"

"I told you. Go on, man, answer."

"The—the farm providing the weather remains foggy all the way there."

"Which it is at the moment. If not?"

"*Pennyfields*."

"When will anyone know which?"

"It's the farm unless orders is given to the contrary. It depends on a telephone call from Springham, which would come through about one."

"To *Pennyfields*?"

"Yes."

"Is Larroque at Covent Garden part of the racket?"

"You know everything, don't you?" Although the voice had a sneering undertone to it, there was also genuine surprise, and fear. "I don't know why you worried to pick me up."

"Who's head of the racket? Matcham?"

"Him!" Plunkett's laugh was scornful.

"Your brother?"

"He'd like to be." There was malice in Plunkett's voice.

"Who, then?"

"Stallybrass." The answer was spitting, vicious.

Terhune laughed. Stallybrass! That tiny-built inoffensive, dry-manner, stooping-shouldered scholar! Stallybrass, chief of a band of smugglers. The idea was too fantastic. The man was obviously lying.

"Who's that in front?" Plunkett demanded.

"Never you mind." To Terhune, "You don't think so?"

"I don't."

"That's all you know," Plunkett asserted in an unsteady voice. "I know he don't look it, but he is. You ask Matcham, or Albert—that's me brother. They take their orders from him. None of the other men know who the boss is. Only me. That's because I have my own ways of finding things out."

"He's a scholar, not a smuggler," Terhune interposed.

"Scholar me foot! I suppose you're thinking of all the books he has in his library? Crikey! Now I know who you are in front. You're that ruddy Terhune; you damned Nosy Parker."

"Shut up!" Murphy ordered.

Plunkett laughed. "If you think he's read any of them books, then you're a blasted fool. He bought the whole bang-shoot from the man what owned *Pennyfields* before Mr. Stinking Stallybrass grabbed it."

The statement shook Terhune. The suggestion of scornful mockery in Plunkett's voice convinced him that the man had spoken the truth. Moreover, he recollected his own surprise that a book-lover, which Stallybrass purported to be, should have been so ready to dispose of his complete library just for the sake of wintering abroad. And this without any apparent qualms of regret or distress.

"Do you think he could be telling the truth?" Murphy asked.

"I did think it strange that he should be selling the complete library—"

"Selling! What's that?" Plunkett demanded in a strained voice. "Stallybrass selling the books?"

Terhune considered that it was his place to maintain silence, which he did. Not so Murphy.

"He's selling it for money, Sam. To go abroad with."

"The rat! The dirty rat!" Plunkett began to rave. "He must have smelled that the game was nearly up and planned to skip so that the rest of us could take the rap. Wait till I tell the boys. He'll be sorry for himself before we're through with him. What's more," he added viciously, "I can tell you why he's waited until now before clearing out."

"Why?"

"An extra big shipment's being landed tonight—three lorry-loads of stuff: watches, lace, silks, perfumes; enough to make a stinking millionaire sit up."

"Does that mean that the whole gang will be used?"

"You bet it does."

"What route are you taking?"

"I don't know. Sometimes none of us ever knows until the last ruddy moment. Stallybrass works it all out, and tells Matcham or Albert last thing." A note of admiration crept into his voice. "He's got more tricks than a monkey up his sleeve. He can lead you coppers up the garden path right enough."

"Perhaps! Now about Kitchen's death—"

"What about it?" Plunkett shouted.

"He found out about the smuggling, didn't he?"

"Yes."

"How?"

"God knows! The Devil must've told him."

"The night he was killed—he knew there was going to be a run, didn't he?"

Plunkett did not answer.

"Didn't he?" Murphy repeated.

"Yes," the other man admitted in a hoarse mutter.

"You told him?"

"I had to. He was going to arrest me if I didn't tell him. Me, his own brother-in-law, blast him!"

"How did he find out which route was to be taken?"

"I telephoned a certain number as soon as I knew myself."

"What had he planned to do?"

"What you mean?"

"You know what I mean: you're no fool. You and he rigged up some plan between you, didn't you? Didn't you?" the sergeant repeated in a rasping voice. "What made him tackle the job single-handed instead of letting the C.I.D. know?"

"So as how I could cut loose when he ordered the lorry to stop."

"*You*? Then you were one of the men on the lorry that night?"

"I—I was at the back."

"Go on. What had the two of you fixed up?"

"I—I said I'd let him know what road we was to take that night. The idea was that he was to step out in front of the lorry. When that happened I was to call out 'Beat it, boys, the coppers are here'. Then I'd hop out and run, making the rest of us do the same. Then Tom was going to climb into the lorry, drive it off to the nearest police-station, and say as how he had stopped it single-handed, but the driver got away. He reckoned he'd get all the credit, while giving me a chance of getting away."

The story sounded feasible, and his hearers believed it. "What went wrong?" Murphy demanded in a harsh voice.

"George wouldn't stop," Plunkett gasped. "He went and run over the poor bastard."

"George Smiles! Was he driving?"

A strangled "Yes" was the reply.

The police-car came to a stop. "The telephone, Serge," Thompson said.

"I can go now?" Plunkett asked eagerly.

"Go where?"

"Free, of course."

"No ruddy fear, me boy."

"But you promised—"

"Nothing."

Plunkett was almost in tears. "I've told you everything. Why can't you let me go?"

"So you can give warning to the rest of the gang? Not on your sweet life. Tomorrow, maybe, depending on what the Chief Constable says."

Murphy alighted. "Hold on to him, Raines; he's a slippery customer, if I'm any judge of character." The words floated back to the car as he disappeared into the fog.

2

In a large, oak-raftered barn not far from the Dymchurch-Willingham road Terhune met the Chief Constable of the Kent Constabulary for the first time. Colonel Agar was of medium height, square-shouldered, broad-chested. His hair was snow-white; so was his challenging moustache. His eyes were bright, penetrating. His chin was pugnacious.

" 'Evening, Terhune," he greeted, with a handshake which made Terhune wince. "Heard a lot of you. Glad to meet you. Been doing some useful work, what! Many thanks. Hear you would like to stay here and see this thing through. Don't blame you. Might be exciting."

"I should like to, if I shall not be in the way."

"It's unusual to have anyone else about. Very. But if it were not for you none of us would be here. Deuced cold and clammy, what! Fog getting thicker, d'you think?"

"It's much the same as it was. Patchy, of course." Terhune grinned: the Colonel's habit of conversing in short, clipped sentences seemed to be catching.

"Like to hear how we propose to catch these smuggler fellows?" Apparently the Colonel took it for granted that Terhune did, for he went on: "Come over here. Have a large-scale map of the Marsh, as you can see." He pointed his walking-stick towards the far end of the barn, where a large road-map of the district had been nailed up. Clustered about the map were a number of men, some uniformed, some in plain clothes. Several of them were already known to Terhune: the two superintendents, Drake and Boil, Detective-Inspector Collins, the two detective-sergeants, Murphy and Raines. Standing on the right was a uniformed policeman with a walkie-talkie radio apparatus. At the far end of the barn were a number of mobile policemen.

"Now, gentlemen, every road leading out of the Marsh is being guarded," the Colonel explained to the assembled company, waving his stick about as he indicated points on the map. "As they were last time, which was a pretty successful operation, what! Here, here, here—wherever you see the post number written up. We have six men at each post. The moment we give the alarm every road will be barricaded off. That's the first move.

"See these posts—here, and here, and so on?—police-cars are stationed in hiding, one at each post. They, too, are lying low until the general alarm is given. When it is, each car will tour every road in its own area. The moment a smuggler's lorry is spotted, the police-car in question will begin to shadow it, meanwhile radioing headquarters. Headquarters will warn us on the walkie-talkie, at the same time advising the other police-cars by radio to converge on that area.

"As soon as we know for certain which barricade the smugglers are making for, that post will be advised to be ready for action; and reinforcements of uniformed police will be rushed there, by lorry, from the nearest reserve centre outside the area—here, and here, and here.

"We have thirty men at each reserve post, fifteen of whom will be sent to help the original six; the second fifteen will remain in reserve. Thus we shall have twenty-one men at the barricade to deal with the smugglers in addition to the mobile police following behind the lorry, an ample number, I suggest, gentlemen, to deal with the contraband runners. Any questions?"

"Yes, sir." Murphy was the speaker. "Even if the men do not spot the police-cars following them, they may turn off at the last moment, and try to leave the area by a parallel road. For instance, suppose you are advised that they are making for post seventeen." He moved closer to the map and indicated the post in question. "If they were to turn off at the last moment, along the road to the right—here—they would reach post eighteen before you would have time to send reinforcements there."

The Colonel presently nodded. "A good point, Sergeant. To guard against such an occurrence at the two or three points where it is possible, it might be as well to send the other fifteen men from the reserve post there. Anything else?"

"Yes, sir," Collins said in his brusque way. "There won't be a police-car on every one of these roads at any one moment, will there?"

"Unfortunately, no."

"Then it would be possible, through bad luck, for the smugglers to reach one of the barricades before there had been time to give the warning to the reserve police to go there."

"Yes. Possible, but unlikely." The Chief Constable dismissed the idea with an impatient wave of his hand. "Any more questions?"

There was an embarrassed silence. The police seemed chary of speaking up. For his part, Terhune was not satisfied with the plan worked out. After some hesitation, he began, tentatively, "If I may…"

"Naturally." The Colonel was geniality itself.

"How will you know when to give warning to the mobile police to move? I take it that they will not do so until you are sure that the stuff has been landed, and loaded into the lorries."

"We have police stationed along the roads here, to advise headquarters by telephone what happens."

"Wouldn't it have been surer, Colonel, to have surrounded them nearer the coast?"

"No. Making allowances for the smugglers' making direct for *Pennyfields* instead of Springham. If they do we shall close in from the outer circle of barricades, and arrest them there."

"The barriers will be—efficient? Not just poles across the road?"

"Why not poles?"

"I think that the lorries would crash their way through."

"You believe the men to be as desperate as that?"

"I do."

"Set your mind at rest, Terhune. We are using farm carts and old lorries filled with brick rubble, and other weighty material. Any vehicle which attempts to charge them should suffer. Doubt any driver would care to risk his neck."

"Will the police at the barriers be armed?"

"Some. Do you anticipate firing?"

"Frankly, yes. I also anticipate that the men will have their hands and faces blacked."

"Plunkett denied that they would be armed or disguised."

"I think he lied."

"Why?"

"I am convinced that the man who organized the gang—Stallybrass, according to Plunkett—has proceeded exactly on the lines of the smugglers of last century, except that he is using modern equipment."

"And the old-time smugglers used arms, and blacked their faces?"

"Yes."

The Colonel smiled politely, but it was obvious that he was not impressed by Terhune's argument. "The police have instructions to be ready for all emergencies."

"One more thing—if I may—"

"Grateful to you for your ideas."

"I think the smugglers will take to their heels across the fields."

"Quite. Criminals often run when cornered. Prefer running to fighting. The police will pursue them."

"One last question, Colonel. Will the mobile police be on the look-out for broken glass on the road, cattle turned loose in the road, and heaven only knows what other tricks they may have up their sleeves?"

"You have a boundless imagination, Terhune, but, must admit, an efficient one."

"The smugglers may be more than ever on the alert as a result of Plunkett's non-return to *Pennyfields*."

"True—true! But the mobile police have been instructed to watch for every possible trick to stop pursuit. Particularly the two you have mentioned." A pause, "Nothing more?"

Terhune shook his head. The others remained silent.

"Then we will wait for zero hour," the Chief Constable announced.

Chapter Twenty

From 10.30 p.m. onwards radio reports began to reach the Chief Constable of the movements of vehicles and people in and out of the area. There was very little traffic; without exception every vehicle was a private car. A few walkers crossed in both directions; a few cyclists. But no lorries.

Midnight arrived without there having been anything of consequence to rouse the company from the sleepy lethargy into which the majority of them had fallen, pending the time when events would demand their instant attention. In fact, the policeman whose duty it would be to mark the movements of the smugglers on the road map by means of tiny flags sat on his stool, leaned against the wall, and quite frankly slumbered with his chin buried in the fold-over of his overcoat. A few of the men moved about to keep warm; the rest, Colonel Agar among them, clustered about a coke brazier which somebody had thoughtfully provided.

By this time Terhune had learned several facts concerning his own whereabouts. The barn the police were occupying was well within the cordoned-off area: approximately half-way between the two most distant barriers, and a mile south of post eight, which, in turn, was situated at the foot of the sloping hill leading up to Great Hinton.

Behind the barn, and effectively concealed from the road, were two police-cars, and a hired lorry which was there to rush the ten reserve uniformed policemen whom Terhune had noted in the barn on his arrival there. In fact, the more he had talked the operation over with Murphy—in carefully guarded murmurs—the more he had had to admit to himself that the Chief Constable, in spite of his seemingly off-hand manner, had organized a first-class trap. There were weaknesses, of course, but when Terhune tried to think of some practical method of overcoming them, he appreciated the impossibility of doing so without the help of a far larger number of men than were likely to be available without calling in the military.

Prejudiced by his study of the past century, he felt inclined to be critical of the Colonel for not having asked the Army authorities for man-power. The authorities in the bad old days had not been ashamed to seek the assistance of both naval personnel and a company of Dragoons to help overcome the large body of men organized by George Ransley. It was a pity, he felt, to spoil the ship for a ha'p'orth of tar! For all that, it seemed fairly sure that the smugglers were not going to find it easy to avoid being arrested before a new day dawned.

One o'clock and no report that mattered. One-thirty and still nothing. Some of the senior officers woke up and began to look worried.

"I think we ought soon to be having news of a lorry or lorries coming south to pick up the stuff," Drake commented to the Chief Constable.

"What's the greatest distance from the perimeter to St. Mary's Bay?"

"Probably not more than five miles as the crow flies, sir."

"Means nearly double on Marsh roads," the Colonel retorted with dry humour. "Any time now, should think."

"Unless—" Boil began, doubtfully.

A snapping, "Unless what?"

"I was remembering what Mr. Terhune said earlier about the gang being alarmed by the disappearance of Plunkett, and wondering if it was altogether a wise move on our part to arrest him."

"Too late to cry over spilt milk. What's the latest news of fog?"

"Bad enough outside."

"Ask headquarters what it is like further north."

Boil spoke to the radio operator. The reply soon came back.

"Visibility sixty to seventy yards, sir, but patchy."

"Perhaps going carefully on outward journey," Colonel Agar pointed out with reason.

The fog was bad enough: one did not have to go outside to know that. It filled the barn, and turned all the hurricane lamps yellow.

Two o'clock, and still no news. Not one report of anything moving had come through for more than an hour. The majority of the faces looked disconsolate, even the Chief Constable's. Then 2.15.

"They must have called the show off, sir," Boil suggested, as he glanced at his watch. "It's that blasted Plunkett."

"Perhaps he was lying," Collins snapped.

"I don't think so," contradicted Raines. "He was a frightened man."

"According to him the stuff should be landing now. Where are the lorries to pick it up?"

"Something coming through, sir," the radio man called out.

The barn became very silent.

"Point twenty-four reports one lorry proceeding south, believed coming from direction Burmarsh. Impossible to see registration number because of fog and no rear light."

"No rear light! That's one!" Murphy called out.

"Only one!" Collins snapped. "I thought the consignment was to be an extra large one."

"Where's the lorry come from?" Superintendent Drake asked.

The radio operator again. "More news, sir. Lorry moving north has just passed point twenty-two. No rear light visible to show registration number."

"The cunning devils!" Collins exclaimed with grudging admiration. "They reckon two lorries might cause suspicion where one wouldn't."

"But where have they come from?" Drake repeated.

"They must have come from Springham during the day to avoid suspicion, sir," Collins replied. "They might have been parked anywhere meanwhile."

The men in the barn waited for the next report with tense interest. The minutes passed: fifteen of them, but the radio remained silent. Another five minutes, and then:

"Point twenty-three reports vehicle moving slowly eastwards towards coast road: fog too thick to distinguish it from post, but engine sounds like lorry engine."

"*East!*" Colonel Agar exclaimed. He sounded surprised. "Check whether east or west."

"It must be a *third* lorry, sir," Collins told him. "From still another direction."

Drake laughed "By God! They're taking the stuff away in relays."

The Chief Constable's expression was grim as he surveyed the ring of police officers about him. "Did not reckon on relays travelling different routes, gentlemen. May cause breakdown of our plans."

"How, sir?" Boil asked.

"If second lorry sees first being tailed, may double on tracks and try alternative route. If too near, may not have reserves left."

"We are going to have fun," Murphy murmured in Terhune's ear.

"Coming through, sir," the radio operator called out.

Immediate silence followed. A few seconds later: "Point twenty-three again. Vehicle now going west. Sounds like same lorry. Officer there wonders if it merely turned into main road in order to reverse."

Agar and his officers studied the map. "Why the deuce should it turn?"

"It may not be the same lorry, sir," Murphy called out. "It's probably the first lorry loaded up and leaving by a different road."

"Right!" the Chief Constable agreed with a snap. He traced the road with the end of his walking-stick. "It's bound for Broadway, to begin with, but where after that? Deuce take it! Looks like St. Mary's, Blackmanstone, Newchurch, to Willingham. Tell headquarters to radio police-car at Brooklands to patrol area."

Raines spoke up: "Excuse me, sir."

"Well! What is it?"

"If I were driving the lorry I should by-pass St. Mary's and Newchurch by turning right at Broadway, left at the next fork, then right—"

"Or left at Broadway," Collins joined in. "Then left again, right, right, then left—"

"All right! All right! Can see for myself. Four ways out. Which one? Shall have to wait report from police-car. Tell headquarters advise points seven, eight, nine and ten lorry heading north. Will send orders for reserves later."

The radio operator passed on the Chief Constable's orders. Silence followed. All eyes were fixed on the large-scale road map. Puzzled, anxious eyes they were for the most part, for many present began to realize, for the first time, how the maze of roads, criss-crossing the Marsh at that point, made it a simple matter for the driver to select— without diverging to any great extent from his original course—any one of four roads out of the Marsh. Moreover, by the time they could be reasonably certain which road would be taken, the lorry would be little more than two miles from the barricade.

"Cannot afford take chances," Colonel Agar announced unexpectedly. "Order all barriers across all roads."

"All roads, sir?" the operator queried.

"I said *all*," the Colonel snapped. "Any vehicles wanting to enter area must wait. Should not be any this hour of the morning."

Within a few minutes the radio operator reported, "Message has gone out to all points, sir." And, two minutes after that, "Lorry has passed point twenty-four, heading in direction of Burmarsh."

"Returning by different routes, by Gad!" the Chief Constable exploded. "If we had relied upon mobile police alone, might have been lucky to capture one out of three. Advise mobile police in that area to move."

"You did right to order all barriers across the roads, sir." Superintendent Drake stamped on a cigarette he had only just lit. "Even if the men take to the fields and escape, we shall get the goods."

"Want the men as well," the Colonel snapped. "At least the majority of them. Must have them. This smuggling must stop."

"Of course, sir."

The tension in the barn increased. Somewhere in the area two lorries loaded with contraband were heading for police traps. A third lorry was due at any moment to follow suit; somewhere in the same district mobile police-cars were hunting for the first two lorries. At any moment news might be coming through of the first clash between the smugglers and the police...

This unnatural, eerie silence was broken by the voice of the radio operator contacting the radio headquarters.

"Lloyd listening, Lloyd listening. Over..." And presently, "Message understood, standing by..." To the Colonel: "Mobile car seventeen has picked up a lorry, sir, on road to Broadway. Is tailing it as instructed."

The Colonel pointed his stick at the policeman with the small flags.

"Quick, man. Flag that car. Must see what we're about."

Lloyd's voice was heard again. "Lloyd listening. Lloyd listening. Over... Message understood. Standing by." For the first time that night a note of excitement underlined the man's voice as he called out, "A second lorry has passed point twenty-three, heading west and travelling fast."

"Gad! If it travels too fast it will catch up with car seventeen."

"Unless it piles itself up, sir. Even the smugglers can't take too many chances in this fog."

"Nor can we, Drake," the Colonel muttered grimly. "Mr. Terhune has told us how fast the lorry travelled which killed P.C. Kitchen. With those poor devils in car seventeen between two lorries, no knowing what will happen."

In gloomy silence the men in the barn stared at the road map. Before anyone could offer a suggestion, the radio operator's voice was heard again, first listening to headquarters and then signing off.

"Car seventeen reports that it is tailing lorry closely for fear of losing it, sir. Visibility very poor," he called out.

The Colonel hesitated as he looked at his officers. His eyes were worried, his expression grim.

"Your suggestions, gentlemen, please?"

"If it remains too close it will risk being seen by the men in front. Not only that, it would have no room to manœuvre if the smugglers take evasive action."

"You mean such as throwing out empty bottles as they did to Mr. Terhune, Drake?"

"Yes, sir."

Superintendent Boil laughed with grim humour. "If we don't want to take chances with the lives of the men, there seems only one thing to do, sir. Order them to take whichever fork the lorry doesn't—they should be getting there soon." He pointed to a place on the map which showed the road dividing.

The Chief Constable's expression hardened. "The men knew they might have to face hazards when they joined the force, gentlemen," he declared in a grating voice.

An awkward silence followed. "Yes, sir," Boil muttered.

Lloyd sang out, "Car seventeen reports that lorry in front is increasing speed."

"It's been spotted." There was more than a suggestion of distress in Drake's exclamation.

"If I order it to fall back the lorry behind may catch up with it," the Colonel stated.

Collins nodded. "Most probably, sir," he snapped.

"Second lorry may intend taking alternative route. Must know where lorries are heading," the Colonel continued. He called out, "Order all cars west of line Willingham to St. Mary's to converge on roads north of Broadway; those east of line to converge north-west of Burmarsh."

"Lloyd calling Rankin; Lloyd calling Rankin. Over... Order all cars west of Willingham-St. Mary's to converge roads north of Broadway; two lorries heading north; all others north-west of Burmarsh one lorry heading that direction. Over..." A few seconds' interval, "Message understood, sir; going out to all cars."

A minute passed; one tremendous minute of sixty other minutes. Then the voice of Lloyd.

"Lloyd listening, Lloyd listening. Over... Good God!..."

The police stiffened with apprehension, fear.

"What is it, man?" Chief Constable shouted.

"Message understood. Standing by." Lloyd signed off, harshly unintelligible. He stared at the Colonel. "Car seventeen reported liquid being sprayed on road from rear of lorry—"

"Go on."

"Next, that the road was on fire all around them, sir."

"God! Petrol!" The shoulders of the Chief Constable lost their normal rigidity; he looked suddenly quite old.

Lloyd swallowed. "Contact ceased."

"The ruddy swine!" Boil shouted.

"The men may have jumped out in time," Collins suggested. His voice remained unemotional, but there was an expression in his eyes...

"The Lord willing," muttered Murphy.

"It was my fault, gentlemen," the Chief Constable began, in a quietly agonized voice.

But Drake interrupted: "It was their duty, sir. It will be our duty to see that the men in the lorry… pay…"

The slackened shoulders stiffened again. "You are right, Superintendent. Send out a general call. Let every police officer on the Marsh be told what has happened. They must know what to expect—and what to avenge."

Lloyd sent the message over the walkie-talkie apparatus. As soon as he had done so the Chief Constable spoke again.

"Must not rely on receiving news which will enable us to know beforehand at which point lorries will try to leave the Marsh, gentlemen. Personally think one of the two here"—he paused to rest the ferrule of his walking-stick on the spot approximately where the police-car must have been when it became enveloped in flames—"will make for one of these two points." He moved the ferrule up the map and touched points eight and nine. "The other will probably make for ten or eleven. Think we cannot afford to hold our reserves, but should post them to the four points immediately. Of course it will mean splitting our forces. What do you say, gentlemen?"

The two superintendents began a hurried discussion with the Chief Constable, to which Terhune listened with only half his attention. The other half was pondering on the incredible thing that was happening before his eyes. It was too like one of the old Drury Lane melodramas, or a slick gangster film, to be real. Who, witnessing the scene, could possibly believe it was taking place in a quiet rural district of a country at peace? In his wildest imaginings he would not have dared, he realized, to invent such a fantastic plot for one of his books. For the realistic readers and critics of his day and age would dismiss so improbable a story with the intolerance of a blasé generation who would not allow themselves to remember that history does sometimes live up to its reputation of repeating itself: that there could still exist desperate men who were willing to run a cargo of contraband goods for the sake of a pocketful of money: that within the memory of people still living a battle had been fought between criminals and the military in the heart of London's East End.

Lloyd's impersonal voice disturbed his reverie. "News from point three, sir. Lorry brought to a halt by barrier. Before police could surround eight men jumped from rear and ran across fields. Although pursued, seven men escaped in fog—"

"Damn!" Colonel Agar exploded. "What about the eighth?"

"Arrested by mobile police-car number eleven. Man had face blacked, and wore long mackintosh."

Agar glanced at Terhune. "So you were right about the smugglers being disguised. And taking to their heels across the fields. I wonder if—"

What he was wondering was never known. "Lorry reached point eight, sir. Police tried to board it, but were repulsed by men inside who fought with heavy staves. One constable was knocked unconscious but not otherwise seriously hurt: another was knocked off running-board, and is suffering from broken leg and concussion."

"The lorry—"

"More coming through, sir." A slight pause, and then: "Not enough police to arrest men. Lorry has reversed, and is making off in a southerly direction at high speed."

"Means they intend trying another way out. Warn all points."

"Yes, sir." The man spoke into his apparatus. "Lloyd calling Rankin. Lloyd calling—"

"Listen!" Collins snapped.

With the exception of Lloyd all the men in the barn stiffened into inactivity. Presently they heard a faint drone of an automobile engine.

"Maybe one of the police-cars—"

"That's a heavy engine, sir," Raines contradicted. "That's no car. It's a lorry."

The hum grew louder.

"Begod! and it's this way it's coming. Past here, sir!" Murphy called out.

"Right!" Agar turned and addressed the waiting police. He issued his orders with the snap and precision of the successful military commander. "Draw barriers across road, then station yourselves to catch the men as they jump out of the lorry. Hit first; we will ask questions afterwards. Remember what happened to your comrades." They began to hurry off. "You armed men, wait." They halted, six of them. "Fire at the headlights as soon as the lorry comes within range. Without lights it will be helpless: we shall be on more even terms."

"The lorry might not be one of the smugglers, sir," Drake pointed out.

"Certain to be," Agar snapped. But he nodded his head. "We will take no chances. Put that red hurricane lamp in the middle of the road fifty yards north of you. If the lorry comes past, fire. Understood?"

A sergeant saluted. "Yes, sir."

"Off with you. At the double."

The eager men needed no encouragement to move. They ran out of the barn; all but one of them with right hand instinctively on gun holster.

With envious eyes Agar watched them leave. "Should like to be with them, gentlemen, but..." He waved his hand at the map: the third lorry was still unaccounted for. "Superintendent Drake, you will take charge outside."

Murphy saw Terhune's expression, and chuckled. "Which for you, sir? Inside or out?"

Terhune listened to the drone of the engine growing louder. "Outside."

"Quick, then."

The two men followed Drake and the others out of the barn. The moment they stepped into the darkness they realized how warm, in comparison, was the barn which they had thought so cold. The salted fog brushed against their faces; its clammy touch was icy—or so it seemed for a time: later they realized that it was more unpleasant than icy.

It was impossible to see a step ahead. Fortunately, both men had a torch. They picked their way along the muddy track to the road, listening meanwhile to the noise of the approaching lorry, now not far off. Yet nothing was to be seen when they reached the road. Just here and there, in the light of their torches, the ominous shadow of a waiting policeman; the distorted outline of the farm wagon which had been drawn across the road; and, a short distance along the road, a red point of light.

Then, in the near distance, they saw a small yellowish-white smudge of light grow visible. It moved towards them in a tortuous dance, weaving in many directions, but all the time growing larger.

A quick reflection passed through Terhune's thoughts as the yellow smudge approached the red light. If the scene within the barn had been fantastic, the scene without was weird; more unreal than a Disney nightmare. Then the yellow glow and the red light mingled; the red vanished; the yellow smudge separated into two entities, two yellow eyes...

A crackle of explosions, a series of stabbing orange flashes, both magnified and distorted by the fog. One yellow eye disappeared; then the second. A squeal of brakebands; a shout of fear and agony; the hideous grind of crumpling metal; a dull, ominous thud...

2

"Two men got away in spite of everything," Murphy told Terhune some time later. "We have the rest; a bit battered but otherwise whole. With one exception. The driver's had it. Steering-wheel went clean through his chest. Know who it was, when we wiped the black off his face?"

"Smiles is my guess. Unless it was Matcham."

Murphy nodded. "Smiles it is. He won't last long, but he's talked. He says he was not driving on the night Kitchen was killed, and I believe him."

"Who was?"

"Sam Plunkett. Smiles usually drove but Plunkett wangled the job for the night. He didn't mean to take any chance of Kitchen's not dying."

"Any news of the third lorry?"

Murphy's face turned grave. "It got away."

"Good lord!" Terhune stared at the sergeant. "I shouldn't have thought it possible. What happened?"

"Colonel Agar received information that it was heading for point ten, so he ordered the barriers to be removed."

"He did what?"

Murphy's expression relaxed. He chuckled. "It should be plain to you, sir, why he gave such an order."

It was, too, when Terhune gave the matter thought. "He wants to make certain of finding evidence at the fruit farm when he raids it?"

The sergeant nodded. "Which will be soon after the lorry has been seen arriving there. Enough time for the men to get into bed, and fall asleep without waiting for the other two—"

Terhune yawned. He felt very much relaxed after a night of nervous tension and excitement. And the mention of bed didn't help matters much...

THE END